I0744247

# ALSO BY ANNE RENWICK

Elemental Web Chronicles

*The Golden Spider*

*The Silver Skull*

*The Iron Fin*

*Venomous Secrets*

Elemental Web Tales

*A Trace of Copper*

*In Pursuit of Dragons*

*A Reflection of Shadows*

*A Snowflake at Midnight*

*A Ghost in Amber*

*A Whisper of Bone*

*Flight of the Scarab*

Elemental Web Stories

*The Tin Rose*

*Kraken and Canals*

*Rust and Steam*

# A WHISPER OF BONE

AN ELEMENTAL WEB TALE

## ANNE RENWICK

*To Glory*

THANK YOU TO...

Glory, a most superior canine whose backyard New Haven antics with the local groundhogs drove her human, Joss, to the brink of insanity and inspired this story.

Sandra Sookoo, my wonderful editor who mercilessly ferrets out weaknesses and sets my work on a better course.

My husband who puts up with all my strangeness as he patiently waits for my next book to take shape.

My mom and dad who instilled in me a love of both reading and travel.

Mr. Fox and his red pen.

# CHAPTER ONE

*New Haven, Connecticut*
*June 1885*

Special Agent Ryan Nolan rolled his shoulders and knocked again.

"Open the door, Mr. Alcantra." He tossed the brass key and its fob, letting them jangle and clank as they slapped back into his palm, his message clear. "There is no escaping this discussion."

Taking a room at the expensive and exclusive Sea View Hotel was the water rat's first mistake. Escorting loud and giggling paid female company through the lobby in broad daylight was his second. Mothers pushing wide-eyed children behind their skirts while fathers directed their ire at the hotel manager was never good for business. Complaint after complaint had been registered. But it was the many rough-sided crates the Spaniard carted through the lobby to his room that twisted a final knot in the manager's cravat. He'd dispatched a kinetic chiroptera, an official cry for help.

The hotel's mechanized bat had flapped its way to central New Haven, dropping a message down the Customs House chute, alerting the agents within to the peculiar behavior of a certain hotel guest they might wish to investigate. All notes were ignored until the third or fourth such missive arrived, whereupon Ryan imagined the receiving agent sighed heavily before flipping through pages listing the names of known and suspected smugglers. The half dozen red flags beside Mr. Francisco Alcantra's name had snapped that agent wide awake. Soon, electrical signals traveled along south-bound wires to the Improbable Biologics Investigational Service—IBIS—and the resulting telegraph message landed on Ryan's desk in the predawn hours alongside a train ticket and a sealed envelope.

The name inside was that of a Spanish man recently over-heard bragging about the ungodly sum he'd been paid for his latest job and hinting at the existence of a *cuélebre*.

If there was any truth to this report at all, any positive proof of the giant, winged serpent-dragon of Iberian Celtic mythology's presence on U.S. soil, the Spaniard was in for a world of pain under the Rare and Emergent Species Act of 1862.

Excitement had zipped through Ryan—no cryptobiologist could be indifferent—until he'd noted the destination.

*New Haven.*

Struck by sudden ossification, his heavy, cold heart had dropped to his toes, momentarily depriving the ice-cold blood in his lungs of oxygen.

Really, it had only been a matter of time. He'd forced his jaw to unlock and his diaphragm to drag in a deep breath. Any city with a port was bound to have trouble arrive on its shores. His hometown was no exception.

By the time the steam train chugged north, and an omnibus deposited him on Beach Street, the strain of mollifying affronted guests had taken its toll on the hotel manager, now bug-eyed, sweating bullets, and desperate to rid himself of "that Spanish scourge".

With no more than the gold flash of a badge, a few hushed words, and a grateful glance from said manager, Ryan gained unfettered access to the smuggler's room.

"There is a vile odor emanating from his room, but he refuses to let anyone enter." The distressed man had shoved a key across the counter. "Please remove him, his guest, and the rest of his baggage."

A decided possibility. But that would depend upon what Ryan found within.

The walls of the hotel hallway pressed in on him. At its end, a damp, salt-infused breeze drifted in through an open window carrying with it the garish sounds of the carousel. It wasn't that he disliked New Haven itself—or in this case, nearby West Haven. Not exactly. Rather, associated memories forced him to confront certain uncomfortable truths of his existence and reminded him of local family members owed a visit.

But such dark musings were irrelevant to the task at hand. Time to roust the man who fancied himself a modern-day pirate.

Within, the low murmur of voices mixed with faint, if frantic, scrambling noises. It wouldn't be the first time he'd rousted an undressed couple from bed. He smirked. In most circumstances, catching a man with his trousers down, distracted and off guard, made an arrest that much easier.

Ryan rapped on the door and called out, "Last chance, Mr. Alcantra."

Inside, glass clinked. A thud sounded. Still the door didn't open. Instead, he heard the rattle and scrape of a window sash rising. The Spaniard attempting a jump from the second floor?

Cursing, Ryan jammed the key home and twisted.

The door slammed open as a loud crack split the air—the report of an air gun discharging.

Ducking, he rushed into the room, quickly assessing the situation. Amidst a backdrop of open crates, a scatter of imported goods and general disarray, there was a woman collapsed upon the floor, laughing. A man slumped in a chair. And a third hooded individual leaned out the window with a grappling hook gun in her hands and a six-shooter in a holster belted low on her hips and tied securely to her thigh.

*Her.* Or so the curve of hips beneath close-fitting trousers suggested. A fashion choice he'd grown to appreciate during his days in the western territories, especially as worn by one particular woman. The one that got away.

A reflection that cost Ryan a precious moment.

"Stop! U.S. Customs!" He drew his Eagle B29 sidearm and ran forward.

The woman glanced over her shoulder offering him a glimpse of dark eyes framed by long lashes and lips that pulled in a smirk as she tossed something onto the floor that snatched his feet from beneath him to send him careening, arms wind-milling. *Crash!* He landed—hard—atop a scattering of small, round seedpods. Embarrassed victim to a classic delay tactic. Yet one that granted her all the time she needed to secure her grappling gun, clip a hook to the front of a five-point harness strapped about her body, seize the handle of a large canvas bag and leap.

He pushed off the floor, lunged for the window and took aim.

Suspended from a wire cable, the woman zipped through the air, a dark blur soaring over the crowds of people below. Hoots, hollers, and screams of delight erupted as tourists caught sight of the figure overhead, numbering her flight among the many spontaneous performances that drew visitors to Savin Rock Park.

Was it wrong of him to take dark pleasure in disabusing them of that notion? He squeezed the trigger—*bang!*—firing a dart that skewered the woman's thigh and guaranteed her a world of pain.

The crowd gasped, searching for the source of the sound, not quite convinced they'd heard the report of a gun. Especially as the fleeing figure gave no indication she possessed any nerve endings.

A string of curses fell from his lips as she drew a knife from her boot and sliced through the rope from which she hung, dropping to the ground in a crouch. Plucking the dart from her leg, she sprinted along the tree-lined path and climbed into a waiting steam carriage. Within moments, the vehicle lurched into motion and disappeared from view.

Wonderful, a criminal with a sky-high pain threshold. She ought to be on the ground, writhing in agony. An unsettling beginning. *Dammit.* He clenched his jaw, both annoyed that he'd not pursued her yet secure in the knowledge his primary directive was to apprehend one Francisco Alcantra. Speaking of...

"Who is she?" He turned toward the man at the table, reaching to shake the man's shoulder, to wake him from his silent stupor.

But his hand hovered in the air and his next words caught in his throat as he reassessed everything about this assignment. There was a bullet hole in the man's forehead, one so recent the trickle of blood between his eyes had yet to dry. All while the woman on the floor laughed and sang a song of sixpence.

The scene before him was both disquieting and absurd. He didn't relish informing the hotel manager of the violent death that had occurred on his watch. The resulting histrionics would be the least of his problems.

Ryan tipped the dead man's chin up, making a positive identification from the tintype included with the IBIS directives. He sighed heavily. Of course it would be the Spaniard, Francisco Alcantra, the man responsible for this landslide of events. The complications and questions just kept piling up. He'd located the smuggler, but now hunted a murderer and possible thief, given the bag gripped in her fist as she jumped from the hotel window. His sole witness a warbling madwoman.

By how many minutes had Ryan missed the sound of a pistol's discharge? For this hole in Alcantra's forehead was not the work of an air rifle, but a handgun. Had the death shot been fired by the woman who'd leapt from the window? Likely, given no weapon was readily visible in the room and the female on the floor appeared all but insensible. Not that he had entirely discounted her. Yet.

He holstered his weapon and ran a hand through his hair. So much for an open and shut case. Was it too much to hope that there would at least be evidence of a dragon species tucked somewhere inside one of the many crates lining the walls? Given the dead man's occupation and the oversized canvas bag hauled away by a likely murderess, the contents of this room would need to be inventoried and thoroughly searched to discover what was taken in hopes of determining why the meeting had taken a deadly turn. Was it as simple as a dispute over the agreed upon fee? Or had the woman desired something Mr. Alcantra refused to sell? And so on.

Regardless, before the rude interruption of the Spaniard's death, it appeared the threesome had gathered about the table to take tea. Two empty cups, a third untouched. *Wait.* Not tea. At least not of the *Camellia sinensis* variety. Ryan squinted at the green-tinged liquid that sat cooling in footed Spanish silver colonial teacups. He plucked the lid from the kettle that hung over a small burner. Inside, bits of cactus floated.

Peyote. A powerful hallucinogen.

Unwise, consuming a mind-altering substance during a business negotiation. Then again, Mr. Alcantra's whispers about his imports—such as a *cuélebre*—had landed him on a list of wanted smugglers. Shrewd, he was not.

Ryan considered the sights before him. Everything spoke

of confidence. From the casual manner in which the scene was set, he suspected the Spaniard believed the meeting a mere formality. That the murderess had arrived to collect her goods, only to discover the man wished to entice her into an additional transaction. A fancy hotel room with a large bed. Two pretty women in attendance. A little mescaline to lower barriers and enhance the overall sensual experience.

But the water rat had badly misjudged and had paid for it with his life.

Still, many questions remained. And, as the situation reputedly involved a rare or emergent species, IBIS protocol dictated that Ryan remain in New Haven until the case was solved. So much for a brief visit to his childhood home. Against his screaming instincts, he would stay with family, kill two birds with one stone.

The tea did, at least, explain the state of his single witness. The half-dressed, cackling woman sprawled upon the floor, blonde curls cascading over the deep, red pile of the carpet, was oblivious to all save the images conjured by her drugged brain that were, seemingly, projected on the ceiling. A victim of circumstance? Spared an end similar to the Spaniard's by Ryan's timely arrival? Given her befuddled state and the precise placement of the bullet in the Spaniard's forehead, she ranked low on his list of suspects.

A niggling sense of recognition gnawed at him. Then her head turned, and bright blue eyes met his.

"Well, Polly, put the kettle on!" She grinned up at him. "If it isn't Ryan Nolan."

His eyebrows crashed together. "Rose?"

Of all the women in New Haven, what were the odds he would find his ex-fiancée here on a hotel floor, drugged?

He glanced at her hand—a wedding band. Married.

In their youth, she'd been known as the Wild Irish Rose. Suitors had trailed behind her in Wooster Square, a dozen deep. Confident of his prospects, Ryan himself had courted her, presenting her with bits of sea glass and heart-shaped rocks collected on the shore. And it had worked. He'd slipped a ring on her finger, fulling intending to make her his wife.

Until his world unraveled. The morning of his mother's funeral, at the very moment Rose ought to have stood with him graveside, she'd been sighted returning from Long Wharf after spending the night in Captain Donovan's stateroom.

After that, the bloom was off the rose, with all of Wooster Square Society focusing all attention on the wild. As for Ryan? He extended her the benefit of the doubt, sat in her family's parlor for hours awaiting an explanation. But none ever came. She'd returned his ring, refused to speak with him. Taking that as a tacit admission of guilt, he'd left for Ireland three days later and never returned to New Haven.

Until today.

As to her eventual fate? He'd assumed her father would buy her a suitable husband—but married to a smuggler? To Francisco Alcantra? That didn't sit right.

There was one person who could answer all his questions involving local society. Not that the woman he called grandmother ever bestowed her knowledge freely. No, the vain, rapacious old woman filed away every dusty rumor that struck her as curious or valuable in that knife-sharp mind of hers, storing it until its revelation would inflict maximum effect. He could ask, certainly, but the price of such information would come at a steep price. One he refused to pay.

With a heavy exhale, he asked, "What do you know of Mr. Alcantra?" Given the drug she'd imbibed, coherence was probably too much to expect. He bent to lift Rose off the floor, grateful she was mostly dressed, freeing him from any later implications of impropriety.

"Cisco?" She patted his cheek. "A large seagull pecked his eye out."

"A seagull?" Confusion wrinkled his brow. He set her down on a tangle of sweat-stained sheets, a questionable improvement over the floor. "A bird." Had the mescaline given the murderess wings in Rose's mind?

She flapped a hand. "The one that flew away. Out the window. *Voomph!*" A statement made with much conviction and a roll of the eyes. As if *he* were the unbalanced one. "Vicious demons, those salty feathered fiends. But no worries, Cisco will sort it out with an eye patch. All the ladies will sigh."

Over a dead man? "Including you?"

"Me?" She giggled and winked. "Never. But more will make him all the merrier!"

He thought of the three teacups. Of the possible assumptions implied therein.

"Is that so?" Something oily and fetid twisted through his innards. How deeply was she entwined in this mess? Openly cavorting in a popular hotel with a known smuggler who may or may not be her husband. Sipping peyote tea in the presence of a murderess. What more disappointing facts would he learn?

Pity was an uncomfortable sensation when it lodged against suspicious disapproval before backing misplaced loyalty against a wall.

*Aether*, there was little hope of extracting any useful information from Rose until she was in possession of all her faculties. Which might be quite some time, judging from her flushed face, dilated pupils, and the irregular pulse throbbing at her neck.

He couldn't let her go. But he couldn't keep her here. Not like this.

"And where are you residing these days?" Fingers crossed there was a responsible adult to whom he could deliver her.

"A house on Olive Street serves as a proper birdcage."

Not far away, then. But a birdcage? He knew both relief and worry simultaneously. "And what is its number?"

"Why? Wouldn't you rather stay here? With me?" She lifted a leg and pointed a stockinged toe toward the ceiling, tracing a lazy circle of invitation in the air. Petticoats pooled at her hips as she slid her palms from her corseted waist upward to frame her breasts.

A move that left a bitter tang in his mouth. "Not an option, Rose."

Her lips pursed into a pout. "I'll do anything you—"

"No." He turned away, hiding the curl of his lip.

A number of agents might mock him for failing to take full advantage of such an opportunity, but Ryan found such behavior distasteful. He was no monk; he merely preferred the women in his bed not to arrive there for the purpose of negotiating a business exchange. He refused to trade sex—or anything else—for the protection of a potentially complicit witness.

He studied the room. Open crates lined its edges, their lids propped against their sides. Packing material—various dried tropical leaves—littered the floor. Ignoring Rose, he examined one import item after another, wrinkling his nose at the foul odors of preservative that wafted upward, all while keeping his eyes peeled for a possible murder weapon.

There were bottles of thick and opaque glass, each corked, sealed with wax and labeled with a twist of twine and a brown-paper tag. Within floated dark and shadowy shapes. As he read the scrawled ink on each, he mourned the loss of life caused by those who believed severed parts of an exotic animal would cure ailments their physician could not. Much as he wished to stop his inventory, to leave the task to another, such was his job. It had to be done. He needed to know exactly what had been imported.

A few bottles held tantalizing clues to the existence of creatures not yet listed in the Linnaean classification literature and he set them aside for closer study. Such were the moments that defined his ambition and drove his career. Far too late for the individual animal sacrificed to provide the raw ingredients, but not necessarily for the population that provided them. IBIS would investigate and, if located, protect those who remained in the wild from a similar fate.

For now, he moved on, continuing his inspection of the

room's contents while Rose sang breathily, "*Birds of a feather flock together, And so will pigs and swine.*"

He found boxes filled with peyote buttons, with various seed pods. Bottles of tequila and mezcal. Packets of powders and pills. Rolls of musty furred, feathered, and scaly skins. Entire wings of brightly colored birds. Assorted eggs with both leathery and rigid shells. Dry bones. A bag of monkey feet. And entire dried animals—fish, turtles, lizards, snakes.

Only one creature still lived. An irate, hissing iguana locked inside a cage far too small. Perfect. His brother Liam, in one of his many efforts to guilt Ryan into a visit, had written at length about his son's fascination with all things dragon-like. Meaning Owen, his ten-year-old nephew, was about to receive the gift of a lifetime. A smile tugged at his lips. The creature was bound to upset everyone else in the household, an unexpected bonus.

Archaeological artifacts were also among the collection. Ornaments of beaten gold and carved jade. An assemblage of ancient pottery.

Every last item in this room would interest and inflame all who worked within the walls of the Peabody Museum at Yale.

But they were Mexican exports, not Spanish goods.

So much for finding evidence of a *cuélebre*. Or the murder weapon.

Wait. What was that?

He tugged at a box shoved beneath the bed, pushed the lid aside. The box was only half full, its contents wrapped in newspaper—he unwrapped a gold torc, blinked and dragged his stunned gaze away to the top of the newspaper page—from

Gijón, a coastal city in northern Spain, dated a few months past. Next, he unwrapped a bronze spearhead. Followed by a stone fragment with an eroded carving.

He almost set the stone aside when the sunlight pouring through the window cast curious shadows across its surface. He squinted. Tilted it back and forth. Was that a feathered wing protruding from a dragon's back? His heart soared—a *cuélebre!*—then took a swan dive into a dark pit. If this was the *cuélebre* the smuggler had bragged about, then his mission was complete. There was no actual cryptid—living or dead—only a fanciful artistic rendering of one.

Still, all three items were Iberian, artifacts from continental Europe, likely modern-day Spain. Not even the same hemisphere as Mexico. Yet tucked among Mesoamerican commodities. Why?

He set his jaw. Several crates were only half full. What inventory was missing? What was in the canvas bag whisked away by the hooded presumed murderess? Was she the competition, a cryptid hunter sans ethics?

He straightened. "Have you met many of Mr. Alcantra's customers, Rose?"

"Met the chickens," she said. "But not the rooster."

He sighed. So they were back to birds. "And where might this chicken coop be?"

"Oh? What's good for the goose is good for the gander? As if I'd send a fox to chase the geese." She cackled. "They bite, you know. Such pretty feathers but they'll nip off your nose." She dropped the back of her hand against her forehead and waggled her fingers.

"Rose," he exhaled, frustrated and wishing to be free of this nonsense. There was a murderess to hunt.

"Fine, fine. As we are speaking of ruffled feathers and eggs, when not in his counting-house, the king has provided a home in which I roost." She pushed herself into a sitting position and reached for a day gown. "It's quite the nest, you know. If we must take wing, drop me at Sixty-Five Olive Street?"

Finally, her inane blather had coughed up a proper address. Perhaps tomorrow she could converse without quoting a mishmash of Mother Goose. One last task, though, before he faced the next steps of this nightmare.

Ryan turned back to the dead man who stared blankly across the room, blissfully beyond Rose's inane avian-themed prattles. He dug through Francisco Alcantra's coat pockets, searching.

There. Worn leather and paper met his fingertips.

He tugged free a small book and flipped through its pages. Code. He'd expected nothing less. Thankfully, it appeared to be a simple substitution cipher, nothing he couldn't break with an evening's work. With luck, it would contain all the man's local contacts. Including the true identity of this aforementioned chicken coop where his customers might—

Ryan jumped back, his hand falling upon his weapon.

Mr. Alcantra's eyes had shifted. Ryan could swear the man was looking directly at him.

But no. The hole in the man's forehead negated that possibility.

Ryan fished a loupe from inside his coat and held the optical device to his own eye. Ignoring the jump in his heart rate and the curdle in his stomach, he peeled back the Spaniard's eyelid and leaned closer.

Something small, ridged and wormlike swam beneath the Spaniard's cornea.

He grimaced. So much for a clean death and a simple death certificate. The Customs House authorities would be extremely put out when they were forced to employ the autopsy services of a pathologist.

Mr. Alcantra might be dead, but the creature in his eyeball was not.

HAND CLUTCHING HER THIGH, Maria writhed on the floor of the jolting steam carriage, cursing as an unknown drug burned through her veins and arteries.

She'd know the face of the man who had shot her anywhere. More than one framed photograph of his visage had graced the fireplace mantle of their American host. Handsome enough and good with a weapon.

The timing of his arrival, however, left much to be desired. She'd long since given up any hope that an IBIS agent might be persuaded to aid their cause. Not that they needed him anymore. The canvas bag beside her held key artifacts, if ones that had taken far too long to be liberated from storage, and the greedy Spanish smuggler with his unreasonable demands was no longer a problem.

If their luck held, she need only endure a few more months in this god forsaken country.

# CHAPTER TWO

Charlotte Reid bent at the knees and heaved. The shovel arced overhead, catapulting the dead and dismembered victim of violence over the fence and out of her yard.

"Bury your own dead!" she hollered, then side-eyed Glory. "Must you always involve yourself with the groundhogs?" This was the seventh such oversized rodent to breach the border in as many days. What they were fleeing, she wasn't certain, but they arrived bloody, wild-eyed, and frantic. Which served only to fire her dog's bloodlust. "*Must you?*"

Glory had the good sense to feign remorse. Fiercely protective and easily bored, the large, thick-furred canine intimidated most with her aloof disposition and steady stare. Indeed, they had just cause to worry as Glory was quite capable of dragging an adult human down the street. Not that she'd tried. Yet.

Her neighbors, however, would make excellent test subjects. If only they'd emerge from the house long enough.

Not only did she not know their names, she was not at all certain she could pick them out in a lineup. Two men, a dark-haired woman, and their cook. Charlotte had tried introducing herself. But the cook had opened the door, stared at her as she spoke, then grunted something in an unfamiliar language while flapping a hand at her in a universal motion for "go away".

The rest kept to themselves. Lights appeared and disappeared in the windows. Curls of smoke rose from the chimney. Mysterious individuals came and went, almost always at night and wrapped in hooded cloaks. Absolute ridiculousness.

She'd introduced herself to the owners of the other home bordering these odd neighbors, but Charlie Tims and his wife hadn't been able to tell her much at all, save the strange owners had arrived a little over two years ago. The neighborhood had grown accustomed to the curious bird calls and no longer paid it much mind. Though they too were, understandably, also concerned about the sudden appearance of mangled groundhogs in their own yard this past week.

"Who burns coal and wraps themselves in wool in the middle of a heat wave?" She huffed. "Are they cold-blooded reptiles?"

Glory sighed. As one forced to wear a fur coat year-round, she was in complete agreement.

Their neighbors were insane. Quite possibly criminal.

This was what came of letting her brother find her a rental property. In the midst of wrapping up an excavation in the Dakota Territory, she'd wired ahead to inform him of her new position at The Peabody Museum of Natural History, asking that he find her suitable accommodations. For her. For Glory. For her fossils.

Hiram had chosen what would have been the perfect house, going so far as to inform her of the aviary on the adjacent property, assuming her enthusiasm for all things feathered would make her fast friends with like-minded neighbors. She didn't mind the chirping, warbling noises. Or even the faint smell of bird droppings. But the humans? They were an obnoxious mystery.

Which meant she'd been spending her evening hours working at a table in her kitchen, crank fan blowing over a bowl of ice, watching for movement out of corner of her eye, field glasses at the ready. Not just watching, mind. Academic papers didn't write themselves and C.S. Reid had a fast-approaching deadline to meet.

In nothing but her sleeveless cotton shift—the heat was oppressive even at this late hour—she stalked back to the house to the accompaniment of odd chirps and whistles. How right her brother was that the birds housed next door would intrigue her. Which made her situation so very annoying and frustrating. No matter the window from which she chose to peer at the occupants, the woven grass mats wrapped about the aviary's walls blocked her view.

Inside, Charlotte washed her hands to remove any trace of groundhog, then dropped into her chair. She touched match to wick, igniting a small flame that reflected in a concave mirror to send light pouring into a microscope, then slid a fossil under the lens and adjusted the focus. Tonight's task involved composing a description of beautifully preserved microstructure of fossilized feathers and their attachment sites. As her paper, should it be accepted for publication, would upend and shake the bedrock of paleontologists everywhere, it had to be perfect.

Hands poised above the keys of her typewriter, she glanced out the window. Traffic had decreased due to the impending storm, making it all that much easier to spot any irregularities. When the canvas-roofed Stabinsky Steamer car arrived at dusk, she'd chalked it up to another bizarre visitation by a mysterious guest. But no one had emerged from its interior. Nor had a neighbor exited the house to climb within. A strangeness heaped upon eccentricity.

Miserable, Glory flopped at her feet and moaned her displeasure. The poor pup.

The weather this past week made Charlotte long for the heat of summers out West where the air was so dry it sucked water out of your pores, where a full canteen was the only thing that kept you from turning into a desiccated mummy. Temperatures might not rise so high here in New England, but this sweltering heat wave combined with the lack of a breeze stuck cloth to skin and sent strands of her hair curling every which way. Of late, men had taken to loosening cravats and misplacing waistcoats, while women abandoned all but their thinnest petticoats and sought refuge beneath wide-brimmed hats and broad parasols. The most fortunate among them fled to Long Island Sound seeking the relief of a cool, offshore breeze.

With luck, the dark thunder clouds building on the horizon would soon pour buckets and put the city out of its collective misery.

Her gaze drifted to the faint cracks of light that seeped from between the heavy curtains drawn over the latched windows of her strange neighbors. Had everyone within died of heatstroke?

No matter. She willed her focus back to the typewriter in front of her and forced her fingers into motion. *Raised bumps on the ulna may represent quill knobs, anchor points for wing feathers...*

Years of bone hunting in the Dakota and Wyoming Territories for the likes of Edward Drinker Cope and O.C. Marsh had left her with a respectable nest egg. But she wanted to be an acknowledged paleontologist in her own right. To leave her own indelible mark in the field.

Many had laughed, scoffed and ridiculed, labeling her goals as impossible. But persistence had pried open classroom doors and arranged for library access in the East while fossil hunting out West had provided both practical field experience and thesis material. Not that there would be an official doctoral degree. Women—of any color—weren't permitted such lofty aspirations. Degree or no degree, she'd nonetheless won a position at Yale's Peabody Museum and was all but done with her first monograph.

*Fine.* There might have been a *smidgeon* of extortion, a little arm twisting and a vague, unsubstantiated threat.

Professor Marsh was a curmudgeon to the nth degree,

hostile to females and a known tightwad. Except he'd owed her a favor. And so, when she'd volunteered *not* to collect a salary, he'd grudgingly granted her permission to work in his laboratories, to scrape rock from fossils, to arrange, catalogue and label the surfeit of specimens various bone hunters sent his way. Was hers the short stick? Perhaps. Still, credentials were credentials, and when she published, she'd be damn sure to list her research institution as Yale.

All of this possible because she'd had enough of the increasing hostility between two certain paleontology parties and, in a fit of temper, severed ties and set about leading her own group—a cook, a guide and a few trusted men along with the necessary horses, wagons and assorted equipment—into the Dakota Territory, far from the simmering drama.

There, they'd hit pay dirt.

Among other specimens, she'd found and sold a large, impressive, and nearly complete hadrosaur skeleton for a handsome figure, enough to encourage her to arrange another expedition. The following year, she'd again headed out into the Dakota Territory, into areas not yet explored. At first, their time in the field had felt doomed. Then, as winter approached, lightning struck. They'd found a cache of amazing specimens. Ones that put dollar signs in the eyes of her men. The next day, she'd all but stumbled upon the fossil remains of a caenagnathid, a bizarre, bird-like dinosaur.

She'd dubbed it Anzu, the chicken-from-hell, named after the bird-like demon of ancient Sumerian mythology. Roughly eleven feet long, nose to tail, and five feet tall, its jaws sported a toothless beak and its head a rounded crest—not unlike that of a cassowary—while its neck and legs were more reminiscent of an ostrich. There, however, any resemblance to modern flightless birds terminated. Its forearms ended in sharp-tipped claws, and it possessed a long, powerful tail. Most surprising of all? There were fossilized feather impressions surrounding those appendages, ones unlike any found in North America *and* in possession of alternating light and dark striations.

Not an archaeopteryx—the branch leading to birds, small creatures with a broad wingspan capable of gliding if not actual flight, as discovered in Germany in 1861—but a large carnivorous dinosaur with decorative feathers and clear reptilian traits. Unheard of. Yet there it sat at her feet.

And if, perchance, she could produce evidence that the striations were indications of color? Actual melanosomes, color-bearing organelles, fossilized within the partially degraded feathers and filaments? Such would be the making of her career.

When her head stopped spinning at the long-reaching implications, Charlotte had set about excavating every last remnant of the chicken-from-hell, carefully documenting each fossil fragment before shipping them East to her brother in New Haven. She'd worked though as much of the fall as possible, holing up in a nearby town for the winter, only to resume her dig with the spring thaw.

By early summer, she'd arrived in New Haven and settled into a routine, toiling at night to study Anzu, turning the fossil bones into a data set to support her first monograph. She worked in utter secrecy—sharing her private scholarly pursuits with no other museum employees. A necessity that many adopted while in O.C. Marsh's employ, given the professor's reputation for publishing the findings of his underlings as his own—blatant theft.

The typed pages of her monograph lay stacked beside her upon the kitchen table. Nearly complete. An editor at the *American Journal of Science* had agreed to review her paper and awaited her submission. She only needed to decide how much of the feather data to include, and what she ought reserve for a separate, more detailed publication. Her brother had promised her the use of his aetheroscope, that she might closely examine the structure of the possible melanosomes, and then—

A scream cut through the heavy blanket of thick night air. Glory's ears perked as she raised her head, calculating the potential entertainment value multiplied by the heat then divided by the energy required to stand. The cry came again. Not human. And, this time, more a prolonged screech.

The dog leapt up barking and Charlotte snatched up her field glasses, lifting them to her eyes.

*Bang!* Her neighbor's back door slammed open, casting a crooked rectangle of light onto packed dirt and weeds, and revealing a shadowed silhouette of a stout woman chasing a squawking chicken. The protesting poultry ran beneath a low bush, eliciting a string of curses uttered in that strange, unfamiliar language. The woman's arm darted out and a second later, she yanked the bird from the undergrowth and hauled its flapping form back inside.

Nothing more than tomorrow's dinner escaping the cook.

Disappointed, Charlotte swung the field glasses toward the steam car. A face stared out from the window. A familiar one. A visage she'd never thought to lay eyes upon again. Her breath caught in her throat.

"Well, well, well. If it isn't Ryan Nolan. Of all the streets in all the cities..." Anyone in the know and calculating the odds would report the chances of neighborhood cryptozoological shenanigans had risen by one hundred percent.

Did he still work for himself? Had he joined a private firm? Attached himself to a government agency?

Glory lifted an eyebrow.

"You're absolutely right to be suspicious," she informed her pup. "He's most definitely involved in that nonsense next door. The only question is how." And she'd have answers. Tonight. Even if it meant the effort and misery of dressing to the bare minimum of socially acceptable standards.

She stalked to her closet, yanked out her old split skirts and tugged them on. Buttoned a thin blouse. Laced her sturdy camp boots and slid in a sharp knife. As cotton and canvas fused to her skin, she sighed at her hair in the mirror. The past was past. Ancient history. So, if there was no point in making any special effort, why was she standing here contemplating hairpins? The storm might break at any moment and that meant rain. She grabbed her Stetson instead.

He must be suffocating, sitting in that steam car. A thought that made her smile. She'd take him tea, but that would involve boiling water which required a heat source—and there was zero chance she would voluntarily elevate the temperature inside her home for anyone.

Water?

No. This reunion required something stiffer.

Whiskey.

Throwing open a cabinet door, she reached for a bottle of coffin varnish collecting dust in the back. A toast to old times. She stuffed two shot glasses into her pockets. To soak up the booze, she grabbed a tin of hardtack and headed for the door where her guard sat, anticipatory and expectant.

"Stay, Glory." The dog turned sad eyes in her direction. "Sorry, sweetie. You can chew on him another time."

Careful to secure the door latch behind her, she stalked to the Stabinsky Steamer and threw open the passenger side door. Only to find herself staring down the barrel of a strange weapon.

"Charlotte?" Her name both a gasp and a sigh as he lowered his arm.

Quite satisfying. As was his damp collar and the limp cravat tucked into his waistcoat. Cravat. Waistcoat. Her lips twitched. Such were new sights. Sadly, they conspired to deprive her of what she knew to be a splendid view. The hollow of his throat. The strong flex and limber shift of muscles moving beneath shirtsleeves. All hidden by the trappings of civilization. How willingly had he donned so many layers?

Out West, he'd refused to wear such a noose. Or cut his hair. Or trim his beard. From top to bottom, he appeared a new man. Hell, there was even a shine to his shoes. Not that she was complaining. East Coast Ryan's polish was appealing, no matter the sheen of sweat on his brow. But for the miserable weather, she might have wished she wore a bustle and skirt.

Unbidden, old feelings clamored, demanding she unlock the corner of her heart where they'd been long-confined. Lust, in particular, flared to life—a flame flickering in the inky darkness reminding her of long-ago evenings that had held so much promise. But that was what came of lowering one's defenses. Best to keep the wall in place, the gate locked.

Fences were also useful. If, perhaps, not so very effective at keeping out the neighbor's oversized rodents.

"You'll catch flies with your mouth open like that." She pushed his wrist aside and climbed in. "I come bearing gifts." Shot glasses clinked as she uncapped the whiskey and poured. "Cheers." She touched her glass to his, then tossed back her drink. After a moment's hesitation, his movement mirrored her own.

Rain drops plopped, with heft and weight, upon the canvas roof. Lightning flashed—a brief moment of stark illumination followed by a crash of thunder. *Finally.* The cold front couldn't move through fast enough.

Such an expressive face, Ryan's. In a flash his visage might morph from amused laughter to ice cold command. The dark slash of his eyebrows would lower, and the light blue of his eyes would freeze. Laughter would fall away from his lips as they narrowed into focused concentration. It was a deeply disconcerting experience to witness, like watching mercury solidify and wondering if hell was about to freeze over.

He was also the most uncooperative man she'd ever met, which was saying something. And the most observant. You wanted him with you, not against you. Sneaking up on him was a near impossibility. Which was why Charlotte hadn't even tried.

But surprising him? Quite satisfying. And she decided she wasn't done yet. Grabbing his cravat, she yanked his mouth close, her kiss desperate and punishing, much like the bite of coffin varnish on his lips. How dare he raise her hopes of a future together, then abandon her when she'd needed him most? How dare she still miss him, miss the rough scratch of his beard against her skin, miss his company every single night the sun began to set on the horizon?

In a flash of movement, his hands gripped her hips and hauled her into his lap, deepening the kiss. Heat flooded her body, filling her with rising need and frustrated desire and—

He pulled away, his breath ragged. "When I returned to Cheyenne, you were gone."

She gasped as his teeth nipped at her neck, branding her skin with a heat that never failed to burn straight through to her soul. Impossible not to tip her head, to invite further attentions. "I left word with the doctor."

He lifted his head. "He had no message for me."

A gust of cool air slipped through the open window. Welcome relief, no matter how it struggled to slip through the woven cotton fibers of her blouse. *Boom. Flash.* The skies cracked open, and rain poured down, fast and furious.

She cursed the doctor. Had the hateful man deliberately sabotaged any future with Ryan? "Medical options are limited in a mining town. I decided my chances of a full recovery were better elsewhere." Gritting her teeth, she'd made arrangements, then took the next train out.

"Elsewhere?"

"San Francisco, the closest city." She lifted her leg to drop her booted heel upon the dashboard. "It's never been quite the same." Never could be. "My ankle."

"I should think not." His broad palm smoothed over the curve of her hip, found the placket of buttons that held the lower garment closed, toyed with them as had been his habit. "But how many can blame a stiff ankle on the sudden and unexpected weight of a large, carnivorous dinosaur?"

"Stiff?" She snorted. "Bit of an understatement, what with all the nuts and bolts and metal plates it took to shore up the fractured bones."

"You needed surgery?" He swallowed. "I had no idea it was that—"

"Bad? How could you?" Charlotte interrupted with the wave of a hand. Irrational of her to hold a grudge, especially now. A man couldn't be expected to follow a woman who'd disappeared into the sunset. "No matter, I've done fine on my own. I'm working at the Peabody Museum now." Bragging, perhaps, but her announcement elicited a satisfying level of wide-eyed awe.

Guarding her heart, her mind, was second nature. Rarely did she lower her defenses. In her experience, only family could be trusted. Not that they were much help, scattered as they were about the four corners of the globe. Risk falling in love? With a cryptobiologist who chased after imaginary creatures? Out of the question. An unacceptable risk. No matter that Ryan would always occupy a corner of her heart, such men were prone to sudden disappearances. Foolish of her, dreaming of more. A mistake she refused to make again. It had hurt too much when her world came crashing down.

Deep into an argument about the predatory capabilities of *Tyrannosaurus rex*, they'd snagged lanterns from the campsite and marched out to the dig site to point directly at the evidence while arguing their respective viewpoints. A perfect excuse to remove themselves from the company of others. Not that the bone hunters were under any illusion—given the eye rolls and head shakes that accompanied their departure—as to why the two of them wished to step beyond the light cast by the campfire, alone.

Ryan maintained that the giant lizard was no different from a snake or a monitor lizard, that the intramandibular joint would have been flexible, allowing the creature to hold tight any struggling prey. Charlotte, however, held fast to the conviction that only a stiff lower jaw could exert enough force to crunch directly through bone.

Scientific debate heated the air between them, to the point where, right or wrong, they played devil's advocate merely to prolong the dispute. Their lips had met, skin already on fire, a convenient blanket tucked into a grassy hollow not far away. A habit that offered them far more privacy than the thin walls of tents pitched closely together.

Not that they'd made it to the blanket that night.

As she'd reached with her knife to point at a particular angled bone, the ground rumbled and shook. Just enough warning for them to turn away, but not enough time to run.

The cliff above them crumbled, showering them with a cascade of rocks and dirt and dust. They'd escaped the worst of the landslide, but the terrible lizard's jaw had dislodged and landed on top of her ankle with the entirety of its mineralized weight.

Charlotte had fought back sharp tears of pain as Ryan carried her back to her tent. Sprained, it would be days before she could put any significant weight on her ankle.

With it wrapped and propped on a rock beside the campfire, he'd handed her a tin cup of whiskey, then set about hunting for a suitable stick to serve as a crutch. Which was the moment a man on a clockwork horse galloped into camp with news.

The light of the campfire had danced across Ryan's face as he listened to the rider's words. Never mind she couldn't hear what was said, the light that sparked in his eyes told her all she needed to know. He wasn't a bone hunter like her, not really, but a cryptozoologist. He'd come West hunting for hints of mythological creatures, of beasts long presumed dead that still roamed the wilderness, undetected. But out here a man had to earn his rice and beans, hence his work with a shovel and pick.

Face tight, he'd nodded, then crossed to her side. "Remember that old, abandoned mine I told you about?" His voice pitched low. "The short, shadowy figures and missing tools and unexplained banging?"

Her heart sank. She did indeed. Such was the bedrock of every real argument they'd ever had.

Were there strange creatures in the world? Certainly. But did all myths and fairytales surround a nugget of truth? She'd argued against, he'd argued in favor, the core of their disagreement centering around the existence of proof. Kraken and pteryformes and so on were well established and known species. Save cryptids were exactly that. Cryptic. Not yet proven to exist. Dinosaurs, on the other hand? Bone hunters were hauling them to museums by the hundreds.

"This is your chance to prove me wrong," she'd said, swallowing her irritation. "You need to go."

A frown had carved itself into his face. "Your ankle—"

"I'll manage." She always did. Out here, one did not admit to any weakness. Among such hard-boiled men, emotions were to be hidden lest they be exploited. Best not to examine or name the unhappy feelings that roiled and churned inside her chest. Besides, she knew something about grand dreams. She'd not be the one holding him back from the possibility of an amazing discovery even if she did think he stood a far greater chance of finding an untapped seam of gold. "Go."

"I hate leaving you here like this."

"But?" She'd raised an eyebrow at his pinched expression.

"There's talks of setting off a charge to collapse the shaft where the noises are coming from. If there's any chance of taking the creature alive..." Roughened palms had framed her face as he'd kissed her. "I'll be back by tomorrow evening."

"I'll be here." Still, out West, a sudden shift in circumstances or fortune could grind the best intentions to dust. Best not to make any promises.

With a final look of regret and longing, he'd mounted his own horse, pointed its nose toward the Black Hills and disappeared into the dark night.

Charlotte hadn't seen Ryan since. Shouldn't feel her pulse leaping and racing now that he'd reappeared. Ought not blow the dust off their past to begin again. Alas, she could not bring herself to walk away from this chance to breathe life back into their unfinished romance.

# CHAPTER THREE

"Did you find it?" Charlotte's gaze was firmly fixed upon her foot. Outside the rain poured down in sheets. "A Tommyknocker?"

He frowned. Doubts about the merits of his profession had threaded through many of their spirited discussions. Was she weighing the value of a cryptozoological find against the pain and suffering she must have endured to shore up her ankle? "Don't deflect. Metal screws in bone are no small thing. And that's ignoring risks of infection."

"It's neither here nor there," she answered. "Neither of us had any idea how badly it was damaged." A rueful smile tugged at her lips. "Let's leave it at 'attacked by a carnivorous dinosaur and lived to tell the tale'."

She'd done more than survive. Through the grapevine, he'd learned of her recent expedition into the Dakota Territory. That she'd wintered over, no less. He wasn't certain if he ought to be terrified or impressed by her persistence at all things paleontological. To this day, it baffled him how much effort was expended to acquire the fossilized bones of the ancient and extinct when extant wonders still walked this earth.

Yet he'd gone and fallen head over heels for a woman who'd constantly poked his cryptozoology arguments full of holes, forcing him to defend his position with logic, not pie in the sky hopes. Every message he'd sent, every inquiry he'd posed in an attempt to pin down her location had slipped through his fingers like sand. As soon as a reply arrived, she'd moved on—often beyond the reach of a simple telegram. Fate, merciless and unkind, thumbing its nose at every opportunity. Though he'd not given up, it was a twist of fate that brought them back together.

Now she was in his arms, her soft backside upon his lap. No corset bones caged her torso, no layers of gathered skirts or petticoats blunted the outline of her hips or legs. Nor were tonight's hat or hairpins fully up to the task of containing the beautiful twists of curls she so rarely set free. Every last inch of her contrived to tease forth provocative memories.

He fanned his fingers over the thin cotton of her blouse, felt the rise and fall of her chest beneath his palms. Not just his own breath quickened with anticipation. He swallowed back the beginnings of a groan, forcing his body to a guarded still-ness. Sparks still leapt between them, but were they enough to rekindle their past romance into something more lasting and permanent? He hoped so, for it was lowering to find himself envying the stray lamplight that dodged harsh raindrops to illu-minate the graceful arch of her eyebrows, the soft curve of her cheek, the inviting bow of her full lips.

*Inviting?* Ryan caught himself leaning forward and gave himself a mental slap. *Focus.*

He glanced out the car window through the driving rain. The house was silent, and traffic had dropped sharply. Only the few souls who had no choice were still out and about, the wheels of their carts and carriages splashing through muddy ruts.

No lights, no movement since a brief flurry of activity occurred in the backyard. An incident that had also caught Charlotte's notice. Had her arrival at the steam car drawn the attention of the occupants, silencing them out of an abundance of caution? Possibly. Not an optimal surveillance outcome. Then again, their enthusiastic reunion was as convincing a cover as they came.

"Who's deflecting?" Charlotte pinched him. Despite their kiss, her frown informed him he was not yet forgiven. "Set aside your guilt for the moment and tell me what was in that old mine."

*Ouch.*

"We found one," he answered. "But not alive."

"Really? How bitterly disappointing. And yet?" Her simple words were a nudge, an invitation to share every last fascinating detail. Interest and amusement and doubt danced in her wide, brown eyes.

"No one has ever been able to produce evidence that Knockers migrated to the United States with Cornish miners. Or with the Welsh as *Coblynau,* mischievous spirits of the coal mines."

Until his find, there'd been no physical proof of their existence at all. Anywhere. Merely stories and rumors and general superstition. The basis for many a campfire's debate.

"I remember."

Taking a deep breath, he pushed aside a niggle of irritation —now was not the time for a stale argument—and launched into the details of their discovery.

Deep in an abandoned mine shaft, the strange, misshapen corpse wore a tattered shirt and old-fashioned knickers with boots that just reached bony kneecaps. Seated on a short, three-legged milking stool, the cryptid was not far from a number of items reported missing by miners—both recent and from years past. In his hand, an old German beer stein decorated with lusty scenes, its contents drained, the faint scent of hops hanging in the stale air.

Of short stature and possessed of an elongated nose, pointed ears and overlong arms, the cryptid also wore a beard stretching past his knees. The white of his whiskers and the weathered face carved with deep wrinkles suggested a natural end to his lifespan, whatever that might have been. The deep disappointment lay in the Tommyknocker's humanoid form; Ryan remained convinced they were capable of speech, the creature's death nothing short of a tragedy.

Crushing though it had been not to find the cryptid alive, the discovery of the Knocker had been the making of Ryan's career, the hook on which he'd hung his hat, and validation that his years of study at Trinity had not been a waste of time or family funds. The Smithsonian Museum had been thrilled to accept his donation in exchange for a position within IBIS. To this day, the body remained under intense scrutiny.

A cryptozoologist could spout legend and lore until he was blue in the face, formulate hypotheses and write long academic tracts consuming vast sheaves of paper and an enormous quantity of ink, but such compositions were nothing more than inscribed nesting material for scholarly rats unless one could produce cold, hard data.

A point upon which he and Charlotte were in total agreement.

Kraken and pteryformes and even dragons—despite her expressions of doubt—were all valid and established lines of scientific inquiry. But creatures without a designated flesh and blood type specimen were considered unproven.

Which was all a long way of justifying why he'd not returned to her side the next day. "Finding a coffin and arranging for the Knocker's shipment took far longer than it should have. I didn't want to risk losing or damaging the only type specimen ever located. I'm so sorry I—"

Her fingers fell atop his mouth. "Look," she breathed. "A neighbor just stepped onto the porch. Hooded and caped, as always."

A tall, muscular figure paused to open an overlarge black umbrella. Ryan had severe doubts about the accessory's ability to protect its owner from a deluge that might just serve to float boats into low-lying parts of the city, but the man seemed committed. Perhaps it was a weapon in disguise? In Dublin, he'd learned not to trust the superficial appearance of parasols. Many contained blades hidden within. Why should an umbrella be any less deadly?

Charlotte slid from his lap back into the passenger seat, a

practical if disappointing move. "As you swore up and down you'd never return to New Haven, there must be some sinister plot brewing next door. Something to do with suspected cryptids. But I'll have you know that while I've witnessed plenty of strange, I can only report escaped chickens and mangled groundhogs."

*Mangled groundhogs?* More telling than she might think. It occurred to him they would serve as tasty morsels for a *cuélebre.*

"You've been watching them?" He glanced at her as he reached for the fuel handle and pulled, dropping coal into the burner. The water in the boiler was still hot—he'd been careful to maintain a low level of pressure in the event he needed to move with any speed.

"For weeks." Charlotte tossed him a grin. "Lucky you, to know their neighbor."

"Is that an invitation to conduct surveillance from inside your home?" Anticipation buzzed through his veins. A neighbor. And a partner. Perhaps even a romantic partner. What had he been thinking, wishing this assignment had fallen to another agent when the task before him had led him back to his long-lost love?

"Is *that* what we're calling it now?" She leaned back, crossed her arms. But a light danced in her eyes. "Depends."

"On?" A low hiss accompanied the turn of a knob. Steam seeping into the engine, raising the working pressure. They were prepared to follow the man at a discrete distance, swiftly if necessary.

"If you'll loop me in on whatever bizarre activities are going on inside that house."

Charlotte was already aware of Ryan's vocation, if not the specifics of his employment, so why not?

The Improbable Biologics Investigational Service frowned upon involving civilians in surveillance work as they preferred to maintain a low profile while pretending to be nothing more than Customs Agents. Their work was, on the whole, a tedious process of sifting through and verifying endless reports of odd and unusual creatures. Sinuous forms swimming in a river or a lake, wing spans so wide they blotted out the moon, a dark shape with one too many eyes living in a deep forest. Rarely did any leads pan out. More than once he'd referred an individual reporting cryptids to an optometrist and found the problem solved itself.

But not always. On rare occasions, IBIS agents unearthed marvels.

What they were chasing after here in New Haven, if anything, was unclear. And Charlotte's assistance, no matter the angle from which he examined it, was an asset. She was smart, capable, and determined. Not to mention the proximity of her residence to the individuals under investigation. More-over, she would cast doubt upon each finding, forcing him to meet exacting standards by sweeping aside any bias or wishful thinking.

Her job at the Peabody Museum might or might not prove an asset. He'd thought about consulting the anthropologists and zoologists therein but couldn't chance that one of them might have been the smuggler's customer. Impartiality and integrity were of the utmost importance. He'd heard back in the affirmative from an expert archaeologist with the Smithsonian who, even now, travelled north from Washington, D.C. on a train. The zoologist had cited other pressing responsibilities, leaving him a team member short. Charlotte's background in zoology was first-rate and he trusted her.

Who was he to reject this sudden windfall of good fortune?

A steam cart pulled down the street, pausing briefly before the house. The umbrella carrying man leapt onto the bench beside the driver, and the vehicle lurched back into motion.

"Agreed." He waited as their quarry passed a few wood frame buildings. When the cart turned the corner onto Jefferson Street, he pressed down upon the car's brake, releasing it. Wheels spun in the mud with a loud whirr, then caught hold, throwing them forward.

Charlotte braced herself on the dashboard, wide-eyed, as the steam car wobbled and jerked down the road. At her feet, shot glasses clinked against the whiskey bottle. "Have you operated a Stabinsky Steamer before?"

"Drove it here, did I not?"

Water streaked across the windshield, blurring his vision as the vehicle's wheels skidded around the corner. This model might be all the rage among society gentlemen and capable of great speeds, but it would never catch on in wider society. Not if rain threatened the safety of its occupants. It needed better tires and an automated, motorized device to whisk water from the front window.

"One cannot rent such a contrivance." She snorted.

"Chances you own a car at all approach zero, let alone one in New Haven. Does your brother know you stole his toy?"

"Stole?" He huffed a laugh. "That's a harsh assessment." A zig, a zag and they were on Chestnut Street, a consistent southward route that pointed them at the harbor. "But, yes. I expect by now he knows his shiny new set of wheels have escaped the safety and security of his carriage house."

And so very satisfying it was, snatching away his brother's newest toy to zip about the city, checking the addresses he'd decoded in the Spaniard's notebook after enduring a long, largely silent and judgmental dinner with his family. The only improvement from his last such meal being his father's absence.

His sister had sat, eyes downcast, seemingly unwilling to talk about the preparations for her upcoming wedding—a red flag in and of itself—and his grandmother had gloated, pleased as always to see the wayward grandson taken to task. All while his sister-in-law's expression grew increasingly pained as her husband posed one pointed, unpleasant question after another, followed by emphatic pronouncements about what Ryan ought and ought not do.

Why had Ryan not visited earlier, weeks ago, when he first sent word of Father's condition? Did he not realize the patriarch's time left on this earth was severely limited? That the responsibilities of managing the factory would soon fall to them? Ryan would be a co-owner of the Patrick Nolan Shoe Company and needed to behave accordingly. Plans must be made. His resignation tendered. Enough of this nonsense, running about the country chasing after myths and legends.

There were no polite answers. What he needed was time to speak with his brother privately, to inform Liam of the twisted branches grafted onto their family tree, to disabuse him of the notion that the man they called Father would ever leave the slightest fraction of the family business to Ryan, and to repeat, ad nauseam, that he was a cryptobiologist in the government's employ with no intention of focusing on shoe leather over pursuing any and all leads that hinted at the existence and/or location of dragons.

Only one thing about visiting his family this evening brought with it the slightest degree of happiness and satisfaction: passing the care and feeding of the hissing iguana into his nephew's hands. As predicted, his brother Liam had glared at Ryan with the heat of a furnace hot enough to smelt iron, silent and unable to bring himself to douse his son's delight.

Ryan had declined cigars and brandy, pleading exhaustion, and escaped to his bare and soulless room. From there, he'd employed the timeless technique of climbing from his window onto a low roof over the kitchen's entrance. He'd jumped to the ground before sneaking through the shadows to the old carriage house to make off with Liam's brand new, shiny Stabinsky Steamer.

The first address had led him to the home of Hobart Bigelow, owner of The National Pipe Bending Company. Nothing suspicious had leapt out at him, but the man's factory was located near the railroad—perfect for transporting illegal goods. Ryan would circle back later. The second address didn't exist—decidedly disreputable, but what could he do with such information? Nothing. Which had taken him to a third address on Lyon Street—all but depositing him upon Charlotte's doorstep. Her very presence redeemed everything New Haven had thrown at him this day.

She laughed, yanking him from his musings. It was a bright sound he'd missed far too much. "You'd best be chasing after a golden-egg laying goose. You'll need collateral for when you snap the axel of this steam car. Poor Liam," she teased. "What has he done to deserve such treatment?"

All these years, and she remembered everything he'd ever revealed about his family? A warmth filled his chest. Only with her had he ever risked sharing the details of his youth. He cast his mind back. What had he told her about his mother? Out West, walking the canyons together beneath the bright stars in the night sky, had he mentioned his parents' unhappy marriage, the infidelities that had set them at each other's throats making the lives of their children a misery? That after his mother's funeral, he'd headed left New Haven with plans to never return?

Most likely. Falling head over heels in love tended to loosen a man's tongue.

Even now, the final chapter of his family's saga was being written. Would there be more sordid details to share? Not unlikely, given his sister's apparent misery. Something he'd have to get to the bottom of before returning to Washington, D.C.

But back to Charlotte's question. Why *did* his brother possess such a fancy machine? The Stabinsky Steamer was an extreme luxury, even for a shoe baron. Was it Liam's receding hairline? The anticipation of adding yet another child to his burgeoning nursery? Or was its purchase simply a way to blow off steam—pun intended—under the pressure of escalating business responsibilities?

"Beyond being a self-righteous, sanctimonious killjoy? Nothing. At least, not yet."

He hadn't cared for the disapproving frown that etched itself into the corners of Liam's mouth beneath the curl-tipped ends of his waxed mustache as his brother mentioned his many contacts within New Haven's Customs House. If his brother thought to interfere, attempted to terminate Ryan's career... Well, it wouldn't work. But numerous pointed questions might disabuse the other agents that Ryan's investigation was anything other than bog standard.

The cart turned right on Greene Street, heading into his old neighborhood: Wooster Square. He followed but steered straight after the driver took a left onto Wooster Place, heading instead for Academy Street, the next road over that ran parallel, but on the far side of, the green-grassed square. Their quarry was wise to pass through the fashionable neighborhood, to take advantage of the numerous gas lamps that lined the park for a quick check to see if they had a tail.

Ryan would do the very same thing if he spotted an unfamiliar vehicle idling outside his home that then followed in a rainstorm—if he intended activities of a nefarious nature.

She snorted. "Afraid to pass by the family homestead?"

"Not at all," he lied. "Merely keeping the pursued from detecting their pursuers. A home field advantage maneuver, if you will."

Still, he glanced across the park to his family's home with

its bright squares of light. Windows that served as beacons, warning him away. But also a stark reminder that the price tag on this steam car was more than a year of his government salary. If the cart continued in the same direction it now headed, it would wind up at the docks. Possibly Long Wharf, a rough area of town where driving a Stabinsky Steamer was as good as sounding a foghorn to announce one's arrival. Not to mention Liam would gut him and drag him through the streets by his intestines if the steam car was damaged.

"Keep your eyes on the target." Ryan did his best to keep the sigh from his voice as he slowed the steam car down, pulling to the side. He flipped a lever, diverting the engine's source of propulsion. "But follow me. We're appropriating alternative transport." He threw open his door and raised his hand, hailing the driver of an old-fashioned, clockwork horse-drawn carriage.

"Timmy!" He swung up onto the high seat and dropped a heavy hand on the boy's shoulder. "I've need of this vehicle."

"Mr. Nolan!" Wide-eyed, the boy blinked. "But the O'Conners. I'm to fetch them from the theater."

"And so you will." Ryan flashed the gold of his Customs agent badge and pointed at the steam car, doing his best to ignore the rain soaking into the tweed of his cap and streaming down the side of his face. "That's an official order. Take my ride. Then return it to my brother."

"No way!" A bright smile stretched Timmy's face. "You want to trade this old heap for a Stabinsky Steamer? In this storm?"

Not in the least. "Quickly now!"

The boy leapt down and ran to the steam car as thunder boomed and lightning flashed across the sky.

"Are you insane?" Charlotte yelled as Ryan tugged her up to sit beside him. "Does he have the first idea how to operate that thing? Do the words 'electrical storm' mean nothing to you?" Soaked through, the thin white cotton of her blouse presented a captivating and contoured view of her skin. Regretfully, there was no time to enjoy it. He ripped his gaze away, tracking the progress of the steam cart around the square.

"He's a smart kid. He'll figure it out. The Stabinsky is too noticeable by half." He glanced overhead. "As to the storm, you need not ride beside me." He hooked his thumb over his shoulder. "There's room inside." The corner of his mouth kicked up before his next words slipped free, knowing they would ruffle her feathers. "Or you can stay behind."

She clamped her hat on even tighter and glared at him. "There's not a chance you'll be rid of me so easily this time."

He grinned, even though it made her narrow her eyes. Yep, still vexed about Wyoming. But it meant she still cared. A conversation for another time. "Hold tight!"

As the steam cart hooked a right onto Chapel Street, the passenger's face flashed white beneath the umbrella, scanning the square for moving traffic. Finding none, the muscled man turned face forward, his hand still white knuckling the handle of his accessory. Gun? Knife? Sword? Ryan hoped they'd not be finding out, but aware was prepared.

True to his predictions, the cart turned onto Brewery Street, a straight shot down to Water Street where an abundance of warehouses, docks and boat slips often hid all manner of misdeeds. It only remained to discover which vice was on tonight's agenda.

He pushed a lever, unlocking the horse's clockwork mechanisms, then tugged on the reins to resume the chase, thrilled to set off on another adventure with her by his side.

# CHAPTER FOUR

Charlotte tugged the broad rim of her Stetson lower. Not that it did a lot of good. Her white blouse clung to her skin, revealing far too much, but the split skirt meant the pounding rain wouldn't turn the garment into an impediment should they need to leap from the carriage. At least it cooled her down. Only with Ryan would she embark upon such madness, agree to sit upon the driver's perch in the middle of a thunderstorm, held aloft and exposed to the elements while racing down muddy, waterlogged streets.

But for the screeching of a deranged chicken, she would—even now—be detailing the intricacies of feather impressions left behind in sandstone formed from long ago coastal sediments deposited at the edge of a large, shallow Cretaceous sea. An activity that was of far more value in furthering her career than chasing after shifty neighbors with no notion of their proposed wrongdoing save that Ryan's appearance meant a cryptid was involved. Or had at least been mentioned.

Vaguely. Possibly in the back corner of a dark pub under the heavy influence of alcohol. Such was enough to trigger a quest.

Paleontologists rolled their eyes at this kind of behavior. Not so your average cryptozoologist. They sought adventure and discovery in a manner forever at odds with paleontology. If anything, sneers accompanied the very thought of working with incomplete skeletons, unknowable physiology and not the slightest chance at understanding the habits or social structures of a petrified, bygone era.

Disinclined to conceit, Ryan was an anomaly among his own kind. Though he'd traveled to the West to hunt living curiosities, he'd been happy to work in the dinosaur boneyards learning all he could, convinced that a solid understanding of the past might hold clues to predicting what future forms might emerge from the shadows. After all, what were the pteryformes or kraken but atavistic throwbacks?

No so, she'd argued. Of the kraken, she knew little save they tended to clog brackish waterways and rather diminished the appeal of seaside bathing. But pterosaurs, the flying dinosaurs of yore? Those she'd studied in painstaking detail. The court of popular opinion might have convinced most that the fossilized winged creatures were closely related to the pteryformes that soared through European skies due to the number of superficial features they shared, but not her.

Both pterosaurs and pteryformes possessed an elongated fourth digit on their forearm that supported a wide membrane stretching from hand to hindlimb, true. But pteryformes were in possession of five digits on their hindlimbs—a feature never —not even once—found in the fossil record of the pterodactyloids. Evolution tended toward digit loss, not gain. Moreover, when comparing their skeletal structures bone by bone, numerous other characteristics proved non-homologous. Therefore, she maintained that the European pteryformes deserved their own branch on the tree of life as a new, emergent species, first documented in the scientific literature in 1756 soaring above the fjords of Norway.

Such was only one of many topics she and Ryan had argued about. Endlessly. Hour after hour. Like opposite poles of magnets, they'd been pulled into each other's orbit, circling ever closer as perpetual pedagogical discourse drove others away. Until, one day, professional crossed the line into personal and a moonlit quarrel over the function of the three horns and frill of the triceratops skull ended in a heated kiss, forever altering the trajectory of their relationship.

Which was why, for all her dedication to the unchanging certainty the geologic record provided, she now sat in the driving rain beside the one man whose very presence seemed to erase all logical thought from her brain. Everything dry, dusty, and academic forgotten as she dug her fingers into the edge of her seat, grinning as he took the corner on two wheels. Threat of death by sudden electrocution aside, there was nowhere else she'd rather be. Or with. She welcomed this temporary insanity with open arms for it made her feel alive.

Water gushed from the gutters of ever-larger and evermore commercial buildings as they approached the harbor and its profusion of wharfs. "What—and be very precise—" she shouted over the rattle and clank of unbalanced wheel rims, clomping steel hooves, and driving rain, "do you know about my neighbors?"

"That their address, alongside two others, was recorded in a known smuggler's notebook." He downshifted the horse, slowing as they neared Water Street, hanging back. The steam cart clipped steadily on in a southward direction past the lumber yards, along a road that edged New Haven Harbor.

"And this smuggler refuses to cooperate?"

"He's dead. Murdered by a thief who leapt from a hotel window and escaped with an overlarge satchel in her possession."

"Her?" Charlotte blinked. "The thief?"

Ryan nodded and out spilled a bizarre story that began with the suspected transport of a *cuélebre* specimen—some kind of mythological dragon recorded in the myths and fables of northern Celtic Spain—and ended with an assortment of Mexican goods, a dead smuggler with a curious worm in his eye, a murderess, and a hallucinating woman of some local notoriety.

"And this woman, Rose, can shed no light on what happened?" Why did that name sound familiar? And significant?

"Her physician promised to send word when she wakes, hopefully with a sound and clear mind. Meanwhile, though it's unlikely to help my case, an autopsy has been arranged for tomorrow morning." He shrugged. "Until then, I search for suspects with no clear idea of what exactly was stolen or what to expect, other than nefarious activities involving illegally imported materials."

"That's it?" she yelled through the driving rain. "That's all you have to go on?"

"That's all."

It never failed to impress her how Ryan would chase after the slimmest of clues. "If the people at those addresses paid for and received an item your smuggler brought onto our shores," Charlotte observed, "one would presume they were satisfied customers, disinclined to theft and murder."

"Correct."

"What of the other addresses?"

"One belongs to a seemingly upstanding citizen, a wealthy individual known to buy the occasional antiquity. Tomorrow a proper Customs agent will pay him a visit, for all the good it will do. The second address does not exist. Your neighbors are the third and, as yet, the most suspicious. Not that I can justify raiding their house. Yet." He slid a glance at her. "Unless you can shed incriminating light on your neighbors' activities?"

"They keep to themselves, maintain a private aviary. Receive many deliveries, rarely go out. I could only identify the cook, the woman who chased after that chicken as it made a break for freedom." Her brow furrowed as she thought of Glory's recent outdoor recreation. "They're up to something, though. An alarming number of damaged groundhogs have squeezed beneath the fence of late." She rolled her eyes. "Don't give me that look. They can't possibly be hiding a live *cuélebre* on that property. There is simply not enough room."

*Was there?* No. Absolutely not. So why did doubt flutter in her stomach?

Ryan did not overtly disagree, but his silence meant he wasn't yet ready to rule it out.

"Their backyard is a tangle of wild vegetation," she elaborated. "Perhaps a hawk of limited skill has claimed the space as a hunting ground? Regardless, my yard is no sanctuary. Glory puts them out of their misery, if not always swiftly, leaving me to deal with the aftermath."

"If you've a dog hunting on your behalf, why not turn them into groundhog stew?" The corner of his mouth kicked up at the memory of past campfire meals. "Cook was a dab hand at turning all those prairie dogs into dinner."

"Cook?" She laughed, clamping a hand atop her hat to keep it in place as storm winds picked up closer to the water. "During a heat wave? Not a chance. No matter the sad eyes when I reject her offerings."

They rumbled across railroad tracks, heading further south toward Long Wharf, a non-residential, non-genteel section of New Haven Harbor. A constant influx of silt dumped into the bay by the Mill and Quinnipiac Rivers motivated the continuous extension of the exceedingly long wharf ever further out into the harbor in search of deep water—a feature that appealed to ocean-going ships as well as large freight dirigibles by way of providing open sky. Along its length stretched an array of utilitarian buildings. Warehouses filled with building supplies. Others held livestock, wholesale butchers and a meat packing plant.

It was onto this wharf—and into wet gusts that snapped across Long Island Sound whipping up white-capped waves—that Ryan steered their carriage. Ahead, the steam cart stopped in front of the offices for Sperry, Barnes and Bass, a meat packing plant. The enormous structure was comprised of several buildings of various designs and sizes, each stuck to the last as the company expanded.

But before they reached that hulking pile of brick, Ryan pulled the clockwork horse into a hard right turn and came to a sudden stop between a shed and a roofing company, mercifully cutting off the howling wind.

"We'll take the rest of this on foot. Still with me?"

"You need to ask?" She elbowed him in the ribs. The only parts of her still dry were the crown of her head and the tips of her toes. "You think I'll stay behind? Not a chance. I want to know what's going on next door as much as you."

Ryan leapt from his seat onto the dock and held up a hand, offering assistance. She accepted, grateful when her feet skidded across the saturated old wood.

The storm had put pause to the unloading of cargo ships and dirigibles. All transport vessels were quiet, dark shadowy hulks with nothing but a few lamps swaying in the wind to mark their location. All save one. At the very end of Long Wharf, there was a stir of activity surrounding a single rough-looking airship. A captain intent upon unloading cargo in this weather? Unusual.

A number of men in waxed canvas coats fought the wind and rain, cranking the numerous winches necessary to secure a large freight dirigible to the end of the dock, to anchor it firmly in place. Others worked to extend a long, ridged ramp from the belly of the dirigible's gondola.

Here, nearer to solid, if not dry land, bright lights and

raucous sounds emanated from a dilapidated warehouse turned temporary shoreside bar. Sailors had abandoned their ships—however temporarily—to pass the night carousing with loose women who appeared equally enthusiastic to drink and make merry, if only to relieve the sailors of their pay. A few cast curious eyes in their direction.

Annoyance prickled under her skin. She braced for the usual unwelcome and suggestive comments, readying to fend them off. By force if necessary—her fingers itched to pull the knife hidden in her boot. Ryan pointedly slung an arm about her shoulder, drawing her close, marking her as his. His proximity was welcome, if not the need for male protection. The eyes slid away.

"We'll hug the buildings, try to draw close enough to hear —or at least see—what brings our man here on such a miserable night."

Together, they eased past warehouses, moving beneath the overhang of roofs, all while keeping a close eye on dock activity.

The man with the umbrella stood beside the steam cart outside the offices for Sperry, Barnes and Bass, staring expectantly at the hustle and bustle on the dirigible as the ramp was lashed to the dock.

As he'd arrived with a vehicle designed to haul crates, it was unlikely he waited for a passenger. The sleek and polished luxury dirigibles that carried the elite up and down the eastern seaboard rarely moored in New Haven. Those lines traveled between Washington D.C., Philadelphia, New York City and Boston. Smaller, individual Cormorant Class airships tethered to the docks along Water Street adjacent to Harborside Park where there was a small but thriving industry that catered to those wishing for private coastal air travel of short distances.

No, this stretch of New Haven Harbor was for freight of the bulky, dirty, and noisy variety—not fine goods. Which didn't mean the shipment wasn't a precious or perishable commodity.

With the meat packing plant at their backs, Charlotte expected a herd of cattle or a drove of pigs to emerge. But why would her neighbor slink through the night in a storm, checking over his shoulder for a tail, if he was merely here to pick up Sunday's roast?

"If he goes inside," Ryan began, "there's a door just past the icehouse that doesn't latch right. From there, we can follow a somewhat gruesome path through connecting doors to reach the offices. I know the perfect location to eavesdrop."

She raised an eyebrow. "Should I ask how you know that?"

His answering grin was a touch wicked. "It wasn't only dragons that caught my childhood imagination. By a certain age, the possibility of mermaids held appeal. And a rumor ran about that one had been captured and imprisoned in a tank on Long Wharf..."

"And you just had to see for yourself." A laugh escaped her lips imagining Ryan as the young trouble-making imp he must have been.

"Sadly, nothing but a rumor." A spark danced in his eyes. "As were reports of a sea serpent. But the deep-sea kraken they dragged in once was a sight to behold. Thirty-foot-long tentacles and—"

She held up a hand, shuddering. "Stop. Please. The contents of the ocean are off-putting enough already. Ignorance is bliss."

"Ignorance? You left that back at the carriage." His head shook with mock sympathy. "There's no way for me to lead you through with your eyes closed."

"Ugh. Such stomach-churning aspects of your career remind me why I prefer dry fossils and delicate feathers." Yet his presence alone was a siren's song and there was no denying her fascination with either the man or his career.

As angry black thunderclouds scudded away to the east, the rain slowed to a drizzle. A loud clang at the top of the ramp sounded and the hatch in the dirigible's hull slid open. Someone opened the door to the meat packing plant, revealing a barn-sized interior room. A whistle pierced the air, and the sailors stood back from the dirigible's door, clearing a pathway along the wharf.

A raucous squawking and stomping and hissing accompanied the appearance of large, wild eyes set in tiny heads that bobbled on the end of sinuous necks. A sailor used a long hook to throw open a metal gate, and an enormous bird burst forth.

A man rode on its back, legs cinched about the round bulk of its feathery form, hands dug deep into plumage. For all that it appeared a rather precarious position, the rider knew his business as—without saddle or reins—he steered the giant biped down the ramp and across the wharf, pointing the over-sized fowl in the direction of the open warehouse door.

Thundering close behind was an entire flock of the crea-tures. Hundreds of them all hissing and flapping their undersized wings as they stormed into the barn and into what Charlotte could only assume was certain doom. The door slammed shut behind the birds, muffling their cacophony and sealing their fate.

"Why would anyone go through all the trouble to import ostriches all the way from Africa?"

"They're an exotic delicacy," Ryan answered. "About one-hundred and ten pounds per bird. Each ounce sold at a premium price. Imagine the display a whole bird would make atop a table. Quite the social statement to serve at your dinner party."

"The wealthy have no shame." She shook her head, then snorted. "Imagine the hostess sporting a gown trimmed in their feathers, no matter their common color, while bragging about the meal they hauled in from distant lands."

But their target still stood beside his cart—a live ostrich not on his agenda. He waited patiently in the light rain, until a dockworker pushing a handcart emerged from within the gondola. The umbrella man lifted a hand, hailing the worker who made his way slowly and carefully down the metal ramp transporting three stacked crates as if they contained hand-blown Venetian glass. Boring. Dull. Routine. Then, just before the second crate was loaded into the back of the steam wagon, a man in a dark coat burst from the office door, waving a clipboard and shouting. His words lost to them on the wind.

The umbrella man launched a counter argument, gesturing to the cart. The office man shook his head. More heated words she couldn't make out were exchanged, then together they stomped off inside the building.

"Follow me," Ryan hissed. He turned, leading them around to the back of the warehouse. They passed between a pile of coal and a line of smoke houses to reach a low window. "Broken latch," he breathed, lifting the sash, cringing at the loud creak of protest from its wooden framing. "Been a while." He climbed in first, then pulled her in behind him.

The gruesome path he led her along was strewn with offal, hooves, hunks of what might be cold fat and, given the metallic smell of blood that assaulted her nose, the dark stain upon the floor could be nothing other than that. And she didn't wish to contemplate what filled the various cloth-covered buckets that lined one corridor. Ought she be grateful for what the low light level hid or worried about what it failed to reveal?

Thankfully, the twists and turns soon stopped. On the other hand, they'd come to a halt inside a cold storage room, one that was far from empty. Carcasses, both whole and in parts and pieces, hung from hooks alongside links of sausages were cast in disturbing shadow and reframed her earlier queasiness about disposing of a single groundhog. Meat was off the menu, at least for the foreseeable future.

Swallowing back the bile that rose into her throat, she crouched, joining Ryan as he bent an ear to the narrow crack of an ever-so-slightly open door, stealing occasional glances across a hallway and into an office that was near-to-bursting from the paper crammed within its limited walls. Documents of all kinds—contracts, invoices, bills of lading—littered every surface, many in towering stacks that could topple at any moment.

"...paid in full."

"Unacceptable." The umbrella man coughed into his hand, cleared his throat, and continued. "The price was agreed upon prior to shipment."

"Costs have increased," the office manager insisted from behind his overloaded desk. "There was a storm off the coast of Africa. A bad one."

"Your company's failure to provide sufficient packing material to ensure that fragile objects shipped long-distance and internationally arrived undamaged is not my responsibility. Weather is inherently unreliable. The contract makes no mention of an allowance for additional fees. The agreement was for immediate delivery. All three crates go with me. Now."

"Two of the three," he countered. "The third crate of ostrich eggs stays here until—"

"Unacceptable. They are required *now*. The delay caused by the storm might mean many are already past the point of usefulness." Umbrella man slapped his hands upon stacks of papers to lean forward. When he spoke again, his voice was low and foreboding. "Do *not* make me send Maria to renegotiate."

There was an audible gulp. "Fine. Take all three." Then the man apparently remembered he was a vertebrate. "But that fulfills our contract." He stomped past umbrella man, heading for the docks. "If she wishes to purchase any more eggs from our on-shore brood, the price has doubled."

"Nothing short of a miracle would make them lay under such conditions such as these." Umbrella man sniffed. As he turned to exit, Ryan tugged her away from the door and into the shadows.

A distant door slammed.

"Ostrich eggs?" she whispered. Imported from Africa with special intent. But for what reason? Consumption?

"*Fresh* ostrich eggs." A grumpy annoyance twisted Ryan's lips. He'd hoped for much more nefarious. "After all, who would wish to eat rotten eggs? It appears we've been on a goose chase that led to birds of a larger size. I'll check with Customs tomorrow, see if it's all above board."

As they left the slaughterhouse, climbed into the carriage, and commenced the drive back to New Haven proper, Charlotte's mind refused to let go of the puzzle. Could all the next-door nonsense be nothing more than a small band of odd individuals attempting to establish a rare foods company catering to the strange, inexplicable desires of the wealthy to eat the exotic?

If the eggs were fertile, did that mean they intended to set up a breeding colony? On their property in New Haven? She pondered the noise, the smell, the upkeep. The lot size. No. Not inside city limits. Or, at least, not for long. Mature animals would need to be housed elsewhere. The aviary wasn't large enough, but it might serve as a nursery. And the need for an incubator could explain the plumes of smoke pouring from their chimney in midst of summer.

If so, she expected there would soon be more than feral chickens bursting from the kitchen door into the yard. Entertaining at first, perhaps, watching them attempt to wrangle juvenile ostriches, but the smell and noise would overwhelm. On the other hand, ostriches were omnivores, known to eat snakes, lizards and small rodents in addition to roots and seeds.

Perhaps they might also be coaxed to put an end to her groundhog problem?

She glanced at Ryan beside her and, though drenched and drained by the evening's events, she tipped her head back and laughed. He was a man who would leave no stone unturned, no matter what crawled out from underneath. The days before them might be a wild ride, but one way or another, there would be answers.

# CHAPTER FIVE

Returning late last night, he'd slipped through the front door and crept up the stairs, shoes in hand, confident that the rasp, whistle, and wheeze of the patriarch's breathing machine would cover any sound of his ascent. He wanted nothing more than to peel off wet clothing and crawl between crisp sheets where he could contemplate the confusion of today's events in peace and quiet.

But there was no escaping a determined sister who laid in wait. When he misjudged his step by one stair, the creak of a board gave him away. A moment later, she emerged from a faint glow of lamplight seeping from Father's room.

"You never answered my letters." His sister's voice issued a hushed reprimand. "Not one. Captain Donovan, is he my father as well?"

Why this mattered to her after all these years, he could not fathom.

Regardless, he'd accepted the inevitability of this most

uncomfortable conversation. During dinner, he'd stared at her across the table, knowing she'd demand a response. He'd cataloged each of her features in turn and, still, he could find no one character trait that would mark her clearly as a Donovan. Nor was there one that screamed Nolan. Not the slightest of hints existed.

Truthfully, Ryan himself didn't know for certain that the affair between their mother and Captain Donovan was responsible for his own birth. His pitch-black hair was an anomaly among his relatives, but not unprecedented.

All he had was his dying mother's word.

Ryan heaved a put-upon sigh. "It's impossible to know. On Mother's deathbed, she admitted to the affair, urged me to speak with Captain Donovan, to accept his offer to pay for my education."

The man had been famous for his global travels, for the collection of oddities he'd hauled home. Ryan had sought the airship captain out when he was a young boy, curious to learn if the captain had ever encountered a dragon, if it was true he possessed a dragon claw and a handful of fireproof scales. Alas, though no such items existed inside the captain's home, there had been many other treasures to pour over. And he'd found a mentor. For years, the captain had quenched Ryan's thirst for all things cryptid by handing him artifacts of dubious origin, regaling him with stories and providing him with books addressing fact and fiction, myth and lore.

When Trinity's acceptance arrived, he'd proudly taken the letter to his father—where it was met with scorn and derision. Studying cryptids, he'd been informed, was a ridiculous waste of time. When secondary school ended, Ryan was to start work in the shoe business full time. Immediately.

Without funds, he could not hope to attend Trinity.

Then Mother's dying revelation shifted the very earth beneath his feet.

In the ensuing argument, his enraged father informed him that, should he honor his mother's wishes, he would be cut off, unwelcome to set foot across the Nolan threshold forevermore. In turn, Ryan countered that he would be attending Trinity regardless of his orders, that it only remained to be determined who would pay for his education. Incensed, Father had written a bank check with the understanding the matter was to be swept beneath the parlor rug and never spoken of again.

"But you didn't. Father stopped you." Ellen blushed a furious red as she addressed the eight-hundred-pound elephant in the room. "I was born after you. And now the captain's dead."

"So you were and he is."

"Then it follows I too might be Captain Donovan's daughter." She glanced over her shoulder at the slumbering form of her maybe-father who dragged each rasping breath into his chest only with great effort and force. It was a testament to the tenacity of the patriarch's autonomic system that it refused to concede defeat, even in the face of fluid-filled and tumor-ridden lungs engendered by decades of tobacco use.

"There's no way to know if Father abandoned his marital rights after my birth or tightened the noose about Mother's throat to ensure no further infidelities occurred." Ryan was in no mood to mince words. "Save to ask him."

"I can't possibly!" The words emerged on a horrified gasp. "But Grandmother seems to suspect it and won't let me take the parlor clock to my new home. She's ruining my wedding!"

He held up his hand. "What does it matter, Princess Slipper?" Her lips pursed and he immediately regretted his quip. Daughter of a wealthy shoe factory owner, the hated nickname had been assigned to her against her will. "Purchase a new clock. After all, you'll soon be married and free of their oversight."

"And squashed like a bug beneath another man's thumb." Vexed and indignant, Ellen spun on her heel and stomped back into Father's room.

He blinked, uncomfortable with her parting shot. Had Grandmother been holding a grudge against her dead daughter-in-law, heaping disgrace upon a young woman who might not be her granddaughter, thereby twisting what ought to be a celebration into a tortured affair?

He released a long, slow sigh. It was entirely possible. But this conversation was best saved for daylight, for when he was rested and better able to address the past with cool-headed rationality. The small hours of the morning were not the time to dive into the convoluted logic of local gossip.

Not with a murderess on the loose and the possible whereabouts of a *cuélebre* in unscrupulous hands.

He made it three steps toward his bed before he was captured by yet another family member. Old as she was, his grandmother's grip about his wrist was still strong, no matter its tremor. Her other hand clutched a silver, enameled pill box. What did the old dragon dose herself with to maintain such strength? Asiatic black bear bile? And how long had she stood there hidden in dark shadows, listening and volunteering nothing?

"You forfeited your place in this family years ago," she hissed. "Do not interfere. Better to take up with that enterprising Rose girl again." An evil light glowed in her dark eyes. "She inherited that house of your father's, 48 Greene Street, when he died last year. Yet doesn't live there with her husband. Smart lass, not daring to claim a spot in local society. To remind everyone of her past. You should follow suit."

Captain Donovan had willed his Wooster Square house to Rose? *To Rose. To his mistress.* Ryan struggled to keep the shock from his face. Upon his death, the airship captain had left her valuable property. But hadn't seen fit to offer for her hand in marriage after he'd publicly disgraced her? His opinion of the man, already at rock bottom, started digging a hole.

He refused to appeal to his grandmother for clarification, for so much as a single detail. Gossips were a dime a dozen in this neighborhood. He'd find someone else to ask how, exactly, Captain Donovan and Rose tumbled into an affair and how long it had lasted. Not because he cared about their relationship. He only needed to know if the connection had introduced Rose to smugglers such as Francisco Alcantra. Perhaps, he'd even manage to uncover whatever whispers were being spread about Ellen.

"Liam disagrees with you about my place here." He yanked his arm free. "Legalities aside, he'll offer me half the business." Not that he wanted it. Or would accept it. He only wished to watch the old woman twist on the hook. Unkind? Very much so. But she'd made his childhood a misery. If his words left her with a case of indigestion, so much the better.

Her wrinkled face contorted with impotent anger. "Then I expect your attendance at the funeral and your sister's wedding."

"My sister's wedding? Most definitely. As to my father, he died a year ago. Any deference I owe your son centers around his past financial support, much of it coerced."

With that, he turned and walked away, shutting his door, attempting to push aside the mental grumbles time with his family generated that he might focus on his assigned case.

He'd spent half the night on his narrow childhood bed wide awake, staring out the window through threadbare curtains at the moon. Some of his thoughts strayed to the past, to Rose and the captain. Mostly he thought about Charlotte, contemplating "if only". If only they'd not argued over the jaw structure of a *Tyrannosaurus rex*, if only there'd not been a landslide, if only his partner hadn't discovered the Tommy-knocker. Round and round his mind went, turning their interrupted romance upside-down and inside-out as if the past could somehow be altered.

Not that the past prevented them from shaping a new future. Together. Would such a possibility interest her? Their steamy kiss indicated it just might. The corner of his mouth kicked up as he recalled her abrupt and bold re-entry into his life.

The activities of her neighbor's house were disquieting. Secretive behaviors. Deliveries. Yet never any visitors or outbound shipments. Fresh ostrich eggs. The umbrella man's insistence on collecting the shipment that very night struck Ryan as extremely odd. If plans were to incubate the eggs, to hatch and raise ostrich chicks with the intent to establish a colony to satisfy the desires of the socially elite to eat their way around the globe, why not simply purchase a breeding pair of birds?

Morning finally arrived and, grateful to escape his youthful prison, he dressed, ran a comb through his hair, and stepped out the front door onto Wooster Square. After last night's storm, the weather was cool and clear—even though the bright sun promised a rising heat that would have men tugging at their neckcloths by midafternoon. He crossed the square on a direct path to Olive Street. By now it ought to be possible to speak coherently with the survivor of a certain deadly tea party.

He hoped a sober version of Rose would remember the specifics of a murderess with whom she'd sat down to take tea. His only worry was that she and Francisco Alcantra had begun to sip at the peyote tea before their guest joined them, that her mind had already been muddled before the woman arrived.

En route, he tipped his hat and nodded tightly to familiar faces, but refused to slow his steps, not even as he passed a particular stately brick house with a mansard roof. There, he'd spent many happy hours in the library, pouring over books detailing the rise of emergent species, absorbing the various hypotheses surrounding the possible shared relation-ships of kraken and squid. Of living pteryformes to the pterodactyls, extinct flying dinosaurs. Of dragons to the overlarge lizards reported to roam the islands of the Dutch East Indies.

Only to have his friendship with Captain Donovan arrive at a sudden and crashing end. Not only because of his mother's deathbed revelation but because his intended bride, Rose O'Donnell, was seen sneaking away from the very same man's personal stateroom at dawn. Scandal erupted. Rose refused to speak with him. And Ryan, upon learning the captain had departed upon his dirigible for an unknown location without any attempt to provide an explanation, had accepted his legal father's terms. Trinity, on the other side of an ocean, far from family and his former fiancé, had been a welcome escape.

He rounded a corner onto Olive Street, jogged up the steps to her door and knocked. The door opened and he found himself face to face with her steam butler.

"Agent Nolan here to speak with—" Only then did he realize he'd failed to learn her married name. "Er. Rose."

Wiry eyebrows rose. Programmed disapproval, Ryan reminded himself, refusing to allow the machine's expression to disconcert him. If anyone was to suffer embarrassment for improper behavior, it ought be Rose herself.

"He's expected!" she called from a nearby room.

"This way, sir." The steambot turned and rolled a short distance, leading him to a well-appointed parlor.

Though dressed in a loose morning gown of buttercup yellow with her hair pinned into a tasteful upsweep, she was anything but the picture of health. Purple crescents arced beneath her eyes and there was a sallow cast to her skin.

"I see no sense in standing upon formalities, given the

bond we share." She sat before a table, cradling a mug in her hands. "Wouldn't you agree?"

*Bond?* The tangle of their former lives was not a topic he cared to discuss. "I would not. Our past relationship is of no consequence."

"Is that so?" She frowned. "Very well. Coffee?"

A silver carafe and cup—complete with mustache protector—awaited him upon a table.

He raised an eyebrow.

Her lips pushed together into a pout. "There was a time when you were overly proud of the waxed and curled hair that graced your upper lip. I presumed. Honestly, there's not much about yesterday I recall."

Lie or truth? He'd long since favored a more trimmed appearance. Was this her way of claiming drug-induced amnesia? Not the best beginning to an interview. "Yet you remember my presence at the Sea View Hotel?"

Offense twisted her expression. "It's hard to forget the man you once pledged to marry."

This again? He stiffened, hoping her statement wasn't the harbinger of an offer to resume their prior relationship, this time on an intimate level. How could Rose imagine she held any personal appeal to him at all? Only yesterday, he'd scraped her off another man's floor as she recited nursery rhymes. And long before that, she'd hurled herself into scandalous turmoil. They were far past resuming any kind of romance.

Not that she seemed to have flirtation on the mind. A regretful smile flitted about the edges of her lips, but failed to gain sufficient ground. She made no physical advances, uttered no suggestive words. He ought to be relieved. Save there was something wistful and slightly downcast about her demeanor. Was she looking for a shoulder to cry upon? A hero to rescue her? Such was not a role he intended to play.

He was here for a civil conversation, as a special agent of the US government to interview a person of interest. Such was the only reason he would ever voluntarily spend time alone with Rose.

"Mmm." He exhaled slowly, then met her gaze. "We both made mistakes. But I'm here to discuss your more recent ones. Let's begin with your married name."

"Mrs. Enzo Rodríguez," she answered, rolling the "R" along with her eyes for emphasis.

He lifted an eyebrow. A husband chosen from outside the tight circle of those who could claim—at least in small part—Irish ancestry? For all her love of walking alongside the docks, flirting with men of any and all nationalities, he had fully expected her to settle down and tow the line. To do whatever was necessary to be brought back into the safe and wealthy Wooster Square fold.

"Wipe away that look of pity," she said, setting her mug down with a thud. "After the incident and your precipitous departure, my options were limited. Rumors and speculation were fast spiraling out of control. My father strong-armed a few men into proposing. None of them prosperous or even well-off." She tossed her hands in the air. "Scrawny. Poor. Possessed of an intractable stutter or a twisted leg. All of them damaged goods."

Precipitous? He ignored the attempt to cast any blame

upon him. "We were speaking of your husband. Not the past." A pointed effort to set the interview back on track.

"Him?" Her lips twisted. "Bait and switch." She gulped down coffee, dropped the mug onto the table with a thud. "A Spaniard from a wealthy shipping family offered for my hand. I'm led to believe their fortune was founded in ironworks. Visits to a fourteenth century castle in Asturias were dangled. I was as eager to escape New Haven as you. Of course I accepted. I leapt at the chance to start a new life. Elsewhere." She slumped back in her chair. "Yet here I sit. Still here. Enzo works all the time, leaving me to rattle about this house. Alone. I'm a pariah in these parts."

Yes, given such details, she would be. Made ever so much worse by what he presumed was frequent indiscreet behavior unbefitting a lady. But suffering her recitation of woes had borne fruit. A Spanish husband. A Spanish smuggler. And a Spanish castle in the very region from whence tales of the *cuélebre* originated.

*Finally*, a possible lead.

"And Francisco Alcantra?" A gentle nudge of encouragement. He needed her to speak the words aloud, though he could almost write the script that followed.

"Occasionally works—worked—for my husband." A sad smile crept onto her lips. "Cisco's outlandish behavior was... refreshing. His imports..."

"Intoxicating?" he prompted, scanning the room. Alas, all decorations conformed to local standards and possessed not a whiff of illegal Spanish imports.

Sighing, Rose slid ever lower in her chair. "I've become the very cliché of the society wives I once mocked."

Ryan's patience was fast evaporating. What she did or did not do to set her marital situation to rights was not his affair. "Tell me about the woman who joined you for... tea."

"She wore black." Her lip curled into a sneer. "And pants."

"Do you know her name?" His voice grew rougher as it dropped, fast approaching an outright growl. "What did she want?"

Rose frowned. Then pushed herself upright. "Things."

"Spanish things?" he demanded. "Mexican things? What *things* specifically?"

"*More* things." Her shoulder hitched upward, dismissive yet defensive. "Things at a better price. I wasn't paying that much attention." Chin jutting out, she looked away, studying the rug with interest.

She was deliberately obfuscating. What wasn't she telling him?

"I need to know, Rose." He reached into his coat pocket and withdrew his badge, smacked gold metal upon the table to reflect the morning sunlight.

Her jaw dropped. "You're..."

"A special agent of the Unites States Customs Service. Francisco Alcantra was under investigation. Now he's dead. His killer is on the run and in possession of items which may be of particular interest."

"A government agent?" She tipped her head. "How very sad. And here I'd hoped your visit was to be a friendly one, full of exciting tales from abroad. Perhaps one of which might involve an account of successful dragon hunts."

"Spanish dragons?"

"Are there such creatures? I've yet to see evidence." Her gaze lowered to fall upon his cup. "I'm afraid your coffee has grown cold. I'd invite you to stay longer, to reminisce, but—"

"Enough of these deflections, Rose. If you can't answer my questions, I'll need to speak with your husband."

"Impossible." She frowned. "He's away on business."

"And you expect him back when?"

She stood, smoothed her skirts. "Impossible to say." Her voice was frosty, all pretense of friendliness gone. "If you'll excuse me now, Agent Nolan."

"Tell me what you know of Mr. Alcantra." He refused to stand, amused by her sudden formality.

"Cisco imported a vast variety of strange and curious items from any and all countries connected to Spain, past or present." She waved a hand at the parlor decorated to what he presumed was the height of fashion. "But as you can see, my nest is adequately feathered. Why visit his room? I think you know. He was an exciting lover, his buccaneer persona entertaining, if fictitious. I will miss him."

"Him? Or the drugs he provided?"

"As stated, I recall very little of that day." Her lips pursed.

Ryan snorted. "I'm not surprised. Search your memory again. The woman who shot him in the forehead. What was her name?"

She swallowed.

Watching her face carefully, he asked, "Might the name Maria trigger any memories?"

"No." Her answer was firm. But he hadn't missed the slight flinch or the haunted look that crept into her eyes. "I have nothing more to add. Thank you for escorting me safely home. Please leave." She turned on her heel, spinning buttercup flounces behind her, and exited the room. "James! See our guest to the door."

MARIA PEERED over her brother's shoulder in awe as he positioned the ostrich egg in front of the bright candling lamp, illuminating the contents within. He pulled on a pair of magnifying goggles and reached for one of the many dental tools he kept handy, this time a rotating cutter. With the flick of a switch, a small motor hummed to life.

Slowly and carefully he cut away a section of the eggshell to expose the surface of the yolk upon which a tiny white disc rested. The germinal disc, a cluster of rapidly dividing cells that, if left undisturbed, would eventually give rise to an ostrich embryo. At this stage, so her brother had explained, the cells had yet to become determined, to have set off on a path toward building flesh, bone, or blood. For now, they were pliant and receptive to his manipulations.

"Perfect," he whispered. "They arrived in time."

Standing, he held a Crookes tube above the egg and pushed a button. Electricity surged through wires connecting the device to a high-powered battery delivering a burst of ionizing radiation. With the transmutation step complete, he set the contraption down and held out a hand without so much as glancing in her direction. "Pass me the micro-injector."

They would begin by introducing the molecular substance Bixby had extracted from the bright green feathers covering the ancient ceremonial shield. She'd pushed the artifact into his hands yesterday, ordering him to work through the night if necessary.

She was proud of her brother's academic achievements. At the age of nine, she'd spent the summer climbing into the many caves tucked into the hillside that surrounded her family's estate to excavate, daydreaming of the *cuélebre* her uncle insisted had once lived nearby. Never expecting—not really—to ever find treasure. But she had. Five golden coins.

The next day she'd dragged her brother along to hunt for dragon bones.

And so it began.

# CHAPTER SIX

Until last night, Charlotte hadn't realized how very dull and staid her life had become. Altered in an instant by the reappearance of a long-lost love, an unexpected kiss, and a wild ride through a thunderstorm to the docks. All to solve the mystery of a man's murder that might well be tied to the baffling behavior of her neighbors.

An invigorating experience that left her wanting more. More adventure. And more than just kisses. Anticipation teased and had her bouncing onto her toes.

Overhead in tree branches, birds greeted the morning with their bright and cheerful songs. Sounds that always made her ponder the soundscape of the Mesozoic. Had those long ago swampy, fern-filled forests rung with a pleasing chorus of velociraptor chirps and brontosaurus warbles? Or perhaps the evolution of the larynx, the vocal organ necessary for such acoustic communication, bore no resemblance at all to the syrinx, a different structure at the base of the windpipe that was unique to birds. Impossible to know.

She always walked with focused purpose as it tended to discourage would-be troublemakers, but today there was a swing in her step. Perhaps even a slight bounce. Both of which were incongruous with her destination. As was the inordinate amount of time she'd spent upon her appearance. An extra hour to comb and twist and pin her hair into a fancy chignon. Fifteen minutes to lace her knee-high boots—followed by a wrestling match with a corset. Then there had been the bustle to wrangle into place.

All that effort so she might don her favorite burgundy gown with its profusion of ruffles, flounces and fringe. Not only did the dress exhibit her curves to perfection, the brass rings and clasps sewn into the full skirt's design allowed her to pull on ribbons to hike her hemline free of the dust and dirt— or in this case, mud—of city streets. Not to mention the murky and repellant puddles of effluvium of uncertain origin that always befouled the tile flooring of the building she would enter today. How her brother Hiram could stand to work there, hunched over dead bodies, day in and day out was a mystery.

She much preferred her position at the Peabody Museum. Once her tasks for O.C. Marsh were complete, she was free to spend her time in the zoology department studying embryological feather development, the closest she'd come to engaging in wet work on a laboratory bench. Tucked away in a corner of the room, she possessed a desk and a light microscope and a tower of wooden boxes filled with fixed and mounted skin specimens upon glass slides.

Her wide-ranging collection encompassed a variety of species, allowing her to compare and contrast the embryological development of reptile scales and feathers while contemplating the relevance of form and function. What was the why surrounding the origin of feathers? Flight? Thermoregulation? Something else?

As it stood, she had no firm answers.

Like her, Hiram spent hours upon hours peering through microscopes at various bits of flesh. But he took wet work to the limit conducting human autopsies. Studying the cause of death in order to understand and, hopefully, arrest or reverse the disease process was a noble goal. And she was both proud and impressed by her brother's endeavors. Still, the notion of spending her days up to her elbows in human remains? No. Not a chance. She'd sooner toil in a tannery or a tallow candle factory. And that was saying something.

Yet observing just such an undertaking would be her very first task of the day, and only one man—certainly not her brother—could possibly have convinced her to attend such an event, much less with any trace of anticipation. She was to meet Ryan at the gross autopsy debrief of the dead smuggler. Fittingly, the building crouched at the intersection of Grove and Prospect was adjacent to a once-convenient graveyard. Originally the location of Yale's School of Medicine, now located on York Street, the old surgical theater had been converted into an autopsy suite for the purpose of addressing more... unsavory dissections. In this case one arranged by request of Special Agent Ryan Nolan.

How grim could the smuggler's remains be? A gunshot to

the forehead was the undisputed cause of death. Yet, though the hiss of rain had drowned out the specifics when Ryan had explained, she'd understood there was something about the man's eyes he wished a pathologist to examine.

Eyes. Removed easily enough from a corpse, even if her skin crawled at the very thought of applying herself to such a task. With luck, the visit to the autopsy suite would be brief, and they would soon step back into the sunlight to where she intended to suggest they make surveillance plans for the evening. Candlelight and wine and a pair of field glasses to spy on the neighbors. Not everyone's cup of tea, but it was certainly hers. And if Ryan agreed to keep her company...

Anticipation drew a smile to her face as she skirted a lamp-post, dodged an omnibus, and wove through a smattering of pedestrians. Summer term meant fewer students, but the usual business of the city surrounding the university carried on with its hustle and bustle.

For most of her life, the summer months had involved travel. She'd been only seven when she'd boarded a ship with her family in Kingston, Jamaica and waved goodbye to teary-eyed relatives on shore. Jobs were scarce on the island, and her father was convinced his fortune lay in the Black Hills of the Dakota Territory. Never mind he'd missed the gold rush by more than two decades. They'd traveled by boat, train, and wagon, heading ever westward. Over the years, the list of jobs her parents worked were endless. Cowboy, grocer, outfitter. Washerwoman, cook, seamstress. To name a few. In the daylight hours remaining to them, they panned a nearby stream for gold.

Leaving Charlotte, along with her brother and sister, to wander the countryside. While Joyce spun pirouettes and Hiram read aloud from whatever medical textbook he'd managed to beg and borrow from the town doctor, she'd stood, throwing her knife into tree trunks, barrels, and fence posts. When her parents finally struck it rich—twenty-seven ounces of gold flakes from a tiny creek buried deep in a hillside—he'd sent his all-but-grown children to Paris for a proper education.

Hiram attended *La Sorbonne*, Joyce enrolled in ballet school and Charlotte wandered the halls of the *Muséum National d'Histoire Naturelle*, fascinated by dinosaur bones and imagining a future where she pulled their massive skeletons from the earth for fun and profit. All while her gold-struck prospecting parents traveled north to the Yukon Territory.

She'd traveled Europe, seeking out the opportunity to broaden her self-styled education in paleontology. Then, once again, she'd headed West, boarding first a boat then a sooty, dusty train to cross the American plains. There she'd stayed. Until a massive jawbone landed on her ankle.

She'd thought that night would be the last time she'd lay eyes on Ryan, but fate had seen fit to toss them another chance. Which had her springing out of bed at dawn without any aid of the rooster next door that screamed as the first ray of sunlight touched the morning sky. And soon she might learn how—or if—ostriches greeted the sunrise.

As feathers and fossils dominated her every scholarly thought, she was more than happy to help Ryan flip over a rock and expose whatever shenanigans her neighbors were up to. To say nothing of indulging in other, more selfish, interpersonal activities for two. A long dry spell had followed their separation.

But first, an autopsy.

Pulling on the handle of a heavy door, Charlotte stepped from the bright morning light into the entryway of Yale's shadowy past, and she shuddered. Corpses had passed its threshold at midnight, albeit via a back door, borne on stretchers from the nearby graveyard to educate medical students. Still did, though no longer of the variety intended to remain six feet under.

She'd been here once before. Proud of his appointment as attending pathologist, Hiram had insisted upon giving her a tour. That day, however, the gurneys and slabs had held no "patients". Such had been a condition of her visit.

She made her way through hallways and down a set of stairs to reach the old surgical theater, a windowless room tucked in the far back of the building and half sunk into the cool earth where fresh air for the living took lower priority than a damp chill to preserve the dead. There was a scattering of stained wood chips across the floor. About the room's edges, a raised wooden balcony with an iron railing provided audience seating. Once, medical students would have sat in daily attendance, pencils and notebooks in hand. In an era when health and hygiene did not necessarily equate with sanitation and disinfection, the space would have hosted both dissection and surgery.

Today, a body occupied a table in the center of the room. A Y-shaped incision split the dead man open from stem to stern. So much for a simple examination of the eyes.

Beside the corpse, Ryan conversed with Hiram. Her brother, garbed in an apron covered with a multitude of overlapping stains in various shades of nauseating reddish-brown, was pointing at an array of fluid-filled jars. One held the smuggler's eyes. The others held his heart, sections of his liver, intestines, and lungs.

Charlotte took a deep breath. Reminded herself a dead body was a dead body, whether animal or human. She was a woman of science. No need for her heart to leap as it did, to bounce along a tad irregularly as if ghosts might linger in the flickering shadows cast by the gaslight fixtures. "Good morning, gentlemen," she said, stepping onto the wood shavings and into the circle of light.

"You came." Ryan brightened at her arrival, his mouth forming that sexy, crooked smile she'd missed so very much.

"You doubted I would?" She tossed back a grin. Yes, even in the presence of death and her pathologist brother. Hadn't her brother and her sister-in-law been hounding her to consider marriage, dragging her to one "family dinner" after another complete with an unexpected and eligible guest?

Rejected, all of them. Her heart had made its choice years ago out West on the bluffs and plains. No man could hold a candle to Ryan. Only the logistics of how they would frame a life together gave her any pause.

"Ick and squick, you once termed the medical profession, so I wasn't certain."

Hiram cleared his throat. She ignored him.

"You did name me a partner in this investigation," she replied. "I take my responsibilities seriously. Even," she turned to face Hiram's disapproving countenance, "if I must endure my brother's involvement. I see you two have finally met."

Ryan nodded.

Hiram, however, was not impressed. "Him? *This* is the man who left you, injured, with a broken ankle, to chase after some mythological creature?"

"Not mythological, Dr. Reid," Ryan defended, bristling. "The Tommyknocker's remains are housed within the Smithsonian Museum."

"He had no idea the break was so serious," Charlotte said. "And you'll recall, I insisted he go. Such opportunities rarely present themselves, if at all. A rare anthropomorphic specimen like that belongs in a museum, not sold to some traveling side show where its care and condition would rapidly deteriorate. A responsible cryptozoologist has an obligation to ensure a specimen of such scientific value reaches the Smithsonian Museum where it can be examined by experts and their observations entered into formal records."

And sad though she'd been, but for their parting, she'd have never set about running her own expeditions, never journeyed into the Dakota Territory, never discovered her chicken-from-hell. While there was much that was positive about the experience, it had also been a lonely existence, surrounded as she was by men who traveled with her for nothing but monetary gain.

Her brother's mouth opened. Closed. "And why has its existence been kept from the public?"

"Given the number of remarkable anatomical similarities Tommyknockers share with the human race, the creatures might be capable of speech, might possess a culture all their own. As the species lives deep within caves and mines, we must induce they are not keen to mix with humans. Announcing their reality paints a target on their back. Rifles would be loaded, and expeditions mounted in an effort to hunt one down. I'll not be responsible for causing their extinction." He lifted his eyebrows and leaned forward, offering a faintly conspiratorial smile. "If you'd like, however, I can arrange for a private viewing at the Smithsonian."

Hiram slid his sister a sheepish glance. "I would, actually."

She shook her head slowly at him, pretending disappointment. "You are won over all too easily by a dead body."

"I'll speak to those in charge and make it happen." Ryan's voice grew somber. "You should know it pained me to leave Charlotte. Hurt even more to learn she'd left Cheyenne for San Francisco when I needed to return East. When I tried to find her, none of my inquiries ever managed to provide me with a timely postal address."

He'd searched for her? Warmth spread through her chest. "My former employment meant it was rare for me to stay in one place for very long."

"Exactly." His gaze slid over to her and threw heat like glowing campfire coals. "So imagine my surprise when she accosted me in the street yesterday. All this time I believed her still out in the field, collecting. Not once imagining she might accept a job involving doors and a roof, let alone a skirt."

"Certainly not one with a matching bodice." Charlotte lifted her chin and spun about, determined to keep the mood light. "Alas, museum work forces me to abandon comfort in the name of professionalism."

"Skirt or trousers, both suit you," he replied. "As will academia."

"That's enough." Hiram put an end to their flirtations. He pointed at Ryan with narrowed eyes. "You *will* attend Sunday dinner. I'd insist you join us this evening, but my wife would run me through with a spoon if I spring unexpected company upon her."

"I look forward to it," Ryan replied.

Heat rushed to her cheeks. A gentleman so ordered to sit at the family table by another man was assumed to be actively courting his sister. Marriage would be under consideration. From the way Ryan caught and held her gaze, he fully understood. And agreed.

A heavy ache weighed down her heart. She was wistful for a past they couldn't resurrect and discouraged by thoughts of a future that would be a struggle to build. Ryan lived in Washington, D.C., a city far away from both her family and an academic position she'd worked hard to secure. She found it unlikely that New Haven's Customs House saw enough mysterious, uncanny imports to appoint a full time IBIS agent to their office. And those were only the practical considerations. There were social ones as well.

"Now," Hiram waved a hand, "if we may proceed, I've a long day ahead. Several bodies await examination."

"Certainly." Ryan beckoned Charlotte closer. "Your *brother* completed the autopsy earlier this morning." The look he tossed her was a reprimand. "I don't believe you ever mentioned he was a pathologist."

"I *did* mention he was a physician. While we were out West, he was in Scotland." Discussion of siblings had been brief and superficial. They'd been busy conversing about other things. Truly private moments hadn't involved much speech. "Still in training. His return to the United States, his relocation to New Haven preceded mine by mere months."

"A pathologist," Ryan repeated. "Who was likely in charge of my smuggler's autopsy. You might have said something last night."

She lifted a shoulder. "Things were a bit chaotic."

Annoyed at their lack of focus, Hiram cleared his throat then attempted to course correct. Again. "The proximal cause of Mr. Alcantra's death—a bullet between the eyes—is not under dispute. Nonetheless, despite his swift death, he wouldn't have been long for this world, suffering as he was from a most impressive, and quite likely fatal infestation."

"Infestation?" Not infection. She didn't care for the nuance behind Hiram's word choice. Invertebrate biology made her skin crawl. Bugs had too many legs, worms not enough. Individually or in the wild, she could cope. But collected together in large quantities to the point that they overwhelmed a host to cause disease? No thank you. "By what?"

Bracing herself, Charlotte ventured closer, peering into the open abdominal cavity, grimacing as she did her level best to ignore the skin flaps that hung on either side of the corpse, peeled back from chest and stomach to expose the internal viscera. Amongst the twists and coils of the man's intestines and embedded in his liver and spleen were small, white, C-shaped parasites each ranging from one to two inches long.

One shifted. Writhed. As if struggling to emerge.

Bile rose into her throat. Only Ryan's steadying hand at the small of her back kept her on her feet. "Are those..." She gagged. "Worms?"

Hiram rocked his hand. "Debatable. As I was saying before you joined us, Mr. Nolan's victim suffered from what soon would have been a lethal infestation of tongue worm, though they are more accurately known as pentastomids, an unusual ridged vermiform parasite that feeds entirely upon blood. Not worms, exactly, but they do appear so when existing in their larval form. Adults possess a mouth and four clawed legs at their anterior end, indicating the species may well be a kind of stem arthropod."

*Aether, the distinction failed to improve the situation.* "Tongue?" she squeaked, willing the room to stop spinning.

"So named due to the flattened appearance of some species," Hiram replied. "The formal diagnosis is visceral pentastomiasis complicated by nasopharyngeal involvement." He pulled back the smuggler's lip using a blunt-nosed probe and gestured at a number of raised lines beneath the surface of the skin. "Note the ridges? An infection such as this is usually acquired by means of ingesting water or raw offal containing the larval forms of the—" Her brother sighed as only a long-suffering sibling could.

The entirety of Charlotte's digestive tract rebelled.

Heaved. Threatened to toss this morning's breakfast of straw-berries and cream. She clapped a hand to her mouth.

"Charlotte, do you want to wait in the hall?" Ryan asked.

"No." She hated how her voice squeaked, high and tight, fooling no one. "Please continue, Hiram."

"Very well." He looked doubtful. "As requested, I've exam-ined the contents of a number of pills and powders your unfor-tunate victim had in his possession. This appears to be the source." He waved them over to a brass microscope and nudged at a glass slide resting on the stage. "Given the stylized snake with fangs stamped on the paper packet and its alleged Mexican origin, I'd wager it to be rattlesnake powder."

"Making his condition the result of product contamina-tion," Ryan concluded.

"Is this powder used as a zootherapeutic?" Charlotte asked. There was no end to what humans would consume in an attempt to cure any number of maladies, real or imagined.

Hiram nodded. "Some believe the Tzabcan rattlesnake, *Crotalus tzabcan* to be specific, possesses curative properties when consumed raw. Among other conditions, the entirety of the animal—meat, viscera, and skin—is reputed to treat rashes, rheumatism, ulcers, and even sexual impotence."

*Sexual impotence.* She rolled her eyes. The ridiculous things men would consume in pursuit of harder and longer knew no bounds. Her gaze slid back to the smuggler's body. Had the Spaniard felt himself flagging one day and sampled his own product? Only to find the condition worsened? She imagined playing host to that many not-worms would be draining. How much rattlesnake powder did one need to consume to be so riddled with parasites?

"Though usually administered orally, it's sometimes sprinkled into an open wound with the belief that it speeds healing. Unfortunately, the raw state—particularly the ground, uncooked lungs of rattlesnake—can introduce pathologic bacteria or, in this case, pentastomid cysts. No larger than a fraction of a millimeter, they are effectively invisible to the naked eye." Her brother waved at the microscope. "Take a look for yourself."

Ryan bent and peered through the objective, adjusting the fine focus to study the slide. Then straightened, offering Charlotte a chance to observe the grayish powder sprinkled across its surface.

Determined not to back down from any challenge this case presented, she stepped forward.

At the center of a circle of bright light, various ground snake fragments—including bone—refracted the incoming light. The pointer, a narrow metal wire, directed her eye to a clear oval inside which a darker, coiled shape rested. The cyst, she presumed, a kind of egg. An unhatched parasite waiting to make its way into the warm, moist environment of an animal's unsuspecting digestive tract where it would wreak havoc upon its involuntary host.

"An exceptional case of pentastomiasis." Her brother held out the small jar containing the smuggler's eye. A bit of the devil crawled into her brother's eyes. "I assume you intend to escort my sister to work after inviting her along on this charming, early morning outing?"

Ryan nodded.

"Well, then. Should you wish to incite an argument among the invertebrate biologists at the Peabody, drop this off with a requisition for a precise Linnean classification. If you're interested in their analysis, my sister could show you the way."

Ryan reached for the container as Charlotte took two steps backward. She could swear the not-worm had moved. Bile rose into her throat. She swallowed. Hard.

"I hate you." Skewering her brother with a look, she held up two pinching fingers, almost but not quite touching. "Just a little bit."

Hiram's low laugh echoed through the dissection room and followed them out the door.

# CHAPTER SEVEN

They exited the old surgical theater and stepped back onto the bright, sunlit streets of New Haven. Ryan watched as Charlotte drew in a deep breath of fresh air, insofar as one could term the air of a city powered by coal. Regardless, her skin quickly lost its ashen tone.

"Better?" he asked.

"Much." The word emerged on a hard exhale. "Of all the specialties and subspecialties, my brother chooses to spend his days with death and disease." She stared pointedly at his coat, where he'd tucked the small glass jar with its disembodied eye into an interior pocket. Opened her mouth, then shut it again with a quick shake of her head. "Your interview with Rose this morning. Any luck teasing out relevant information?"

"Yes." His lips twisted. "Though not directly. When I mentioned the name Maria, she flinched. Yet denied knowing anyone by that name. Rose did, however, admit to dallying with the Spaniard, a man occasionally employed by her Spanish husband."

"Dallying and sipping peyote tea." She grimaced. "Let's hope she didn't sample any rattlesnake powder."

He cringed. "Particularly as there is no known cure, though your brother assured me clinical manifestation of symptoms is rare. Fortunately, this particular parasite is not known to transfer from human to human, but instead by ingestion of the infected intermediary host—in this case, rattlesnake."

"Hosts to unknown numbers of larvae and there's not any —" A look of horror fixed itself upon her face. "No. Enough of that topic. I regret my remark. You were saying?"

Not keen to contemplate organ infesting parasites either, he continued. "Rose married into the Rodríguez family, one that made their fortune exporting ironworks from northern Spain. Asturias, to be exact. The very region where tales of the *cuélebre* originated."

"A curious connection." She tipped her head in thought. "A dragon from Spain, but imports from Mexico. The tangled pasts of the two countries means the link cannot be dismissed. Is there such a thing as a Mexican dragon?"

They crossed the street, blessedly dust free from last night's rain, weaving between an omnibus and a man riding a clockwork horse.

"No dragon, at least not from a European perspective," he said. "Ancient Mesoamerican culture possessed a feathered serpent deity known as Quetzalcoatl to the Aztecs, Kukulkan to the Mayans. The motif appears on many ancient buildings and in the Mayan codices—folded books written on paper made from fig tree bark and inscribed with hieroglyphs—only four of which still exist."

"Quetzal, genus *Pharomachrus*?" She glanced at him. "Any relation to the bird with iridescent green feathers and a red belly that lives in the cloud forests of Mexico?"

He grinned. Of course she would know the specifics. "Yes to the plumage." His mind cast back to one of the items found among the smuggler's collection. Sadly, he'd confiscated the entirety of a quetzal's wing. Brilliant feathers that, or so he imagined, had been destined for a lady's hat. "Beyond that, I must admit ignorance."

"A fabled feathered serpent. Part bird, part snake. Not part lizard. And yet the creature sounds like a kind of dragon to me. Any rumor of existing remains?"

He shook his head. "The creature, insofar as I am aware, is entirely mythological. But one could say the same of the Asturian *cuélebre*, also a winged serpent, but officially classified as a dragon of the bat-winged variety."

"So both are serpents and both fly. One with feathers but no wings. The other with no feathers, but a patagium—membranous skin stretched between fingers and the body."

"Er." Ryan blinked, impressed. "As depicted in imagery."

"A smuggler with a habit of eating contaminated raw snake products, a fact that may or may not prove relevant. Regardless, Mr. Alcantra is responsible for the rumors that dragged you here to New Haven." She frowned. "That is far too much coincidence to dismiss."

"I'd little hope of finding a live *cuélebre*," he admitted.

"There was a dust up about dragon eggs near Edinburgh this past spring, something to do with Russians in the Ural mountains."

Her eyebrows flew upward. "Which led you to speculate that you might be dealing with individuals looking to purchase dragon eggs on the black market?"

"The thought crossed my mind." The stone edifice of the Peabody loomed before them. "And yet our chase turned up ostrich eggs."

"Don't give up on them too soon." She laid a hand on his arm and his heart swelled with pleasure. Of her nearness, of course, but also from the joy of speculative banter with someone willing to give credence to the bizarre directions in which his work pointed him. "Exotic. Rare. Unusual." Charlotte imbued the words with dark, layered meaning. "Wait until you hear the cacophony of my neighbor's backyard. From the sound of it, they've an aviary full of birds that couldn't survive on their own in North America. If they set themselves up as purveyors of fine feathers, it wouldn't be hard to mislabel a few dragon eggs, tuck their crates among ostrich eggs and slide them past Customs?"

Ryan shook his head. "Thing is, dragon eggs almost always require a constant source of heat. In captivity, a stone hearth with a roaring fire is best, though I hear they can be transported using a coal-burning brazier. But acquiring a viable dragon egg? Next to impossible." His mood was light. Buoyant even. Time spent in Charlotte's presence had that effect. And he'd missed the pure joy of bandying about various ideas, tossing out those unsupported by evidence while pocketing those that fit for later consideration. He couldn't resist needling her about the one they'd debated for hours. She'd argued in favor, him against. "They're rarer than hen's teeth."

She leveled him a one-eyed squint, mouth pursed. Still, amusement fluttered in her reply. "Tease all you wish. But just you wait. The discovery of archaeopteryx with feathers *and* teeth changed everything. Someone somewhere might someday prove that ground-dwelling dinosaurs possessed feathers."

"Wouldn't that be the find of the century." He laughed. "While there are dozens of winged mythological creatures, most are humanoid. But as we're talking dinosaurs, better to compare to dragons. Yet not a single confirmed sighting has reported anything resembling plumage on a four-legged beast."

"None living." Her eyebrows rose as a shoulder lifted and fell. "None from Europe, in any case."

"You found something." He froze, one foot upon the first step leading into the Peabody. "Tell me."

"Did I suggest there was something to share?" Charlotte offered him an enigmatic smile, then began to climb the stairs. "Now, did Rose mention her husband's line of work?"

She knew something. Something important. "Only that he was away. Traveling for work. Why?"

"Because there's a Professor Enzo Rodríguez on staff at the Peabody."

Shock and surprise rippled through him. "Her husband works here?" Ryan caught her arm, sputtering. "And you were going to mention this when?"

She laughed. "Precisely now. Professor Rodríguez is a

herpetologist and head of the Zoology Department. His research interests lie in the evolutionary dental relationships between alligators, caimans, and crocodiles. If this man is her husband, Rose lied."

"Lied?"

He pulled open a solid wooden door and they stepped into the hush of academic grandeur. In the grand, two-storied hall, a central staircase marched upward, one wide enough to permit the passage of the largest of specimens. To his left and right, grand archways granted passage into rooms filled from floor to ceiling with fossilized bones. From dinosaurs to birds to horses. Professor Marsh had assembled a most impressive collection of creatures that once roamed the face of the planet, yet did so no more, to grace his hallowed halls.

Incomplete or lesser specimens were relegated to the attic, the cellar, or the research floors above.

"Professor Rodríguez returned from Florida last week, from a collecting expedition out in the field." With focused purpose, Charlotte strode toward the stairs. "I will allow exactly one guess as to what items he brought back."

"Eggs?" He kept pace beside her.

"Nailed it in one." Her burgundy skirts flared out behind her as she whirled onto the next rise of stairs. "Come. Zoology is on the third floor."

A glimpse of her trim ankles brought a smile to his face and he wondered how many knives she'd managed to tuck into her boots. Not that he expected she would need blades inside these hallowed halls. On the other hand, if a certain murderess had business with a certain Zoology professor, precautions were warranted.

"We've a theme developing," she pointed out. "Last night it was ostrich eggs. This morning, tiny pentastomid cysts, a kind of egg. And now *Alligator mississippiensis* has stepped on stage. The American alligator lays its eggs in early June."

"But produce no feathers. Leather for shoes, belts, wallets. Also, meat. All consistent with an enterprise in offering the rare and exotic, yet something rings false."

"Agreed."

The ceilings of the third floor were lower and the windows lost their arching curves. Here upon this floor of feathers, fur, and scales there was a fervent busyness, one that far eclipsed the activities of the two below. Inside each room, a multitude of men—and a few women—sat at desks and tables and counters, uncaring of the human activity buzzing about them, each zealous in the pursuit of obscure and detailed knowledge of their chosen phylum, class, order, family, genus or species.

"Miss Reid." A tall, thin, stoop-shouldered man stepped into their path and waved a stack of papers in her face "Where have you been? I can't keep up with the telegraphs. There's a crisis brewing. The professor is fit to be tied. He's learned that Anderson accidentally shipped a box of edaphosaurus vertebrae and spines to Philadelphia, but Cope is claiming no mistake was made, that the bones rightfully belong to the Academy of Natural Sciences, that he has every right to name a new species if and when he sees fit."

Ryan huffed a soft laugh. Only O.C. Marsh and Edward

Drinker Cope could turn an argument over a long-dead sail-backed synapsid into an emergency.

But Charlotte hesitated. "I'm afraid we've a pressing matter of our own, Mr. Peterson."

The man executed a cold and swift evaluation of Ryan's importance and marked as him insignificant, underlining his dismissal by turning away with a sniff. "I might add, Miss Reid, that we already possess the skull and limb bones. Those fossils that have gone 'astray' are necessary to form a complete skeleton. We cannot afford to dismiss this brewing calamity."

She rocked back on her heels and threw an imploring glance toward the ceiling.

Ryan had met O.C. Marsh exactly once. An encounter that confirmed all negative reports. He was a belligerent steamroller of a man who considered the entirety of the Peabody Museum his personal possession. As such, Charlotte, who split her time between ornithology and paleontology, could not afford to risk her position by refusing to pacify its de facto ruler or his minions.

"Wire Anderson. Ask when he was last paid." Her expression hardened, bracing for argument. "If Marsh failed to pay him for the Anchisaurus fossils, this could be a warning shot."

Mr. Peterson stiffened. "I couldn't possibly—"

"Discuss money?" Charlotte snapped. "Anderson is our leading collector. The professor has purposefully delayed payments to him before and Anderson has threatened to take action. Pay him and the 'accident' might be resolved in our favor."

"The professor would have to agree." Mr. Peterson looked as if she'd asked him to swallow a live frog.

"Yes, he would." Her eyebrows rose. "Frame it as a clerical oversight, assign him no blame. Likely he'll grumble and agree there has been some *confusion*. There's little alternative. What do you suppose will happen if Anderson—our top bone hunter—chooses to work for Cope instead?"

The man blanched.

"Exactly. There's a reason the reporters have dubbed their feud The Bone Wars. You're a vertebrate, Mr. Peterson. Time to stiffen that spine and do what must be done. Coax Anderson back to our side or we'll all suffer the gaping maw and sharp bite of the Cope-Marsh-not-so-professional-rivalry." With that witty repartee, she whipped past Mr. Peterson, tugging at Ryan's sleeve. "This way."

To date, he'd only witnessed her brilliant competence during excavations in the bone yards out West. And it lost none of its shine in an urban, professional setting.

Zoology occupied the entirety of the third floor. Herpetology claimed but a small corner. Terrariums with unblinking lizards and coiled serpents lined one wall, their cages resting atop a length of cast iron heating coils. Tall and extensive shelving held pickled specimens—both in part and whole—floating inside labeled jars alongside dried and skeletonized lizards. Seated at various low tables and desks, men wielded calipers, tape measures and magnifying glasses.

At their entrance, the soft scratching of graphite pencils across paper slowed and a number of curious gazes turned in their direction. But not all.

"Dr. Rodríguez?" she asked.

Without looking up, a man in a charcoal suit answered, "He's out today. Talk to Bixby, his assistant."

In two long strides, Ryan reached the man's desk. Bending close, he growled. "And where might this Bixby be?"

"Can't miss him." The herpetologist continued his work. "He's the man burnt to a crisp by the bright tropical sun."

A question that needed no answer. Charlotte was already on the move, heading directly toward a wide-eyed, sunburned man. There was a nerve-grating screech as his chair shoved backward, a crash as it toppled onto the ground. He snatched up a box and darted across the back of the room for a side door.

"Head him off!" Charlotte called, hot on Bixby's coattails. "Run for Entomology! Second door on the right."

Ryan retreated. Dashed down the hall. No need to count doors, he only had to follow the shouts of protest. He burst into a room where insects ruled. The scientists within were in an uproar, exclaiming in horror over the safety of their delicate, precious exoskeletal darlings as Bixby wove between tables, knocking over equipment and specimens. But all his zigs and zags were for naught. Ryan guarded the doorway, blocking his escape.

The man gaped, then spun on his heel.

Ryan's fingers twitched to unholster his weapon. Easy to drop the zoologist with a single dart. But this was neither the place nor the time. A room full of witnesses meant endless paperwork. Besides, Charlotte had this covered.

She snagged a long pole with a netted loop used for collecting butterflies. Without stopping, she yanked her skirts above her knees and hopped onto a chair, climbed atop a table and lunged at Bixby as he circled back.

Out West, he'd seen her scale cliffs, descend into dry riverbeds and navigate rock-strewn canyons with ease. True, she'd been wearing trousers then, but today her skirts, bustle and corset seemed not to hinder her at all. Moreover, he found much to appreciate in this urban setting. The manner in which burgundy ruffles fluttered at her thighs. The enticing pattern of her stockings. The leather-wrapped handle of a knife tucked into her boot.

He marveled at the perfect arc the pole traced through the air, how the hoop dropped precisely over the Bixby's head and shoulders, yanking his torso to a sudden stop. How he illustrated that an object in motion tends to stay in motion, especially when that entity was a guilty man trying to escape the long arm of the law. Alas, he was not dressed for success. The slick leather soles of their newest suspect's shoes skittered on a litter of fallen notepaper, and he crashed to the floor, landing with a heavy thud.

Charlotte jumped from the table and dropped into a crouch beside her captive.

Ryan grinned at her. "Most impressive." He tugged a pair of handcuffs from his pocket and snapped them about Bixby's wrists, looping the chain about a handy exposed pipe to prevent his escape. "We've a number of questions for you, Mr. Bixby."

Muttering under her breath, cursing vanity, her choice of boots and her unstable metatarsal joints, Charlotte yanked the box from Bixby's clutches.

Protests rang out.

"What gives you the authority to barge in here?"

"How dare you confiscate his belongings!"

"Chasing him through here destroyed my *Graphium deucalion* butterfly from the Sunda Islands!"

In response, Ryan flashed his badge. "Special Agent. Customs." The room quieted. "This man may be in possession of stolen material. If he attempts to run again, I *will* draw my weapon." Let them all wonder if that meant a bullet or a dart. "Please step back. We need to examine the contents of his box."

"Do not open that!" Bixby clawed at the netting, his metal bracelets clanging. "You'll destroy all my work!"

"Is that so?" Charlotte set the box on a table and raised its lid. Everyone in the room leaned in to watch as she lifted a ratty green feather from the interior. She rotated the plume in the dusty sunlight, demonstrating an iridescent shimmer. Excitement sparkled in her eyes as she caught his gaze. "Quetzal."

"A feather?" one man called out. "All this over ladies millinery?"

Ryan yanked on a leather cord from around Bixby's neck, exposing the artifact that hung there. "Pairs nicely with the bead of carved jade."

A few chuckles broke out, quickly stifled when the next item landed on the table. "Three jars of," she squinted, "sectioned bone floating in..." She glanced at Bixby. "Enzymes? Acid?"

Bixby's nostrils flared, but he said nothing.

"And a paper sack of several dried snakes, more or less intact. *Crotalus tzabcan*, the Mayan rattlesnake?"

"Who informed you?" Bixby demanded. "I was told—" He snapped his mouth shut and glared at them.

"It was a mistake," Ryan said through gritted teeth, "letting yourself become involved in theft and murder."

The blood drained away from the man's florid, sunburned face, leaving him slightly sticky with sweat. "Murder?"

Ryan lifted his eyebrows but said nothing, preferring to let him to stew. Most men failed to hold their tongues under intense pressure. Bixby might yet accidentally volunteer more information.

The last item Charlotte lifted from the box appeared to be a small aether-chambered humidor, one inlaid with overly complicated controls. Copper tubing snaked about, its various branches diving through the wood to deliver the rare gas into a central chamber. Interlocking brass gears connected to knobs and dials, allowing its operator to finely manage the internal conditions. The faint hum of a motor whirred.

The glass set into its lid revealed four Petri dishes filled with a gel-like substance.

"It's a portable thermoconductive cell culture incubator," Charlotte informed him. Her fingers danced over the smooth surface. "The contents are being maintained at a temperature slightly higher than our own and adjusting atmospheric gas ratios to reflect less oxygen rich conditions. Opening the chamber, exposing them to our environment might well damage the viability of whatever cells grow within."

"Will they survive outside the incubator?" Though he

addressed his question, narrow-eyed, to their prisoner, it was Charlotte who answered.

"For a few minutes."

"Mr. Bixby," Ryan addressed the captive, who had righted himself to a seated position. "Last chance to explain your project before we take a peek."

"Without context, you'll learn nothing." Bixby looked away, fixing his gaze upon an odd display of headless grasshoppers. "Go ahead, destroy them. I'll simply begin anew."

"A difficult task to accomplish inside a prison cell," Ryan observed, then waved at Charlotte to proceed.

"Might I borrow a dissecting microscope?" she inquired of the room at large.

Chairs scraped, papers and specimens were shoved aside. And a small clearing opened in the detritus of arthropods.

"Thank you." She sat down, fiddled with the knobs, waited while the needle on the dial slowly rotated to zero. With the flip of a latch, a slow hiss of aether escaped and the lid popped open. Working quickly, she withdrew a Petri dish, set it on the microscope stage, and adjusted the fine focus. "There are cells growing. Osteocytes, I believe. Bone cells suspended in a collagen-based matrix. Derived from ground snake collagen if I were to guess from the contents of the box."

"Collagen?" Fossil-based as their previous time together had been, it was a new experience to witness Charlotte employ her laboratory skills.

"A connective protein sourced from anything cartilaginous —skin, tendons, bones—by boiling them for an extended period of time, much like bone broth. The resulting gelatinous product is then collected and further purified. Acid solubilization is another method of extraction."

Charlotte slid the Petri dish back into the incubator and removed the next, examining all four plates in turn. Lowering the lid, she flipped a switch and adjusted a dial, restoring their growing conditions.

She leaned back in her chair to stare down at Bixby. "Excellent work, a clever way to provide your cells the ability to grow in a three-dimensional gel."

The praise sent a brief ripple of pride across the man's face before he schooled his expression to boy-caught-with-his-hand-in-the-cookie-jar.

"But to what end?" Ryan inquired, his voice taking on a sharp edge.

She shook her head. "My histology training is of limited scope, focusing primarily on form and function of the developing layers of skin, dermal layers which derive from the ectoderm. Bone originates from mesoderm. It's possible that a developmental biologist might be able to tell us more, but unless Mr. Bixby can be convinced—"

"Not a chance," the man under discussion muttered.

"Or we locate Professor Rodríguez and demand answers—"

"Ha!" Bixby barked. "When he learns you've—" The man's face went bright red.

"Not the best plan." Sarcasm dripped from Ryan's words. "Pointing a finger at your employer."

"You can't leave me here."

"No, we can't. Not indefinitely." He wrestled his annoyance with the man under control. "We'll be back in a few minutes to take a walk over to the Customs House to discuss the origins of that feather and those snakes." He turned to Charlotte. "Professor Rodríguez's office?"

Her eyebrows lifted. "You wish to leave him here? Unsupervised? Among a room full of entomologists who may or may not be sympathetic?"

She was right.

"I need someone to guard Bixby for a few minutes." Ryan pulled the small glass jar from his inside pocket and held it aloft. "Someone with a lead-lined stomach capable of dealing with human remains. I'm told the creature infesting this eyeball is a stem arthropod. A pentastomid, not a worm." He paused for effect. Breaths caught. A few faces turned green. And more than one person shifted on his feet. "I'll require a detailed report. If a monograph results, you will be first author. Are any of you interested in the intersection of international smuggling, invertebrates, and human disease?"

# CHAPTER EIGHT

They left Bixby chained to the radiator, screaming in protest.

A colleague stood over him, hands wrapped about his not-a-worm prize while chaos erupted in a roar of shouts.

She ignored it all.

With the portable cell culture incubator firmly tucked under her arm, she led Ryan back into herpetology and straight to Professor Rodríguez's office. As department chair, he claimed a corner room with two tall windows and far more light than was allotted to most. Not once had she stepped across the threshold.

Soon after her arrival at the Peabody Museum, she'd gathered all her courage and knocked upon his door.

"Yes?" He'd not looked up from the notebook on his desk nor had he ceased writing.

She'd introduced herself, explained her interests, hoping to catch his attention. "I wonder if you'd care to collaborate? The embryological development of both feathers and teeth involves complex interactions between ectoderm and mesoderm. I thought we might conduct an ontological study examining—"

"No," he'd replied. His words fell between a grumble and a tired sigh. "I've no available time for new projects. Nor have my assistants. Moreover, extant birds are only distantly related to crocodilians. Our respective interests share no common ground."

Not the sharpest or most unkind dismissal she'd ever received. Still, it had left her vexed for days.

Following that unpleasantness, their paths crossed only in the halls. There, Professor Rodríguez behaved as if she were invisible. A predictable if discouraging reaction to those of her sex and skin tone. Such did not bode well for her appointment to a formal academic position within the Peabody Museum, no matter the quantity or quality of papers she published. If Charlotte wanted an official title and an office of her own, she would need to seek employment elsewhere, face the dreaded interview where C.S. Reid was discovered not to be white or male.

But now that a chance to dethrone the ruling department head had presented itself, she would grab his academic chair with both fists and shake until he fell to the floor and crawled for the door.

She was getting ahead of herself. They needed to locate the professor. To do that, they required evidence.

Like most spaces occupied by the zoologically obsessed, his office was crammed to the gills—or ought she say gullet—with papers and books and reptilian remains. Skeletal, mostly, but she spotted rolls of alligator leather tucked in cubbyholes beside glass jars of teeth and desiccated leathery eggs.

Ryan plucked one such egg from the shelving, blew the dust from its surface and sneezed. "Not a recent acquisition."

She pressed her hand atop a large, steam-powered egg incubator. "Cold." To be certain, she lifted the lid. "And empty. After all that time in Florida, there appears to be nothing to show for it. Not here."

"No crates, nothing obvious to indicate he is in possession of viable alligator eggs." Ryan flipped through the detritus of papers that littered his desk. "But everyone makes mistakes. So far, we've uncovered two."

"He stepped inside the museum after his return from Florida." She clicked her tongue and shook her head.

"And recruited an assistant incapable of subterfuge." Ryan yanked open a drawer. "Skillful, perhaps, but downright squirrelly. Enfield ought to have slid that box deeper beneath his desk, then escorted us here himself, offering to help."

Charlotte focused her attention on the various grinning crocodilian skulls. She pulled one from a shelf, running a finger across the tops of pointy, conical teeth. Maxilla and mandible. Not particularly sharp but, when paired with strong jaw tendons and muscles, prey found itself in the grip of a deadly bite. Able to grow new teeth when older ones were lost or damaged, she'd often wondered if dinosaurs possessed the same abilities.

"Contemplating his work in the context of our scattered evidence?" Ryan slammed one drawer shut, yanked open another.

She nodded. "Professor Rodríguez studies dental development and differentiation of alligator teeth, with an eye to establishing their phylogenetic relationship to crocodiles, caimans and the gharial."

Dust motes floated through the air glinting in the sunlight. Dust and bones. Dinosaurs and dragons. Ostriches, alligators, and snakes. International imports and exports. Eggs.

An idea coalesced.

"As per your earlier statements," she began, thinking aloud as she turned each puzzle piece about in her mind, fitting one to the next, "there is money to be earned selling rare and unusual items to the rich. Ostrich steaks for banquets and quetzal feathers for hats. But there is also a limit to how long the wealthy find a novelty novel. Others will imitate their so-called betters. Once the shine is off the alligator leather shoe, the affluent will source a new curiosity. Polar bear liver, duck-billed platypus eggs, Amazonian frog legs." She took a deep breath and gave voice to the simplest most parsimonious answer that accounted for the entire body of amassed clues. "Ultimately, however, in terms of establishing a long-term business in New Haven, it does not pay to chase after ever more unique items. Better to develop a product that consumers will return to, over and over. One they can manufacture with relative ease, yet plead scarcity."

"And thus raise the price." Teeth rattled inside a cardboard box as Ryan poked at them, his lips twisted, not quite convinced. Or did he still cling to hopes of uncovering a more compelling plot rife with strange twists and turns?

"Pharmaceuticals are one possibility," she said. "People who believe they 'need' something will pay any price."

He looked up. A speculative gleam lit his eyes. "And will swallow all kinds of tablets, pills or potions to cure what ails them."

"Peddling snake oil is a long, time-honored—and profitable—tradition. Francisco Alcantra clearly believed in his products."

"And look where he ended." Ryan waved at the portable incubator. "Why *grow* bone, an easily procured item?"

"Bone cells grown on rattlesnake collagen." She tapped her chin. "Why go to such trouble? Is it possible that bones of the *tzabcan* rattlesnake are pharmacologically bioactive?"

"Not a question I can answer." He yanked out a slip of paper, stared at it intently.

"What did you find?" She leaned in closer.

"A bill of lading from a shipping company based in Florida. Five crates to a Rose Donovan at 48 Greene Street." He handed it to her. "Concrete evidence that Rose was lying to me. She's involved."

Charlotte's eyebrows scrunched together. It was an address on the illustrious Wooster Square. "Only the first name matches. And did you not tell me Mrs. Rose Rodríguez lives on Olive Street?"

Olive Street boasted a row of stately homes. Ones that faced factories. A black mark against their desirability but perfect for a woman who was not-quite-an-outcast holding fast to illusions of societal acceptance. Whereas a house on Wooster Square meant automatic, unquestioned inclusion.

A muscle jumped in his jaw as he pried his mouth open to speak. "48 Greene Street is—was—Captain Donovan's house."

A fact which clarified exactly nothing. Then she recalled the tale that had sent Ryan fleeing from New Haven all those years ago. "Is that the address of the captain's house, the one with whom your former fiancée—"

"Conducted an affair? It is." Disgust and distaste twisted his face. "Items from Florida shipped to a house that stands empty, to a name that never existed. Hearing Rose's name linked to his when they never married…" It angered him beyond all reason. Rose had known of his close relationship with Captain Donovan, knew that he served as both Ryan's father figure and mentor, yet she'd taken up with him just the same.

She frowned, wondering how delicately she needed to treat the topic. "Why would Rose be in possession of the captain's home?"

He threw a hand in the air. "It seems he left the house to her, or so my grandmother informed me early this morning." Pale, he stared out a window, the bill of lading crumpled in his fist. "I trusted him. Sat beside him, hearthside, year after year, listening to his tales of travel and adventure, let him feed my passion for fantastical creatures and dream of more than manufacturing shoes."

"From a young age, he shaped your future," she agreed. For the better, in her opinion, even if now was not the time to point it out. "You cared. Deeply. Making his actions all that more of a betrayal."

He nodded. Then, spinning away from the window, his

expression shifted and his voice grew tight. "On her deathbed, my mother whispers to me of her affair, of my conception." Pacing now, he dragged a hand through his hair. "My supposed father overhears and explodes with a roar, promising vengeance, all while my sister Ellen cries, wondering if she too is the product of an illicit affair. Rose was to have been by my side in the cemetery that morning. As family. But instead, she was caught down at the docks, exiting Captain Donovan's stateroom."

Her heart squeezed, then twisted in her rib cage imagining the pain of that day. She knew most of this but stayed silent. Something more, something new plagued his mind.

"I've no idea of what, if any, relationship they conducted after my departure." He took a deep breath, exhaled forcefully. "Rose informed me this morning that she married Rodríguez soon after we parted ways, that the man was her best option to quell the scandal swirling about her. All while the captain remained a confirmed bachelor to his death."

Ah, there it was. His idol didn't merely lay broken at the base of a pedestal, it had crumbled into dust and blown away. Charlotte set down the alligator skull and wrapped her arms about Ryan's waist, resting her cheek upon his broad back. "I'm so sorry. Her betrayal cut deep."

"Like a knife in the back." He turned, pulling her against his chest, against the comforting thump-thump of his heart. When he spoke again, she heard guilt in his voice. "Rather than confront her, I left for Dublin soon after, when I ought to have stayed and seen things settled. With her. With my family."

"You were all of nineteen and miserable working in that shoe factory. Leaving for university was the best choice." She tipped her face up and met his gaze. "At such an age, allowances for the pursuit of passions must be made."

"And was youth an excuse some five years later?" Regret pinched his eyebrows together. "When I left you, injured, to chase after a Tommyknocker? I'm still not convinced I should have traded my passion for you to hunt cryptids. I was convinced I could manage both. My heart all but broke when I returned to Cheyenne to find you'd left for San Francisco without leaving me so much as a simple note."

"What?" She reeled back in his arms. "I wrote a lengthy letter and left it with..." She trailed off. A faint memory flared, and she recalled an odd look that had crossed the doctor's face when he'd read Ryan's name on the envelope. Her eyes narrowed. "What are the odds he tossed it in the fire not five minutes after I refused to go under his knife and limped from his office?"

"Doc Jones? High. He had the ego of a peacock. Not to mention he was one among many who would rather not see us as a couple. In any capacity." A wistful half-smile tugged at his lips. "But we're here now. Together." With the back of curved fingers, he stroked the side of her cheek, and something fluttered deep in her chest, filling her with a buoyant hopefulness. "You're still chasing after the mysteries of fossilized bone, and I'm still dreaming of the day I uncover the whereabouts of a live cryptid."

"Both of us gainfully employed." She tapped his chest, her fingertip hitting upon the hard metal of his Customs badge, a reminder that he answered to the federal government. "If in different cities."

"A decided inconvenience." His thumb brushed the edge of her mouth. A poor substitute for an actual kiss. "If there's a way to correct that, might you be amenable to—"

A flash of movement caught her eye. A large step backward restored a respectable distance between them. What had she been thinking? Physical demonstrations had no place in the work environment. Not if she ever cared for a promotion.

The man who'd volunteered to study the not-worm in the dead smuggler's eye filled the office doorframe. "Professor Rodríguez is well-known and well-liked. Escape is being arranged for his assistant, your prisoner."

With a frustrated growl, Ryan tucked the incriminating bill of lading in his pocket and pulled out his handcuff keys and stalked from the professor's office.

With an exhale, Charlotte set aside her own annoyance at the inopportune interruption. She picked up the incubator and followed.

"Time to lock the man in a windowless room at the Customs House and let him contemplate his loyalty to this Professor Rodríguez." He glanced over his shoulder. "I need to head there to meet Dr. Carlos Tetzopa, a visiting Smithsonian scholar from the National Mexican Museum. He traveled here this morning to make an archeological assessment of the smuggler's contraband."

"Not comfortable asking for local expertise?" She let irony drip from her lips.

He snorted. "Hardly, given the number of anthropologists

who work in this very building. Need you stay? Or would you like to accompany me, learn what Dr. Tetzopa has to tell?" A teasing light flickered in his glance. "There are bright green feathers."

The only pressing task today, if viewed through the distorted lens of Marsh and Cope's ridiculous bone wars, was determining the rightful possession of fossil bones belonging to a very specific Anchisaurus dinosaur. Nothing that Mr. Peterson couldn't handle on his own. And there was no chance her mind could focus upon day-to-day tasks, not when the lure of quetzal feathers beckoned.

"Followed by a visit to Greene Street?"

"Yes." He hesitated. "Though it might be best if you don't accompany me to the captain's house, especially with its likely link to a smuggling ring. Somewhere on the loose, there's a murderous woman with a—"

"Gun," she finished. "Yes. I've viewed her handiwork. Safer first to sweep up Rose and press her for answers to our many questions. She might be more forthcoming with evidence mounting against her husband."

Ryan retrieved his prisoner then, humming incubator in hand, Charlotte led a parade that wound through entomology, down two flights of stairs and across the tiled floor to the front door of the Peabody Museum. Mr. Peterson joined them, squawking about telegram delays and rising tensions. A number of young men trailed in their wake. Some protested the prisoner's innocence, others placed bets as to the degree of his guilt, the likelihood of Professor Rodríguez's involvement, and Ryan's ability to prevent Bixby from bolting to the other side of the college campus once they stepped onto the street.

Spectators included all of fourth floor anthropology and archaeology, second floor geology and paleontology, and first floor mineralogy—all peering over railings and around doors.

"What is the meaning of this commotion!" O.C. Marsh demanded, emerging from his laboratory on the ground floor.

Ryan held his gold badge aloft, not slowing his steps. "Suspected involvement in the transportation of stolen archeological materials across international borders."

"Everyone, back to work!" Marsh ordered with narrowed eyes. "Peterson, contact the chancellor. Terminate that man's employment."

"But I'm not guilty!" Bixby cried, a mournful howl that emerged from deep within his chest.

Ryan took no pity, duck-marching him from the building.

Outside, the thirsty ground and rising sun had made short work of last night's deluge. Rumbling wheels and clomping hooves kicked up dust from the streets as they walked down High Street garnering stares as they progressed. Ryan set a swift pace, quickly moving them down the pavement toward the Customs House where they could leave their recalcitrant suspect to contemplate his likelihood of being declared innocent and released.

*Crack!*

Everything happened at once. A horse neighed and bolted, tipping over its cart and sending traffic into chaos. Horns sounded as men hollered, yanking on reins, wheels, and levers.

All as she spun on her heel, and Bixby crumpled to the pavement.

Was that gunfire? Here? In New Haven?

She froze, trying to process the sight before her.

Another shot rang out, echoing off the stone cladding of Alumni Hall. Or was that Dwight Hall? She couldn't quite place the origin.

"Charlotte!" Ryan yelled, dragging his unconscious prisoner behind the relative safety of a stopped omnibus. "Take cover! Now!"

His voice snapped her into action. Options on such a public city street were limited. She ran to a nearby elm tree, pressed her back to its trunk. Shifting the weight of the incubator onto her hip, she reached for her boot knife and wrapped her fist about its hilt. Only then did she twist—ever so slightly —searching for the shooter.

There, across the street, between the College Reading Room and the bronze, robed statue of Abraham Pierson, walked a dark-haired woman. Swiftly. But not enough so to draw attention. Were anyone to notice that her hand was tucked beneath the drape of her overskirt, they would think little of it.

Was that the shooter?

Charlotte bent, lowering the incubator, ready to abandon it to the vagaries of foot traffic in order to give chase, but a sideways glance sent her heart leaping into her throat. Ryan knelt in a pool of blood, hands pressed to Bixby's chest. Eyes fixed and locked, there was nothing to be done. Professor Rodríguez's assistant was dead.

Not so Ryan, though blood bloomed and spread across his chest staining the white linen of his shirt a deep crimson.

Overwhelming dread shot up her spine and gripped her by the neck. This couldn't be how it all ended, with Ryan dying. Not when they'd only just found each other again. Absolutely not.

At a full sprint, she ran to his side, ignoring the wobble in her ankle that sent up a warning twinge. Dammit. Curse vanity and her unstable metatarsal joints.

The incubator hit the sidewalk with a thud, forgotten, as she dropped to the pavement beside him. Pain exploded in her knees. Not that she cared. She scanned Ryan's eyes, his face, his coloring for signs of shock. A bit pale, but otherwise in normal ranges.

She dragged in a breath. "How bad is it?"

He frowned. Had he not registered his own injury?

"Bixby took a bullet straight into his heart. Hard to fault her aim. Did you see her, the shooter? That's the same woman I saw exiting the hotel room. She may well be Maria."

"I did." Charlotte reached for his collar, pulling at his shirt with shaking hands and no regard for buttons. He was still upright, but she'd once seen a man take a bullet, keep walking for minutes, then fall to the ground, dead. Recollections that made her heart leap and thrash against her ribs as if it might burst free. "She fired two rounds. A man is dead and you're bleeding. Where are you hit?"

"Stop. I'm fine." He caught her wrist in his hand and looked into her eyes. His expression reassured her that he was not critically injured. Still, he was far from fine. "The bullet only grazed my neck."

"Not the best shot after all, thank aether." The words rushed out on an exhale. "And you are *not* fine. There's a deep gouge at the base of your throat. In a few minutes it will hurt. Badly. You won't need stitches. Disinfection. A clean bandage." She yanked a handkerchief from her pocket. "Hold this against it."

Accepting the linen square, he released her. Frowned at the blood he'd smeared over her skin.

"It'll wash off easily enough." She inhaled deeply, willing her heart to settle.

He pressed the cloth to the gash. "Why terminate a man growing bone cells on collagen?"

"Or attempt to assassinate his captor?" Her lips pressed into a thin line.

He nodded, wincing at the pain the movement caused. "I can't help but think this is more than exotic pharmaceuticals."

"I'm inclined to agree. But what, exactly?"

"I wish I could say. Whatever it is, it centers around scales, feathers, and bone."

"And eggs." She tipped her head sideways at the small crowd gathering about them, unwilling to make eye contact with a single individual. "We've a growing immediate problem: witnesses and the variety of stories they're bound to tell. Not to mention the approaching police officer."

"Keep an eye out for Maria, I'll deal with the police. I'd hate for her to take advantage of the commotion to circle back and finish the job." Ryan stood and waved his badge at a frowning officer. "The suspect was in my custody," he told the man. "Someone didn't want me questioning him. We require your help."

As questions were asked and answered, Charlotte kept her back to the omnibus, scanning the onlookers for a familiar face and form. But Maria was gone.

An ambulance was summoned, and Bixby's body was carried away. A second body in as many days delivered into Hiram's care. They would hear much of that at Sunday dinner.

Should they manage to last that long.

# CHAPTER NINE

They were beyond late for his scheduled meeting with the Mexican anthropologist. But when a man in custody died on a public street, it tended to send the day into disarray. Despite their use of a side door, their arrival at the Customs House did not pass unremarked.

"Aether," an agent breathed as his gaze jumped from bloodstain to bloodstain, finally landing upon the wound at Ryan's neck.

"It only grazed the skin," Ryan muttered.

"Gouged," Charlotte corrected. "Deeply." She turned to the agent. "If there is somewhere we might clean up?"

Her hiked hemline hadn't spared her ruffled skirts from ruin. Not after she'd dropped to the sidewalk beside him, sliding her boot knife back into its sheath as the dust, dirt, and blood beneath her knees ground into the fabric. The same could be said of his pants. Add to that his coat—arms wrapped about a dying man as he sought cover. And his shirt cuffs as he pressed hands to Bixby's chest in a futile attempt to stem the flow of blood.

And the nick to his throat apparently made him resemble the walking dead.

"Of course. This way." The agent turned on his heel, led them straight to a small washroom and held open the door. "What kind of illegal cargo did you impound that ended in a dispute with shots fired? Stolen, rare or valuable? All three?"

"Mexican rattlesnakes." Ryan grumbled.

The agent drew up short. All blood drained from his face. "They're... you're... will we be expected to store—er—house them here? I'm not sure we have the—"

"*Dead* rattlesnakes," Charlotte clarified, swatting Ryan's arm. "No live animals will be passed into your care. Ignore Agent Nolan's complaints."

"Dead." The agent blinked. "That's..."

"Anticlimactic? In terms of contraband, yes. But the body count associated with my case has now doubled. The man we meant to escort here for questioning was shot and killed on a public street."

The agent opened his mouth. Shut it.

Maria had murdered Bixby—presumably a coworker or a man in her employ—then mere moments later took aim at Ryan. Boldly and openly on a New Haven city street.

Was the murderess protecting a pharmaceutical line? Her actions seemed disproportionally drastic to protect mere pills or potions. Plenty of men made fortunes peddling medicines of dubious benefit and the government did little to stop them. No. Something more was afoot.

Rose was—again—on his short list for questioning.

"Agent Nolan is bleeding and needs to be patched up." Charlotte's tone dragged them all back to his immediate needs. "If you'll bring some bandages and a bottle of the highest proof liquor you have."

The agent looked at Ryan's wounds and snapped to attention. "Does a confiscated 179 proof absinthe qualify?"

"That would be perfect."

The agent left.

"Most of the blood is not mine." Or so he hoped. "It's a mere—"

"Don't." Charlotte held up a finger, throwing him a look that warned of dire consequences. "You know as well as I that shock dampens the sensation of pain. Let me see what we're working with."

She was right. And the agent was back with toweling, bandages, and absinthe—and just as fast exited again, leaving them to their task.

With a heavy sigh and a nod, Ryan yanked off his coat and threw it aside. There was no saving it. Or his shirt. Nothing short of a prolonged soak in chlorine bleach would remove the stains—and that was before addressing the not-so-small matter of the bullet that had torn a ragged hole through the material. Alas, striding through a public building bare to the waist was not an option.

Left alone with the most basic of supplies, he and Charlotte took what amounted to little more than bird baths in the sink, washing dried blood from skin and blotting away the worst of it from their clothes.

Mouth pressed into a thin line, she turned her attention to the deep gouge at his neck with raised eyebrows. "No way around it, this is going to hurt."

Resigned to sharp, burning pain, he unbuttoned his shirt and shrugged a shoulder free from the damp, sticky cloth. And made the mistake of glancing in the mirror. He was not a pretty sight. "At least it doesn't need stitches?"

"Hmm." A noncommittal sound accompanied by the pop of a cork. She poured a generous amount of the green absinthe onto a clean cloth and pressed it to his throat.

All the blood drained from his face. "No infectious agent could survive that," he hissed through gritted teeth, fists clenched.

"That is the essence of the concept." Then her lips curved. She brushed the tip of a finger across his chest, over skin, muscle and crisp curls. "Nice," she hummed. Fire danced in her dark eyes, sparking an answering flame that rushed across his skin, setting every nerve ablaze. "What a shame it was, never catching more than a glimpse of such fine, strong muscles."

With the cold chill of an oncoming Wyoming winter hanging in the air or little to no privacy, their romantic encounters hadn't involved much in the way of bare skin exposed to lamplight. Heat threaded through him. He smiled. In rare, stolen daylight moments, there had been explorations atop clothing, occasionally beneath. Later, under cover of darkness and the warmth of a blanket, they'd managed a single evening together fully unclothed. He remembered the satin of her skin, the scent that was uniquely hers. Pressure, heat, and slick satisfaction.

"Another deficiency from the past we should set to rights," he said, his voice soft.

The burn of alcohol faded into the background as he dipped his head and caught her lips with his. Gentle at first, barely a brush of skin. Then a nip at the corner of her mouth. The soggy absinthe-saturated cloth hit the floor with a wet slap and her fingers, her nails dug into his shoulders—a sweet bite of pain. He backed her against the sink, cradling the curve of her jawline in his hand and deepening their kiss.

Before Charlotte, he would have denied that a woman could impact the thrill of chasing down rumors of cryptids, of turning over rocks in hopes of finding clues of their existence. But ever since their time together in the territories, his life had rung a touch hollow. True, discovery of the Tommyknocker had won him a coveted position within the Customs Agency that granted him access to files for which other cryptobiologists would give their left foot, but... he found he missed sharing the details with someone he could trust, someone who would argue contrary to his conclusions and force him to higher standards—in all parts of his life.

A clatter thud echoed down the hallway, reminding him they were far from alone. Anyone might walk in on them at any moment. And they were late. Very, very late.

"Last night I barely slept," he whispered. With regret, he pulled away knowing that at any moment, the Customs agent might return to shatter this illusion of privacy.

She lifted her eyebrows. "Your brother found a dent in his

car and spent the small hours howling outside your locked door?"

"Please, I would never admit to such a sin." He tugged at a loose curl. "Every thought was of you."

"Of me?" She pushed at his chest, stepping sideways to retrieve the bandages. But not before shooting him a look of teasing doubt. "Or my neighbors?"

"Both," he admitted. "Though everything always circles back to you."

"You'll be conducting surveillance again tonight." A flat statement delivered with only the slightest hint of an upturn at the corners of her mouth. Her hands wrapped gauze over the groove cut by the bullet, around and under his opposite arm. "Might as well take advantage of my kitchen window. It's the best place to view their antics—and less obvious than a parked vehicle." She swallowed. Took a deep breath. "I've a fossil I dug out of a hillside in the Dakota Territory that you'd find interesting."

Why the hesitation? "Dinner and a show?" What, exactly, had she found buried in the earth? He took a wild, over-the-moon guess. "Reconnaissance over wine, candles, and fossilized feathers?"

"You know me so well." She tied a secure knot in the gauze, gave it a gentle pat. Then drew the two halves of his shirt together and slowly pushed each button through its hole. "Yes to dinner. So long as you like tinned beef and hardtack."

He laughed, recalling how her idea of cooking dinner the night Cookie burned his hand was to open a can of sardines and pass out crackers. He plucked at damp fabric. "I'll see if I can't find something better when I change."

She tipped her head. "Stealing from your brother again?"

"Must you be so very precise? And is it stealing if the kitchen is in your family home?" He gave her a quick kiss and shrugged on his coat before scooping up the cardboard box while she lifted the humming incubator. "Let's not keep Professor Tetzopa waiting any longer."

They hastened to the impound room where, clipboard in hand. Professor Carlos Tetzopa was bent over a table, sorting through confiscated items of an archeological nature. Those of biological, perchance pharmaceutical, interest had been set aside. The visiting professor straightened at their arrival. "*Hola*, Agent Nolan. Miss—" The greeting died on his lips. For a moment, his gaze fixed upon the indelible bloodstains that marred their clothing, then he gave a shake of his head. "Tell me the thief is in custody, that you've recovered the missing items."

"I wish I could." Ryan slid the box they'd taken from Bixby onto the table. "Professor Tetzopa, meet Miss Charlotte Reid, friend and partner, from the Peabody Museum. She is both a paleontologist and a zoologist. Her focus is on the evolution of feathers."

Professor Tetzopa inclined his head. "I wish we met under more favorable circumstances, Miss Reid."

"As do I," she replied. "The past twenty-four hours have been... unusually dramatic."

"You refer to the bloodstains?"

"Among other events," Ryan said. "A suspected accomplice

is dead, killed by one of his own." Ryan reached inside the box pulling out one item after another. "We retrieved a carved jade bead, a few *tzabcan* rattlesnake skins, a quetzal feather that has seen better days. And what appear to be demineralized bone sections immersed in acid."

"Bone in acid?" Tetzopa swore in Spanish, passed a hand over his face, then took a deep breath. "Nothing else?"

Charlotte leaned forward, her attention sharp. "Is there something specific you're looking for?"

"Indeed. Come." Tetzopa beckoned them closer. "Before you are a number of items recently stolen from the National Mexican Museum. Not from displays, but from the storage rooms." He tapped his clipboard. "They were kind enough to telegraph me a list, complete with detailed descriptions." He waved a hand. "Zapotec ceramics and figurines, a gold lip-piercing ornament, a sacrificial obsidian knife and so on—all invaluable. This," he pointed at the jade pendant they'd pulled from Bixby's neck, "was on my list of missing items. It depicts the Maize god and was carved by a Mayan sculptor over a thousand years ago, long before Cortez and his conquistadors landed upon our shores. I am glad to see it recovered."

"What else is missing?"

"Three other artifacts." Tetzopa held up one finger. "The fragile fragment of an Aztec chīmalli, a ceremonial shield consisting of ocelot skin, feathers of numerous bird species, and beadwork."

Ryan exchanged a glance with Charlotte, wondering if ancient feathers or ocelot leather fell under the category of "things the wealthy would pay much to own".

She shrugged but lay the tattered feather beside the ceremonial shield. It was a perfect match.

Tetzopa lifted a second finger. "A bone of an unidentified species decorated with Mayan carvings."

Which explained why the man turned a shade of green when the acid was mentioned.

"And three." A final finger rose. "The contents of this pottery," he waved his hand at an ancient Mesoamerican ceramic vase resting upon the table, "with geometrical motifs in red and black."

"It's strikingly beautiful," Charlotte commented.

The archaeologist smiled. "It's Mixtec, terracotta pottery made by an indigenous people in southern Mexico many of whom paid tribute to the Aztecs in pre-Columbian times." His frown returned. "It was found with a lid sealed with a kind of plant resin glue."

On the table lay its lid, cracked in two. Ryan cringed. "Was it still sealed when it was stolen?"

"Not exactly," Tetzopa replied. "It was carefully opened a few years ago that we might study the contents. Parchment was discovered within—a codex with numerous glyphs. Folded, accordion style. After documentation, it was returned to the pot, the lid resealed to keep the contents safe."

"A codex painted on parchment?" Ryan asked, incredulous. "Not on fig tree bark?"

Tetzopa grinned. "You are right to question my choice of words. Many Mixtec codices are constructed from *amate*, fig-bark paper, much like those of the Maya. But the Mixtec are also known to have used stretched deerskin sewn into long strips."

"Any reason this particular codex wasn't celebrated or put on display?"

"The missing codex parchment is unusual. It's long and thin, not sewn together. Not a single seam can be found. And though it is animal skin, it is not that of deer."

Tetzopa had his full attention now. "Is it known which species provided the parchment?"

The professor shook his head. "Not for lack of study. Academic arguments grew ugly with claims that this 'discovery' was nothing more than a modern fake, not pre-Columbian at all. Many pointed to the impossible length of the parchment as proof." He paused, took a deep breath. "And when a handful of archaeologists floated the possibility the skin derived from an extraordinarily large serpent—especially as several of the glyphs recounted the story of the *koo savi* diving into a lake— chaos erupted."

He and Charlotte exchanged glances. Unusually long. Skin from a serpent. If there was any truth to the legend of the Quetzalcoatl or Kukulkan, this could be proof positive. His pulse quickened. Was it possible? The mere belief that it might well be so would drive a black-market dealer to madness attempting to acquire such a rare artifact. One sale might be the making of their fortune. Had Maria killed the Spanish smuggler to obtain this one specific item?

He frowned. What, then, to make of her most recent murder? Bixby had been killed in broad daylight on a public street. He'd known something incriminating, for certain. But what? Merely an address? Or was it linked to the cells growing inside the incubator?

"*Koo savi?*" Charlotte asked.

"The Mixtec term for the serpent of the rain, a plumed serpent that flies surrounded by rain clouds."

"A quetzalcoatl?"

Tetzopa rocked his hand. "Another source of debate. The same god, but in somewhat different forms, is known as Quetzalcoatl among the Aztec, Kukulkan among the Maya. There is much variation in the symbolism involving feathered snakes in Mesoamerican art. This god also takes a human form, shape-shifting if you will. God of the sun and wind, air and learning, he was also sometimes a symbol of death and resurrection." He paused to point at an image on the pottery, one of a skull and crossed bones. "One creation story of the Aztec credits Quetzalcoatl with traveling to Mictlan, the underworld, to locate human bones. Which he ground up and mixed with his blood, restoring them to life."

"Well, that paints quite the gruesome picture," Charlotte commented.

"Mythology often does," Tetzopa said. "In any case, given the arguments, the decision was made to return the codex to the vessel and re-seal the lid until more information regarding its origins could be brought to light."

"The missing codex." Charlotte hooked her finger over the edge of the Mixtec pot, tipping it to peer inside. Was she hoping to find a remnant left behind? "No one thought to chip away a little of the paint from the codex parchment to directly observe the animal skin beneath?"

Ryan too leaned closer, his mind pondering what link there might be—if any—to the Spanish *cuélebre*. Was this the preserved hide of a mythological dragon-like creature? Could it be they'd finally nailed down a precious item intended for a black-market bidding war for the rare and unusual? He imagined a roomful of gentlemen in frock coats and embroidered vests, women in silk evening gowns adorned with feathers of the all-but-extinct, fighting over the codex.

Tetzopa slid an impressed look at Ryan. "Are you so very certain she is not a cryptozoologist, like you?" He turned back to Charlotte. "You wish to posit that the skin is that of the *koo savi* itself? You won't be the first."

"I'm uncertain what to think of this missing parchment." She tipped her head to the side. A measured answer when she was clearly intrigued. Could it be she wondered if the codex might be proof positive of a past cryptid's existence? "If only I could view a section under a microscope..."

"Not possible." Tetzopa shook his head vehemently, rejecting the very suggestion. "The skin itself was prepared with gesso—a mixture of chalk and gypsum—to create a white canvas upon which the Mixtec artist painted, so it cannot be directly observed. Chipping away paint would destroy the value of the scroll. And knowing what kind of skin forms its base serves no purpose. Even were it discovered to be snakeskin, there is no such thing as a feathered serpent. Never mind what Agent Nolan wishes to believe." He paused, perhaps considering his next words. "Myths are sacred tales told to explain the unexplainable. They are not to be mistaken for scientific truths that reflect reality. The *koo savi*, the quetzalcoatl and the kukulkan are myths." He crossed his arms and shook his head. "Imagine a snake flying, feathered or not. Impossible and ridiculous."

Lost in thought, she nodded absently. Was she in full agreement? Ryan wasn't certain.

Tetzopa added, "You seem an intelligent, educated woman. Don't let Agent Nolan drag you into this nonsense."

Ryan smiled. He and Tetzopa had debated the existence of dragons before. Like Charlotte, he demanded clear and incontrovertible proof before he would acknowledge any possibility of their existence. High standards that were invaluable.

"Have no fear, Professor Tetzopa." She offered him a conspiratorial grin. "I don't believe anything that can't be proven with cold, hard data. Fact or fiction, Agent Nolan and I intend to discover who is behind these thefts and murders and put an end to them. Placing ourselves into a variety of possible mindsets is but one approach to uncover their motivation and goals—and one step closer to finding evidence."

"I can see how that might work," Tetzopa admitted.

Charlotte drifted over to the biological materials that had been set to the side. "Do either of you have any objections if I borrow a few of these feathers for closer examination? I'd like to look at them under a microscope."

"The quetzal feathers?" Tetzopa's eyebrows drew together in thought. "I cannot condone their collection for the purpose of adorning hats, but neither are they irreplaceable. So if it helps the investigation, I am not opposed."

She lifted one of the oddly long and thin feathers and squinted, turning to hold it up to the light. A ripple of disbelief crossed her face. Over feathers. What did she see that they didn't? A lot, he expected, given the intensity of her focus. If there was anything informative about the plume, he had no doubt she would discover it.

Leaving the archaeologist to finish his inventory, Ryan escorted Charlotte outside.

"I need to head home, to change." She swept a hand toward her bloody skirts. "And these feathers. There's something strange about them, though I'd rather not attempt to explain it. Not yet." Her expression was thoughtful, her gaze somewhat remote. A scholar sinking into deep contemplation.

"Charlotte," his voice was sharp. "Maria is still free, wandering about with a rifle and aether knows what other weapons." He wished to visit Rose without delay, to change. But couldn't set aside the worry that leaving Charlotte to travel the streets unescorted was a bad idea. "And likely numbers among those of your strange neighbors."

"I'll take a steam cab. Stay away from windows." She huffed. "Really, where else am I to go?"

One bloodied individual would be enough to worry Rose. And he'd not reveal Charlotte's identity to her either, on the off chance she worked with her husband. With Maria. "Come home with me."

Charlotte laughed. "Arrive at your family home covered in bloodstains? No. I'll have a proper introduction or none at all."

"You'll head to your brother's house?" He didn't like the idea of her returning to her house alone. Not one bit.

"I think not." She pursed her lips. "None of the clothes there will fit. And there is the matter of my young niece. I'll not have her or my sister-in-law see me like this. And there's my work. And these feathers. They require my undivided attention. Glory will keep me safe." She lifted an arm to hail a steam cab.

As it drew to the curb, he lifted his eyebrows in silent question. "Your dog?"

"Do you not recall how she's handled the groundhog situation?" Her eyes snapped with humor and confidence. "Be on your best behavior when you arrive tonight. I'd hate to see the two of you off to a bad start."

MARIA STORMED INTO THE HOUSE, slamming the door behind her with a loud thud. She cursed, her fists clenched and her face contorted into a scowl. She had failed. Two shots and only one kill. Unacceptable.

Ryan Nolan and his dark-skinned partner were proving to be a problem. Somehow, they'd uncovered Bixby's involvement, which meant Enzo's cover was likely compromised. Had Rose talked? The woman looked familiar, though Maria couldn't quite decide where she'd seen her before. Regardless, Bixby's incubator had been tucked beneath her arm.

Had her brother's assistant spilled any secrets before she had silenced him? Had she injured the IBIS agent badly enough to buy them time? She hoped so, but they couldn't take any chances. Not now when they were so very, very close to success.

"Romano!" She stomped through the house, heading for

the aviary. Much as she hated outsourcing an assassination, there was much she needed to arrange. Rose would be an easy target for the oversized, musclebound birdkeeper, and he might even manage to eliminate Nolan should the man dare to knock upon Rose's door once more.

With funds low and IBIS on their trail, they needed to cut their losses and head home to Spain. Tonight. There she had a multitude of contacts. Wealthy men willing to pay absurd fees to eliminate competitors, enemies, and other troublemakers quietly and permanently. All without bloodying their own hands.

Easy enough to resume her old profession, to accept a few more contracts. The family estate had been saved. Her parents and siblings lived in relative comfort. Enzo had attended the finest of universities and was a renowned herpetologist on the edge of his greatest discovery. All because of her.

A new laboratory on home soil had always been the plan. They simply needed to accelerate the timeline. Her brother would moan and complain but, in the end, he would agree. Money always had the last word. Always.

# CHAPTER TEN

Her mind was awhirl with disparate thoughts. Time spent with Ryan always threatened to bend her reality into new shapes and today proved no different. First gnome-like creatures from Cornwall, not-worms infesting a dead smuggler, now feathered serpents from Mexico. Not to mention shots fired on a busy city street. Could her day possibly grow any stranger?

She rather thought it might.

When she'd met Ryan, she was drawn like a moth to the flame by the animation and energy he brought to everything he did. Heat rose to her face. Fine. The man had a physique that curled her toes even in tight boots. Hair with a tendency to spike into disarray. Shoulder muscles that rippled beneath his shirt in a way that fixed her gaze. Strong hands capable of both great strength and the most gentle of touches. A nicely rounded backside that stretched downward into powerful legs. She'd drunk from that well repeatedly—without ever quenching her thirst. All while a tiny corner of her mind wondered if the man was quite sane.

Full of talk about kraken and pteryformes and Tommy-knockers and dragons, she'd not known what to make of his cryptid ramblings. Certainly, she'd stood on the streets of Paris, marveling as the shadow of a pteryform slid overhead. Had peered at the stomach-turning contents in jars labeled pickled kraken tentacles—if not dared to try any. But dragons and dwarves hiding in caves and mines? The man seemed to think there was no limit to what might walk the planet. At what point did such interests cross the line into insanity? A man intent upon chasing rainbows would not, ultimately, integrate well with her future plans.

She'd marked him as a passing fancy, one best enjoyed in the wild, then abandoned in civilization.

Yet here she was, corseted, bustled, and employed at a prestigious institution... riding home with bloodstains at her knees and strange green feathers in her hands. The man did nothing but turn her inside out. Feelings. Beliefs. Preconceptions. None of them managed to hold form in his presence, like glass shifting into water and pooling at her feet.

Quetzalcoatl. Both a feathered serpent *and* a god. Believing in the creature itself was difficult enough, the concept that a creature might fly without actual wings was a mental stretch she found herself unable to manage. Without evidence, proof, data, it was asking too much.

Even as she confronted the possibility that the not-quite-normal plumes in her hand might be key to unlocking one of his mysteries. She couldn't risk tucking the rare green feathers into her pocket, couldn't risk a single action that might crush a single vane. To stop her mind from whirling, it was imperative that she pass the feathers beneath the lens of a microscope as soon as possible to confirm what her eyes insisted was the truth.

The steam cab stopped before her home. She paid the driver and climbed down. Pulling a key from her pocket, she slid a glance in the direction of her neighbors. All was quiet, save for the chirping of those poor birds trapped in the backyard aviary, their feathers likely viewed as nothing more than dazzling trimmings for the fashionable.

Feathers held carefully aloft, she stepped inside, managing no more than two steps before Glory leapt toward her, tail wagging and tongue lolling—everything cheerful and bright at the early return of her human, proud to display the fresh blood that stained her muzzle.

"More, Glory? Really?" Charlotte heaved a sigh as she moved through the house to gaze out the window at the mangled cadaver of not one, but two groundhogs. "Look at us, Glory. Your fur, my best dress. We make quite the pair today."

She placed the feathers carefully upon a clean kitchen towel beside her tabletop microscope, then headed into her backyard to heave the groundhogs back over the fence. Glory dogged her heels, proud of her defense of the property, pleased that her workday had resulted in the demise of two invaders and two rodent-sized midday snacks. There was no convincing her otherwise.

The bodice of her dress strained the seams as she heaved with the shovel. Once. Twice. She cursed rabidly as each corpse took to the air, crashing into the dense overgrowth of the neighbor's yard.

Something on the other side squawked in protest. Or was it more of a screeching honk? Charlotte froze, hands still clutching the shovel as she locked eyes with her equally still and mystified dog.

"Was that a bird?" What did it mean that she wasn't entirely certain? Not for the first time, she pressed an eye to the crack between boards, peering through the fence. Thick plant life obscured her view, save for a few flashes of red. Too much red for a small songbird. A scarlet ibis?

She started to straighten when a door flew open, slamming into the side of the neighbor's house. A fit of coughing burst from his lungs. Feet snagged on branches and leaves and Charlotte caught glimpses of the umbrella man lurching across the yard. He came to an abrupt halt. Metal clinked and fabric shifted. Then he dropped to his knees and moaned. Loudly and awfully. He gagged, then vomited. A ghastly, foul fog of a smell overtook her nose and slithered down her throat. Gagging, she spun away, tossing the shovel as she ran for her kitchen.

She slammed the door and fell back against it as she dragged in a deep breath of unpolluted air.

"Why would anyone treat their property as an outdoor toilet when indoor plumbing reached New Haven years upon years ago?" She grimaced, wishing she could wipe the memory of that odor from her brain. Oof. Not at all the kind of particulars she'd wished to glean with her latest, inelegant attempt at spying.

Glory's eyebrows rose in distressed agreement—despite her daily use of outdoor facilities.

Charlotte rolled her shoulders and gave a shake of her head, hoping to disperse the nauseating image, then sat down at her kitchen table before her microscope. Her first priority this afternoon was to thoroughly examine the strange feather smuggled here from Mexico. She angled the mirror to catch the light, reflecting it upward through the stage and into the objective. Sliding the long, thin feather into place, she leaned forward, peering through the eyepiece as she adjusted the focus.

And frowned, utterly baffled. How could this be? This feather was indeed unlike any other she'd laid eyes on before.

She glanced out the window, eyeing the aviary with renewed interest and energy. Did the bird this feather belonged to dwell within? Was it possible a live specimen had been transported from the rainforests of Mexico to New Haven? There might well be a primitive bird caged next door, one as yet unknown to ornithologists world-wide. Her pulse leapt.

Once she showed this to Ryan, he was also going to want to have a look inside that aviary. After dark. Tonight.

Blood heated her cheeks at the thought of soon having him all to herself, alone. Well, at least for a few hours, until dusk fell or something new went sideways. Between the armed murderess at large and Maria's link to Charlotte's odd—now a kind and generous term—neighbors, they would be lucky if they managed an uneventful meal. Perhaps Maria would also fall ill, and no one would notice when they climbed over the fence.

She turned her attention back to her microscope.

Two basic feather types existed, downy and pennaceous. Both possessed a calamus, or quill, the part of a feather that inserted into the follicle of a bird's skin. The feather she'd appropriated from Customs was of the pennaceous variety. Well, at least it looked that way. Superficially.

Normal pennaceous feathers had a round, tube-like rachis that extended from the quill to form the central shaft of the feather. Barbs branched outward from the rachis to shape the vane. Branching from each barb were barbules that possessed tiny hooklets on their tips. These barbules interlocked with those of adjacent barbs, snapping together as a tight, well-organized surface, an arrangement necessary to support flight.

Such was not what she saw beneath the microscope.

Though the overall morphology was that of a basic feather—a central structure with branching elements forming a feather vane—the rachis was oddly narrow and oval, more flat than round. Even stranger, where the feather would have attached to the creature, the not-a-rachis failed to form a tube-like shape. There was no narrowing to indicate it inserted into a follicle.

*And follicles were how all feathers developed and grew. In every single bird species.*

Not only was this not a bird feather, it didn't even belong within the archaeopteryx species. Instead, the tip of this "feather rachis" was thickened and flat. Such as that of a reptilian scale. And the barbules? They overlapped and interlocked. But certainly not in any birdlike manner. Yet, still, she thought the feather just might have a structure that would allow for flight.

Her mind whirled.

Was she was looking at a right-wing flight 'protofeather' belonging to an as-yet unidentified species? So much for a magnified view providing any enlightenment. She was more confused than ever.

What on Earth was this creature? Bird? Reptile? Somewhere in-between? Was it an extant species, one that still lived? Or was the animal now extinct, living long enough alongside humankind in what was now Mexico such that its feathers had been collected and preserved?

Lips twisted with conflicting thoughts, she fell back against the chair, not quite able to believe her own eyes.

This was a breakthrough of untold proportions and there was not a single museum colleague with whom she could share this discovery. Her work on feather development in chickens was common knowledge, as was her unique opinion that the chicken was the closest living relative to *Tyrannosaurus Rex*, with alligators but distant cousins to them all. Most looked askance at her, preferring to point at the ostrich as the most dinosaur-like bird that still walked the planet.

Were she to dare float the idea that the likes of *T. Rex* might have sported rudimentary feathers, she'd be tossed out on her ear.

Only in Ryan had she found a quasi-colleague willing to entertain wild ideas about how dinosaurs might be related to birds. Everyone else scoffed at her theories, barely managing to master the roll of their eyes or the curl of their lips as they sought to inform her otherwise or quickly made excuses to exit the conversation.

To her ever-lasting delight, out West Ryan had shown himself to be an engaging conversationalist, willing to examine her hypotheses, turning each idea over to inspect it from every angle. He didn't always agree, but always presented logical reasons for his position.

In return, she'd forced herself to ponder the possibilities of cryptids, many of which were unexplained animals—but not all. Along with Tommyknockers, they'd debated the probable existence of other creatures with reported anthropomorphic traits—selkies, cat sìth, banshees, lamia, skin walkers and the chupacabra. To name a few.

Nor could she announce the discovery of a protofeather to those same colleagues without also explaining where it originated. Which, at this point, was as much a mystery as the green plume itself.

A vivid shimmer of iridescent green.

Iridescence was a funny thing, relying upon the reflection of light by the barbs of a feather. For example, Blue Jays weren't actually blue. Their coloration was due to Tyndall blue, a light scattering effect easily demonstrated. Hold one of their feathers close to a light source—removing the factor of light reflection—and the feather appeared brown.

The same mechanism underlaid iridescent green. The color was nothing more than a yellow base pigment overlaid by Tyndall blue. Yellow and blue made for green. But hold a green feather to the light and the color was reduced to brown.

Time to test the protofeather. She lifted it before her lamp. And her jaw dropped.

The iridescent green did not disappear.

Excitement built, bubbling to the surface, and tingling as it zipped through her veins like carbonated water. What she held in her hand was entirely unprecedented on many levels. But with only a light microscope, her analysis could not proceed any deeper.

She glanced at the kitchen clock. Hours would pass before Ryan arrived. Plenty of time. She ought to set the odd protofeathers aside, gather her Anzu chicken-from-hell speci-mens and apply herself to documenting the many unique fossil features of the feathered oviraptorosaur.

Would she make any progress with her mind awhirl over the plumage of an undiscovered Meso-American species that might or might not represent an intermediate between reptiles and birds?

Perhaps she might kill two birds with one stone?

For months she'd been entertaining the possibility that the alternating light and dark band pattern of Anzu's feather impressions weren't carbonized traces of the bacteria that had degraded the feathers but were instead remnants of actual melanosomes. And if she were to place a protofeather into the aether chamber of such a microscope?

Not that she could haul any of them to the museum to use the high-powered aetheroscope, a restricted use device requiring a training certificate and registering for a block of time. Something she'd avoided, preferring to hold the details of her discoveries close rather than face the onslaught of a million questions, none of which she could yet—or would—answer.

Instead, she'd leaned upon Hiram, pressuring him to allow her access to his personal aetheroscope. For weeks she'd dialed up the pressure, but there was always one excuse or another as to why he was too busy to train her.

But there must be a how-to manual on his bookshelf. How hard could it be to operate?

An immediate visit to her brother's home was in order.

# CHAPTER ELEVEN

"Rose?" Ryan pushed the door open.

At first, he'd hesitated about arriving on her doorstep covered in bloodstains, a bandage at his neck. Then he'd decided his beaten and disastrous appearance might help loosen her tongue. But after repeated ringing of the bell and a full minute of determined knocking failed to summon the steam butler, an uneasy feeling skittered down his spine.

He jimmied the lock and swung her front door open. "Rose?" A call made into a silent interior before he closed the door behind him and made his way into the parlor. He turned and found himself nose to nose with a deactivated steambot. A palm to the side of the contraption's neck fell atop cold metal. It had been hours since any coals smoldered within.

Muttering words unfit for the ears of high society women, he ventured further into the house. Rose, victim or fleeing suspect? Would he find her cooling corpse in the next room?

Or had she warned her husband the moment he left, setting Maria in motion?

Moving swiftly through the building, he searched for any sign of foul play. And found none.

Not that there wasn't an abundance of strangeness. Most of the rooms were bare. The Olive Street parlor where they'd met earlier this morning was filled to overflowing with decorative elements. Gold-framed pictures, a porcelain mantle clock, china figurines, silk cushions, fur blankets, crystal decanters. Not a single surface was left unadorned.

But the kitchen lacked every amenity. No steam cook stood idle awaiting a programed dinner punch card. Not so much as a clockwork mixer or a hand crank eggbeater lay within. He found only the most basic and rudimentary of kitchen utensils behind cupboard doors or tucked into counter drawers. Odd. He couldn't imagine Rose preparing her own meals.

He located her husband's study, a room easily identified by the toothy grins of an assortment of skulls and a framed photo of the professor, rifle in hand, standing beside a ten-foot-long alligator.

With the man's suspicious absence, his whereabouts unknown, Ryan felt justified prying the photo from its frame. He shoved it in his pocket. Useful, perhaps, if it came down to canvassing the neighborhood. A hasty search of the professor's desk, files and shelves turned up nothing noteworthy. Not that he'd expected Rodríguez to leave any incriminating evidence lying about.

Ryan jogged up the stairs, searching each bedroom and finding each more spartan than the last. When he finally located an occupied bedchamber, he found the walls devoid of decor, the coverlets thin and threadbare. Even more telling, not a single cosmetic or perfume bottle sat upon Rose's dressing table or the corner of a bathroom sink.

She'd run.

At least there was no sign of foul play. A relief, if not a point in her favor.

Something was very wrong here. Were appearances being maintained to conceal poverty? Or had the Rodríguez wealth been consolidated and liquidated? If so, to what end? To bankroll a profitable research project? Finance stock for a biopharmaceutical venture? Fund a swift return to Spain?

And what—exactly—was Rose's involvement?

A suspicious tingle lifted the fine hairs on his neck. Shoulder to the wall, he angled himself to look out a front window into the street below. Sure enough, a figure dressed in dark clothing leaned against the corner of a brick factory building. It was the man they'd followed to the docks the other night, the umbrella man.

Wearing an overcoat.

Last night's storm had dropped temperatures. But only for a few hours. As the sun arced its way through the cloudless sky, women had again raised parasols aloft and more than one man had loosened his cravat. The humidity had crept upward as well. Judging from the pained look upon the coated man's red face, the brick building was radiating enough heat to steam a bushel of clams.

He'd been followed. A quick check out a back window assured him that the man was not working with a partner, that the umbrella man's boiled brain believed Ryan would eventually exit the house onto Olive Street. But he'd failed to account for the neighborhood's arrangement.

Jogging down the back stairs, Ryan headed into the backyard.

Hopping a low picket fence at the rear of the property, he crossed a neighbor's yard to step out onto a street bordering Wooster Square. In a matter of minutes, he could be at the captain's house, hunting for any hint, any clue, any scrap of evidence that would tie Rose or her husband to the shady behavior of Charlotte's next-door neighbor. But the blood-stains on his white shirt dictated he first make a change of clothing.

With gritted teeth, he directed his feet toward his family home. Confrontation was inevitable, but he might, at least, reach his room without notice.

He climbed the outside edge of the rose trellis in an effort to spare the blooms, ignoring the prick and slash of their thorns. Then, bracing against the downspout, he lunged sideways to land on the angled roof that jutted out over the back entrance.

Long out of practice, he almost lost his balance. His shoe leather dug into the grit of roofing tile as he crept forward and raised up on tiptoes to reach for his bedroom window. The sash slid open and, with a mighty pull, he somersaulted into his room, landing with a graceless thud on the bare floorboards.

He shucked his coat, tossed his holster and weapon on the bed. Peeled off the ruined remains of his waistcoat and shirt. Frowned at his stained knees and added his trousers to the laundry pile. Nothing to do about his scuffed shoes as he hadn't packed an extra pair.

Wincing, he peeled the blood-soaked gauze from his throat, relieved to note the bleeding had stopped. As he applied a fresh bandage, worry began to creep in. For all his sang-froid Maria's second shot had been a near miss. And then the umbrella man had appeared outside Rose's house.

His ability to move freely about the city was well and truly compromised.

All they needed was a direct link between the smuggler and Charlotte's neighbors to have cause to raid the property. Top priority now involved searching the captain's house.

He dressed quickly, stuffed the photo of Rodríguez in the pocket of his new waistcoat and exited his room, turning toward the back stairs. He'd make a quick stop in the kitchen and—

"Liam." He drew up short.

Arms crossed, his brother blocked the stairwell. "Do you really think your acrobatic entrance went unremarked in broad daylight?"

"Move," Ryan growled. "I need to—"

"Visit your dying father." Liam grabbed his shoulder and spun him about, shoving him down the hallway toward the front of the house. "It's the right thing to do."

He hadn't thought of the man whose surname he bore as his father in years. He'd have said as much to Liam, but for the whole dying thing. "Not now." Charlotte was waiting and he needed to nose around inside Captain Donovan's house on the off chance the thieves or murderess had left behind a convenient clue. A quick turn and he'd escape via the front stairs. "I've a pressing matter—"

But any remaining hope of flight was cut off by the sight of his sister ascending those very stairs. A hand-painted floral teacup rattled in the saucer she held. Resignation and defeat dragged at her features. From the sag of her shoulders, one might surmise that only an overabundance of stiff and starched clothing kept her upright. A woman engaged to marry ought not spiral into such depression.

At the top of the stairs, Ellen threw a sad, silent glance in their direction, then trudged to her father's room.

"Foxglove tea," Liam explained. "Useful in small quantities, to strengthen the muscle of his heart. Unfortunately, increasingly frequent and large amounts of the bioactive substance, digitalis, eventually becomes toxic."

*And kills the patient outright.* Ryan nodded his understanding. Medicine or poison, it was all in the dose.

With Ellen's wedding on the horizon, he'd been doing his level best to not rock the boat. But perhaps that's exactly what his sister needed? Once Patrick Nolan died, there would be no one left who could decisively answer her question. Hell, he had no qualms about tipping the boat so far it took on water. What did he care if his relationship with the family patriarch finally sank to the bottom and settled into the harbor's muck, forgotten beside mummichogs and bluefish?

"Is Grandmother also with him?" He'd quite had it with the old witch and her son.

"Of course."

An idea began to take form. No more tiptoeing about,

refusing to acknowledge the dinosaur in the room. For that's what this was. A silent argument about Ryan and Ellen's right to call themselves members of this family. He would throw the windows wide open today. Sunshine and air to blow away the contagion of Grandmother's twisted views concerning breeding. Ellen deserved no less.

"Fine," Ryan said. "I'll go. But I'm not begging him for half the shoe factory, even if no strings or shoelaces are attached. That's all yours. If you want help, Princess Slipper is good with numbers, hire her. But making her fiancé Tom Boyle your partner when he cheated his way through multiplication tables? Bad idea."

"I don't care if you ever work at the factory again," Liam growled. "But you'll be polite. You owe me."

*Shit.* Had his intensions shown on his face? Or maybe his brother knew about the scratches on the side of his steam car? Ryan played innocent. "Whatever for?"

"A certain lizard from Mexico."

*Oh. That.* He snorted. "It's an iguana."

"Do I care what it's called?" His brother's grip transferred to the back of Ryan's neck as he leaned in. "Have you looked inside its mouth? Call it an herbivore all you want and go on about how it prefers leafy greens, but with those tiny, razor-sharp teeth it could easily remove a finger. And I could be saving your life by keeping you from the kitchen. Last night, Owen snuck out to the garden to fetch the *iguana* parsley. Ripping it all out by the roots to feed his new best friend. Cook is exceedingly displeased. You. Owe. Me."

"Fine." He would speak with the old man. A few minutes of playing nice, then he'd exit via the front door.

The hum and whirr and rattle grew louder as they approached the master bedroom. There, an oxygen concentrator prolonged the life of Nolan Shoes. When not working, Patrick Nolan's life had been dedicated to indulgence. Drink. Rich foods. An ever-present pipe never empty of tobacco. Over time, his heart had lost its ability to function effectively. Digitalis had helped for a while, but there was only so much the medication could overcome. Patrick Nolan was in end stage cardiac failure and his lungs were filled with fluid.

Liam reached around Ryan, opened the door, and gave him a shove. "A surprise guest to see you, Father!"

Impossible not to notice the enormous hulk of a machine covered in knobs and dials that crouched bedside. It ran twenty-four hours a day, seven days a week, compressing air into a reservoir, then slowly administering the purified gas via a system of pressure regulators and flow valves such that a steady flow of oxygen traveled through tubing to a mask strapped to the old man's face as he lay, propped up by a mountain of pillows atop the four-poster bed wearing a red flannel nightshirt.

The street-facing windows were shut, and the blinds drawn, rendering the space insufferable. The device generated a listless current of air that did little to stir the malodorous cloud of disinfectant and decay that pervaded the room. With the mercury at its midafternoon peak, a sheen of sweat glistened on Patrick Nolan's forehead as he flapped a hand at his daughter's efforts to persuade him to consume a cup of steaming tea, one that added a cloying medicinal note to the overall miasma.

Mere seconds in such a sick room and his own stomach soured. The urge to yank at his cravat threatened to overwhelm. Ryan settled for clearing his throat. Loudly, to compete with the clang of the compressor.

The dying man shoved himself upright and yanked the rubber mask from his face. "You!" he wheezed.

"Me," Ryan agreed. But his gaze was fixed upon his not-grandmother. Swathed in enough layers of black to smother a crow, she sat bedside, motionless, her perpetual frown accentuating every wrinkle as she glared at him with gimlet eyes.

"What are you doing here?" Patrick Nolan demanded. "Studying dragons. Such ridiculousness. I told you in no uncertain terms—" He replaced the mask and sucked in a deep breath of oxygen. "—never to darken my doorway again."

"Not even if I were to tell you their hides make for excellent shoe leather and offer you a sample for the most discerning of clients?"

Patrick Nolan glared. But there was a glimmer of avaricious interest. He inhaled, preparing to fire a retort then fell into a coughing fit and yanked the mask back to his face, dragging in deep gulps of air.

His not-grandmother stood. "Are you here to hasten him to an early grave?"

"To what end?" Ryan answered the old bird, lifting a shoulder. "It's not as if my name is written in the will."

Beside him, Liam stiffened. "Why would you say that? Of

course you're—" He narrowed his eyes at his father. "What have you declined to share?"

Beneath the rubber mask, Patrick Nolan's face took on the hue of an eggplant. A color that spoke to the amount of fluid filling his lungs, preventing sufficient oxygen from reaching his blood.

"That we share a *mother*, but not a father," Ryan answered for him. "While he tomcatted about New Haven, Mother found respite, however brief, in the arms of another man."

"What!" Liam took in the various facial expressions. Not one registered surprise. "How long has this been common knowledge?"

"Common?" He rocked his hand. "Mother whispered in my ear before she died that Captain Donovan sired me. Everyone in this room is aware, save you." He gave Liam a moment to let that sink in before addressing his elders. They'd sort through this here and now. "Were you so keen to be rid of Ellen that you pressured her to accept the first to offer for her hand?"

"Ryan, it's not necessary." His sister set the teacup on the bedside table. "It's just a clock."

"Is it? Most soon-to-be brides smile at any mention of their wedding. Misery overlays your every expression."

Ellen glanced at the door, but abandoned her plans to escape, sinking into a chair instead. Fixing her gaze upon the floor, she gave the faintest of nods.

"What's this about a clock?" Liam demanded.

"The parlor clock," Grandmother clarified. The family

matriarch's feathers were well and truly ruffled now. "Built by my great grandfather with his own hands in Ireland and—"

"—hauled over on the boat when you fled the Great Hunger." Liam rolled his eyes. "Yes, we've all heard the story a million times. If Ellen wants it for her new home—"

"Absolutely not," Grandmother snapped. "It's a family heirloom, one that is not to leave this house."

"But Ellen—" Liam stopped.

"Another cuckoo in the nest," she harrumphed. "I told Tom Boyle as much."

Patrick Nolan yanked the mask from his face. "Ellen is my own blood." Replaced it, took a deep breath, glaring at Ryan. "When I caught your mother stepping out, we struck a deal." He coughed, dragged in more oxygen. "She promised to be faithful." Another long inhale, followed by a raspy exhalation of words that dropped like acid from his lips. "Lest I turn her illegitimate child out into the streets."

"You're absolutely certain," Grandmother huffed, still unwilling to concede she'd made a grievous error, "that Ellen is yours?"

"Mine." A word that erupted as part bark, part croak.

"Very well." The old bird rose, shook out her feathers and lifted her beak. "Then I suppose she can have the parlor clock, if Liam is amenable." Gathering what remained of her dignity, his not-grandmother—thank aether—flounced across the room intent upon making a dramatic exit.

Save his brother stepped in front of the door, blocking her. "Not so fast. The confounded clock is but a symptom." Steam all but poured from his brother's ears. "Is Boyle not to your liking, Ellen?"

A tear escaped the corner of her eye. A second tear joined it. Together they traced a silver path downward across her pale cheek. "He is... was... adequate." She twisted the engagement ring upon her finger, staring at the floor.

"But?" Ryan prompted.

"Ever since he spoke to Grandmother about the clock, since she hinted that—" She exhaled, drew in a deep breath. "Kate is no longer 'at home' to me. Brenda has misplaced the blue, sapphire ring I was to borrow for my wedding day. And Sally sent a long rambling letter full of inane excuses as to why she cannot attend the ceremony."

"So much for the bonds of childhood friendship," he muttered.

"Do you want this marriage, Ellen?" Liam demanded.

She shook her head, scattering the tears. "No."

"That settles it. Call the wedding off. No sister of mine is settling." His brother cleared his throat. "If you'd like, you could work at the factory."

Ryan spoke up. "Better, sign over to Ellen whatever percentage of the business you intended to give me."

Ellen stood, smiled through her tears. "Really?"

Grandmother sniffed. "A fast path to becoming an old maid, that."

"Absolutely not," her father gurgled, eyes bulging as his nose turned puce. Then his eyes rolled back, and he collapsed onto the mountain of pillows, unconscious.

"Look what you've done!" Grandmother cried. "This talk

of his daughter working in a factory is killing him. But it's right and good that you waive your claim on Nolan Shoes." She glowered at Ryan. "All that's left is to sell your half of the house, while you're about it and erase the stain of your birth from Wooster Square."

"Please. I'm not even mentioned in Father's will." Ryan rolled his eyes and turned away. He was done with her nonsense. Time to leave.

"Not *this* house, you numbskull." The old bird squawked. "Did she not inform you this morning?"

Hand on the doorknob, he looked over his shoulder. "Inform me of what?"

An unholy light lit her eyes. "That Captain Donovan left you half his house. The other half went to your sister."

"Sister?" He glanced at Ellen who frowned, equally confused. "Did we not just establish that Ellen is, in fact, a full-blooded Nolan?"

"Oh, such willful ignorance." The old bird's beak parted to reveal yellowed teeth, ones which ought to have been needle-like and glistening with venom, which flashed as a spiteful laugh grated from her lungs. "This is simply too precious. I refer to your other sister, Rose. She's waiting for you now." His not-grandmother pulled a folded note from her pocket and held it out to Ryan.

He snatched the paper from her. Rose's handwriting leapt at him from the page.

*Please meet me at 48 Greene Street as soon as possible. I have important news.*

"His former fiancée?" Ellen whispered, aghast.

A queasiness overtook Ryan's stomach as his mind rewound. Rose's infamous walk of shame from the docks. *Not Captain Donovan's paramour, but his* daughter? It seemed the airship captain had made a habit of seducing unhappy wives.

The old shoe baron rallied and woke, yanking his mask away. "Pills," he gasped. "Tea."

His sister picked up a packet of pills emblazoned with the red ink stamp of a fanged snake and shook one into her hand. "Here, Papa."

"Stop!" With two strides Ryan was bedside. He plucked the packet from his sister's hand. "How long has he been taking these and who prescribed them?"

"It's a common enough prescription, a natural remedy the physician advocated." The old bird snatched the packet away. "It's for his rheumatism if you must know. I myself have found them exceedingly helpful. As have many acquaintances. Age comes with its aches and pains. I see no reason to suffer needlessly."

"What do you, a dragon hunter, know of medicine?" Father popped the gray capsule into his mouth and swallowed, chasing it with foxglove tea before dragging the oxygen mask back to his face.

A new possibility raised its monstrous head.

What was Rose up to? Abandoned by friends and family—including him—had she turned to a life of easy crime? Married a handsome Spaniard with family money only to find he was slightly mad and burning through the family coffers at an alarming speed? Was that the place Cisco had held in her life, drug supplier? Between her insight into local society and her husband's import connections, the ideal clientele would have been easy to pinpoint and target. Aether, had revenge and profit led her to peddle questionable products to her unsuspecting neighbors?

Ryan closed his eyes briefly and pinched the bridge of his nose. "And how long has this been a prescribed therapy?"

"A little over a year," Liam answered. "Why do you ask?"

"My case. This morning I attended an autopsy of a man using exactly this product. His abdominal cavity was riddled with worm-like parasites."

Father gagged, heaving forth the contents of his stomach onto the coverlet, then reached for his mask, gasping for oxygen.

Not technically the cause of Francisco Alcantra's death but let them worry. The residents of Wooster Square would do well to question the quality of the care provided by the neighborhood physician with clear ties to Rose. Another task for him to complete. He would need to alert Customs that they might reach out to local medical oversight committees.

"Worms?" The old bird's complexion grew sallow. The packet of pills she held shook like an autumn leaf in the wind. "From *these* capsules?"

"From a product with the same imprint. The stylistic icon indicates what you're consuming—powdered *raw* rattlesnake. Some recent batches were infested with pentastomid cysts."

"Worm eggs." His brother echoed in a flat voice. "That's what brought you here to New Haven."

Ryan rocked his hand. "Not technically worms, as the

larvae possess hook-like appendages. Connected to my case, yes. But not the precipitating incident." He coughed to cover an inappropriate burst of laughter—he would never forget such a collection of horrified expressions. "Dr. Reid, a pathologist, might prescribe an intestinal purgative, should you ask." Would something such as wormwood or gentian cure an infestation of stem arthropods? "But my understanding is that the most common approach is to hope for the best and wait for them to... pass." He paused a moment while they digested his words. "Now. I must withdraw from this charming family interlude as I've pressing dragon-related business to be about."

The stink of imminent death clung to him as he exited the house. But the oven-like blast of the afternoon heat promised to burn away the stench. Cutting through Wooster Square without regard for flowerbeds or pathways, he aimed for Captain Donovan's house. Former refuge, it was now an unwanted inheritance functioning as a smuggler's warehouse.

He'd had more than his fill today of twisted family secrets. At least he needed no one's permission to inspect the property.

# CHAPTER TWELVE

Hiram would still be at work. Which meant she could use his aetheroscope without him hovering and holding his breath as if his little sister might break his most favorite toy.

To be fair, there *was* precedent. He'd scrimped and scraped and saved endlessly to buy himself an ophthalmoscope. And she'd ruined it the very next week attempting to peer into the eyes of a parrot. Or, to be even more precise, the parrot had ruined the medical device. One ought to approach birds perched on the shoulders of crusty, old aeronauts' shoulders carefully.

But she was an educated professional now and would treat the aetheroscope with the care and handling it required and deserved. She *needed* to use his aetheroscope. She certainly didn't dare operate the Peabody's to complete her independent research. Out of the question. The moment she worked on the

Anzu fossil within the museum's walls was the moment they could insist a supervisor be listed as an author on her paper.

C.S. Reid wasn't about to toss them the tiniest crumb when the work was purely hers.

She would gather her samples, the lithic fragments she'd scraped from the dark stripes of the Anzu's fossil feather impressions, and take them to her brother's house to address the question: were the stripes of pigmentation melanosomes, color-bearing organelles, fossilized within the partially degraded feathers and filaments?

Such was academic work. A necessary step to validate her hypothesis. Only with this data could she finish her monograph and send it to the journal editor on time as promised. Her career depended upon it.

And if she happened to slip a protofeather or two into the aetheric chamber to gaze upon when her examination was done to explore possibilities, what harm would it do? No point in wasting the precious substance, carelessly venting it back into the atmosphere without taking full advantage.

She looked down at Glory and grinned. "Would you like to visit the princess?"

Glory leapt to her feet, tail wagging furiously. An enthusiastic "yes".

Her sister-in-law Isla would be at home with her niece Aileen, an adorable four-year-old who claimed she was royalty, that her prince would soon carry her off to a castle. It possessed a moat, of course, and a drawbridge. And tall turrets and a stable for unicorns. Of which Glory was one. Fortunately, the dog did not seem to mind wearing the paper mâché, rainbow-hued horn Aileen insisted upon tying to her head with a ribbon whenever they visited.

"Let's go." She stood, frowned at the stiffness of her knees, then realized she'd been so lost in the twists, turns, and tunnels of deep thoughts that, for a time, it had slipped her mind her skirts were ruined. Certainly unfit for wear.

Upstairs, Charlotte threw the doors of her wardrobe wide and eyed another of her favorite dresses. This one had a floaty cream skirt atop swags of lace and satin and tulle. Perfect for a romantic evening at home. If one spent peering out of windows. With a man who was the worst possible choice for advancing her academic career. Who led her into situations ending with gunfire on the streets of New Haven. Wildly attractive and anything but dull.

"What do you think, Glory, will such attire overly tempt fate?"

The dog tipped her head in somber contemplation.

"What is life without a little risk?"

Glory sighed and sank onto the ground, looking at Charlotte with impatience, resignation, and somber judgment.

"You're right of course," she said. "A woman shouldn't cast aside all logic just because a man she can't stop thinking about is in town." She tossed the bloodstained skirt deep into the closet and tugged out the pearly fabric. "And yet..."

She would almost certainly regret her decision, but still chose to pair her skirt with a favorite tea-stained blouse. Its embroidered neckline was perfect with her burgundy corset with brass clasps. Her thigh-high stockings, though delicate and pretty, were anchored with leather garters designed to hold her throwing knives. With that in mind, she pulled on her custom-made boots. Then stuck out her leg, waggling her bad ankle back and forth, checking on the internal braces sewn into their sides. Today's mad dash had sent warning twinges to the reconstructed joint. Better prepared tonight than limping and forced to choose between holding Ryan back or being left behind.

A final glance in the mirror, the adjustment of a few hair pins, and she judged herself presentable.

With Glory on a leash and Charlotte's samples and feathers carefully stowed in a shoulder bag, they set out for her brother's house. Which involved prying a few boards from the back fence that she might sneak out through a hole. It seemed wise to avoid any chance of Maria sighting them in her crosshairs. A few rights, a few lefts and they'd arrived. Not too far away to prohibit easy visits—or a quick free meal—yet far enough away that her brother wasn't in the habit of dropping by or appearing without warning. Not with a young one with an early bedtime.

She knocked on the door.

Isla opened it, threw her a wicked grin, and called, "Aileen! Important guests have arrived."

Charlotte's niece came running, skidding to a stop before Glory and throwing her arms about her neck to bury her face in soft fur. All while her guest wagged her tail so hard and fast, she shook with pleasure. "It's been *forever!*"

It had been three days.

"You're just in time for tea, Glory," Aileen pronounced, shifting the ever-present tiara atop her curls back into place.

She detached her matching necklace to secure it about the dog's ruff. "Though sadly underdressed. There, that's better."

Rubies and diamonds glittered and flashed. Paste, Charlotte had first assumed, only to reconsider the very next minute. Isla had a complicated past she avoided discussing. Her education was top notch—as were her kitchen skills. Not that Charlotte cared what social strata her Scottish sister-in-law had been born into. In truth it was Isla's lightning-fast reflexes along with her eyes that occasionally reflected a curious yellow in low light that gave her pause. Could her sister-in-law see in the dark? She'd not yet managed to find a respectful way to ask.

Her niece detached herself from her canine guest to greet her aunt with perfect courtesy and a quick hug. "Would you care to join us, Aunt Charlotte? The queen baked new liver cookies this morning." Perfectly polite, but from the shifting of the little girl's eyes, it was clear she preferred a tea for two.

"Thank you, Princess Aileen." She schooled her face not to grimace at the thought of liver in cookie form. "But I've work to which I must attend."

Arm slung about her drooling guest, her niece escorted Glory into the parlor, cookie tin in her other hand, chattering about the recent rainstorm and the rainbow she'd seen this morning.

"Tea?" her sister-in-law asked while suppressing a giggle. "I do have meatless cookies."

Charlotte pulled a face. "That phrase alone is very wrong. Don't put yourself to any trouble, but tea would be welcome—

after I spend some time in my brother's study." She lifted her samples.

Isla hesitated. "If you break it—"

"I will sell a rare fossil and buy him a new one. An hour and one tube of aether, that's all I need."

Her sister-in-law frowned. "You know it's the newest model, straight from Edinburgh?"

She rolled her eyes. "Complete with an oversized aetheric chamber and an objective that can resolve intracellular structures. Even better, it's coupled to a tintype photographic device that will render a permanent image of whatever the microscope reveals. So he's informed me a thousand times. I'd wait—" a white lie, "—but there are pressing concerns."

Over a fossil. After it spent millions of years in a canyon. Her reasoning sounded lame to her own ears, but there was no explaining the last twenty-four hours. But her sister-in-law was accustomed to the eccentricities of academics.

"Very well." Isla waved her off. "I'll oversee the princess and the unicorn."

Inside her brother's study, Charlotte wasted no time. With the flip of a switch, the aetheroscope's motor began to hum. Battery-powered without any open flames, it was safe for indoor use. She gently tapped the vial of Anzu samples—thin, ashy flakes—onto a glass slide. From an overhead shelf, she lifted an eye-dropper bottle, adding a single drop of the precious and rare cytokeratin stain onto the dark chips she'd pried free from the fossil feather's impressions. She let it sit on a slide-warmer to dry while she prepped the photographic materials for tintypes.

Waiting, she sank down onto a chair, trying to ignore her surroundings. True to his profession as a pathologist, there were various bits of icky, squicky deformed and infested human body parts floating in jars of preservative, tucked into glass-fronted cabinets about the room. Studying the dead for clues to save the living. Noble. Honorable. And really, really disgusting. Proud of her brother she might be, but the decor had the effect of making the room feel far, far smaller than it actually was. And it was hard to shake the feeling that something watched. Even if she spied no free-floating eyes.

She locked her gaze on the shelves filled floor to ceiling with medical texts, schooling herself to ignore her peripheral vision.

A few minutes later, the slide was dry, and she set it inside the aether chamber. Which left plenty of room for the protofeather beside it.

With the small door fastened tight, she vented the air within. Next, the aether. Checking to ensure the seal on the metallic tube had not been broken, she inserted the cartridge and gave it a sharp twist, breaking off the cap. A soft hiss accompanied the release of the gas. She turned on the light and bent to the eyepiece, adjusted the objective ever so carefully, and began to scan the slide. She held her breath as paper-thin butterfly wings fluttered inside her stomach. This was the moment of truth.

Her heart leapt. There. The flakes taken from the Anzu feather impressions lay before her, their secrets revealed. There was no denying that she was looking at microbodies, elongated    pigment-containing    intracellular    organelles embedded in keratin fibers. Conclusive evidence that her fossil, Anzu, the chicken-from-hell had possessed striped feathers!

She jumped from the chair and spun about, hands in the air, hopping up and down. Her grin threatened to split her face in two.

Plenty of questions remained, of course. What was the exact coloration of the fossil dinosaur's feathers? Melanosomes produced a range of color and that was before one addressed any overlying structural color. Impossible to know from a mere feather impression. Still, not a single fossil dinosaur in North America had ever even been *associated* with feather impressions. Not so much as a single one.

She laughed and dropped back onto the chair, squirming with delight. Feather impressions? Find of the decade. Add to that the discovery of preserved pigmentation? Find of the century. Her monograph would be groundbreaking. Her induction into the Academy of the Sciences was all but guaranteed. An event that lay in the future. For now, she could tell no one.

Save Ryan. He would hold his tongue.

First she needed to document everything. With a deep breath, she settled her shaking hands and, over the next several minutes, applied herself to making a number of tintypes, documenting her findings. At last, the task was behind her. Now for this afternoon's second act: examination of a brilliant green feather that should not exist.

She reached for the dials that moved the microscope's stage within the aether chamber to bring the protofeather into view.

Hoping for more than one momentous discovery in a single day was probably asking for too much, but it didn't keep her from holding her breath.

The lens panned over the proto-barbs, revealing their odd shape. One never before documented in a feather—not in paleontology, not in cryptozoology. As was the tip of the proto-rachis, the part that would insert into the animal's skin. It resembled the proximal end of a snake's scale rather than the tip of a bird's quill.

Equally strange, elongated melanosomes lay within the keratin fibers in hexagonal configurations, an arrangement that could account for the glitter and glimmer of the feather.

But when she'd held the plume to the lamplight, the green had remained. That was non-structural color. Were the melanosomes also producing green pigment, a color that could not be obliterated by altering the proximity of a light source? She activated the spectral analyzer to determine the absorbance curve. Heavens, it was exactly as she'd thought: green! Could this be a new, copper-based pigment?

Straightening, she blinked. It was almost too much to take. Almost. Moments like these were as rare as hens' teeth.

In short, this protofeather did not belong to a bird. Nor did it belong to a reptile. And it possessed properties and pigments never before documented. She had no idea what creature could possibly have spouted this incomprehensible plume.

Her tintypes were almost complete when Hiram arrived, his voice booming. "What are you doing in here?"

She startled, dropping the metallic photographs in a clatter. "Work. Groundbreaking work. And you offered to let me use your aetheroscope last week." She narrowed her eyes. "What are *you* doing here?"

"I offered to let you use it while supervised. And it's *my* office." He held up a jar. Inside, a number of disgusting not-worms swirled.

"More of those pentastomids?" She would not gag. Absolutely would not. Swallowing hard and repeatedly was not at all the same thing.

"I compared them to the others we have in a reference library. They possess certain features not seen in other pentastomids."

A library. Of worms. She wasn't going to ask. "And?"

"One I pulled from the liver possesses disarticulated net-like plates, the likes of which have never been recorded." He waved at the aetheroscope. "I want to take a closer look. Some characteristics remind me of tardigrades, others evoke attributes of protostomes."

Never before recorded. There was quite a bit of that going around today. Interesting. But Hiram's findings were curious only to those willing to study invertebrates. A group to which she decidedly did not belong. Still, the day had developed a theme. Ought she share her discoveries with him? No, she would tell Ryan first. To celebrate. Besides, his not-worms and her protofeather weren't linked. Were they?

"I'll leave you to it. I've promised to drop in on the princess's tea party." If only briefly.

Charlotte smiled, looking forward to tonight's date. She popped the release valve, opening the chamber and venting the precious gas. If evidence accumulated against her neighbors, would Ryan make plans to raid the house? She frowned. There were no other IBIS agents in New Haven, or they wouldn't have sent him here. Her heart sank. Which meant he intended go in alone, up against several other people. One of whom was coughing and hacking and running into the far corner of the yard to empty his stomach.

"I've a medical question for you," she began. "My neighbors..."

Hiram closed his eyes. "Them again?"

She described what she'd witnessed today.

"An aviary filled with birds," Hiram repeated. "What could possibly go wrong? So very many things. The first thing that springs to mind is psittacosis. There's a range of symptoms —headache, fever, chills, coughing, diarrhea, and more—that can result in severe pneumonia."

"And psittacosis is?"

"Also known as ornithosis."

She twisted her lips and rolled her eyes.

Her brother snorted. "An infectious zoonotic bacterial disease sometimes also called parrot fever. It comes from direct contact with infected birds—or by inhaling airborne feather dust, feces, or urine."

"That's beyond disgusting." Hiram, always the life of the party.

He shrugged, then pulled open a drawer and handed her a gas mask. One that covered both the mouth and nose, but not the eyes. Built of leather and canvas, two copper-clad filter canisters were affixed to either side.

Her jaw dropped. "That bad?"

He nodded. "Give this to Ryan. The mask will filter out any particulates, keeping them from entering the lungs and lodging there. Goggles would also be advisable. Fatal cases are rare but, from your stories, he'll be unable to resist taking a peek." Then, with a heavy sigh, he produced a second gas mask. "And you. Since you'll not be left behind."

She certainly wouldn't. And given the way Glory had been digging at the base of the fence— Sliding the masks, her samples, and tintypes into her bag, she vacated his desk. "If I bring you a sample of this feather dust?"

"I'll see if I can validate my hypothesis."

"Thank you." Mind buzzing, she exited Hiram's home office. Time to collect her unicorn, head home, and fashion a gas mask for a dog.

# CHAPTER THIRTEEN

Ryan approached the front door, lock picks in hand. Not that they were necessary.

With the twist of a knob, the door swung open upon well-oiled hinges. Inside, an ominous silence greeted him. Weapon drawn, he crept down the tiled hallway, aghast at what lay before him. Or, rather, didn't. Each room he passed was empty of all possessions—furniture, rugs, and decorative elements. Carved marble fireplace surrounds missing. Light fixtures removed, leaving behind bare tubing. Windows that once held intricate stained glass boarded over. All wealth stripped away. Sold to the highest bidder to support a certain Spaniard's enterprise?

Thus prepared, his heart still sank when he stepped into the library to find it devoid of all books, of all the captain's extensive, if odd, collections. Gone was the giant, man-eating seashell, the footstool constructed from a wooly mammoth's foot, the spotted zebra's hide. The narwhal's tusk was missing. The dried cloven hoof of a purported devil, absent. As was the jar in which floated a length of tentacle studded with mysterious curved claws that washed ashore, preserved as a reminder of all the ocean secrets yet to be discovered. The list his mind compiled was endless. All upsetting.

Every last item the captain had collected had been stripped away. All that remained were Ryan's memories, now cast in an entirely different light. Especially one.

Bone. Mayan bone, to be specific. Tetzopa had listed carved bone among the archeological items missing. Upon learning Rose had inherited Captain Donovan's property and the contents therein, his unconscious mind had been at work in the background, searching through the vast inventory of the airship captain's prize possessions until his memories came face to face with the recollection of a Celtiberian bronze carnyx, an elongated war trumpet, once kept propped against the side of the fireplace.

Some two yards tall, the bell of such a war trumpet—most often shaped like the head of a snarling wild boar—was designed to extend far above the heads of warriors, emitting an eerie noise as they advanced. Not so much as a warning, but rather with the intent to cause confusion and panic among their enemies as their army marched onto the battlefield. An early form of psychological warfare.

This particular carnyx possessed a long body ending in a dragon's head, one flanked by two broad wings. Its toothed and hinged maw stretched wide in a silent roar—until one blew through the mouthpiece. Then, an unearthly, haunting bellow spanning a range of sounds from a low, vibrating growl to a high-pitched screech emerged. Impressive enough all on its own.

Eerie noises aside, Ryan specifically recalled that, set into the green-patinated bronze head, were two bone eyes with gleaming pupils fashioned from rough-cut rubies.

*Bone.* In a stylized dragon's head. In an ancient piece collected from the Asturian principality of Spain. From whence hailed both Rose's husband and the mythological *cuélebre* dragon.

Ryan remembered studying the two yellow-white discs, wondering from what animal the bone originated. Cow? Sheep? Possibly a dragon? He'd had long since accepted that the captain's agreement with his speculation was nothing more than good-natured encouragement of a youthful fantasy. Or was it?

Biological material set into a carnyx that had been handed down from generation to generation along with the legend of how it had been sounded as the warriors approached the *cuélebre's* cave on a magical midsummer's night, intent upon killing the creature that they might steal the treasure so carefully guarded by the bat-winged serpent-dragon.

Now an egregiously missing item.

Unlike Rose. Though her presence in the house was a novelty. Not once could he call to mind a single time Captain Donovan had interacted with her, not before the fateful day she'd returned from the stateroom of his airship and severed her engagement to Ryan.

A decided atmosphere of resignation and gloom swirled in

the air with the dust motes as he turned to face the silhouette perched upon the window seat.

"So, little sister, did you gift your husband the war trumpet in exchange for a proposal and a swift wedding?" A suitcase rested at her feet. Beside her, a pile of papers. Her overall expression one of defeat.

"I warned Enzo it was a bad idea to use this address for shipping his supplies. That someone in the neighborhood was bound to notice. But I was wrong. Not a soul commented. No one investigated. Even you had to be prompted." Rose turned her face away to stare out the window. "I'll keep my story short." She dragged in a deep breath. "Upon returning to New Haven, Captain Donovan heard the disturbing news of our engagement and could hold his tongue no longer. He contacted my presumed father, admitting to yet another local affair, revealing my fiancé to be my half-brother. You might imagine the chaos of emotions that followed. My father paced, casting me dark glances while muttering about the questionable paternity of the children on Wooster Square."

Ryan grunted, wondering much the same. Given the two-year gap in their ages, Captain Donovan had lost little time in finding another unhappy wife to warm his New Haven bed.

"I slipped away, tracked down the captain to his airship and demanded answers. He confirmed everything." A tear slid down her cheek.

"You might have told me," he grumbled. "Sent a—"

"Letter?" Her eyebrows climbed high upon her forehead. "I did. The captain wrote to you as well."

There had been many, many letters after he fled New Haven. From her. From Captain Donovan. From his sister, his brother, and his legal father. At the time, he'd been too busy licking his wounds. He'd only opened—and occasionally replied to—those of his siblings. He'd ignored the others, not wanting to be sucked back into their muck and mire. Yet here he was. So much for avoidance saving him pain. Yet had he been remotely aware of the undercurrents swirling beneath the shreds of his past, he still would have avoided this moment.

Hard to wish an alteration of the past, not when it had led him to Charlotte, brought him back to her doorstep.

Even if it did mean he'd once kissed his own sister, a nauseating detail he'd never manage to purge from his memories.

But Charlotte waited for him beside a house that, he suspected, held all the answers to his questions. One guarded by individuals willing to dispatch any interlopers to protect whatever venture they pursued within.

"I tossed them all in the fire," he admitted. "But you had ample opportunity to inform me of our connection this very morning." The tea she'd served him earlier curdled in his gut.

"I almost did, but decided you were best kept in the dark." She flapped a hand at her suitcase. "For your safety and mine."

"Because your husband is up to no good?"

Her brittle laugh shattered any last hopes of her innocence. "I spoke the truth when I told you my disgrace spread like wildfire, that marriage was the solution offered me. Wretched and contemptible choices were presented to me by my legal father." She stiffened her spine. "But our mutual sire knew a man with deep Asturian roots during one of his many voyages who was captivated by stories of the mythological serpent-dragon responsible for his family's wealth. Legend has it that a distant Rodríguez ancestor killed the beast and stole its treasure."

"The source of Enzo Rodríguez's *former* prosperity," he corrected. "Today's investigation led me back to your doorstep."

She nodded. "No doubt you found my home distressingly empty." A faint smile touched her lips, then fell away. The souring of memories? "Tall, handsome, educated—not to mention a most appealing accent—he swept me off my feet. We married in haste." Her exhale was long, forceful and spoke of years of pent-up annoyance. "Only later did I learn Captain Donovan arranged the marriage, providing my husband with a generous dowry to pursue their mutual passion, entangling us all in his family's drama."

"Maria?" Parts of the puzzle began to fall into place.

"Bane of my existence and his twin sister, a woman possessed. Much like her crusader and conquistador ancestors. She'll stop at nothing to restore the former glory of her family's name." Rose tipped her head. "Had you answered Captain Donovan's letters, you'd know he wanted to bind you to her with marriage vows."

And Ryan thought his current family situation was misshapen and twisted. "Because he believed there was a way to locate a *cuélebre*?"

"Locate?" She laughed, rueful. "There's no such thing in all of Spain. Else why would we all be here in New Haven?

Enzo's family might be in possession of a crumbling castle and Asturian heritage, but the story of the mythological serpent-dragon is nothing more than a fairy tale told to children."

No, there was more to it than that, otherwise the captain would not have pursued the connection with such vim and vigor. But Rose was right. New Haven was not the place to go cryptid hunting, not if one wanted a live beast. However, the Peabody Museum where Rodríguez worked was certainly full of the dead variety. *Tyrannosaurus Rex*. Terrible lizard. What was a dragon if not that?

A new and different narrative began to take shape in Ryan's mind. Not one involving the selling of exotic animals to bored wealthy individuals as a means for financial gain, but one that involved pursuing a very specific cryptid.

"And yet your husband is a man who has spent his life engaging in herpetological studies in a focused effort to..." He raised his eyebrows, inviting Rose to finish.

She did so on a heavy sigh. "Install some kind of winged dragon creature upon his family's lands, specifically the caves tucked into the hillside. He's as mad as his sister. Brilliant, both of them. But certifiably insane. What has he to work with?" She threw up a hand. "Alligators with tropical requirements. Ostriches possessed of large, useless wings. They cannot be bred, and a surgical approach will not result in a live animal. Leastways, not for long."

Correct. But Charlotte's neighbors appeared to have a third option in mind, else why pour so many resources, so much effort into their endeavor?

"Yet our mutual father was confident in their success," he prompted. What more might she know?

"Not once did his belief waiver." Rose sighed. "He died a year ago and, with his final breath, begged me to find you, to convince you to return, to aid his cause." She waved a hand, indicating the empty room. "By then nearly everything of value—both here and in my own home—had been sold to fund their joint endeavor. The three of them had descended deep into madness, setting aside every last moral and scruple they ever possessed. By the time I inherited half of this house, it was nothing but an empty shell, a warehouse with an address for the delivery and processing of their menagerie and other supplies."

Ryan frowned. "It wouldn't do to set up an illicit laboratory adjacent to Wooster Square. Not one involving live animals."

There would be too many eyes upon them, too many self-empowered community members who would ask pointed, intrusive and demanding questions that Rodríguez would not wish to answer and could not hide with placating lies.

"Just so," Rose agreed. "As to where, I have no idea. With that pair, it's safer not to know."

But Ryan *did* know.

The Rodríguez siblings had installed themselves in a section of New Haven among hardworking residents with less political clout. In a community that would not demand to know the nature of a neighbor's many shipments, would not ask what creatures flapped and screeched and cooed in their backyard aviary.

Still. Songbirds were one thing. Full-grown ostriches another. But live alligators? For aether's sake, where? The basement?

Rose stood, gathered up the papers beside her and thrust them into his hands. "I must go. All that Enzo and Captain Donovan judged unworthy of selling, I managed to liquidate to fund my escape. In compensation, I've signed my half of the house over to you." She picked up her suitcase. "I want no part in this anymore. You won't be able to find me. Please don't try."

"Wait." He placed a hand atop her arm as the penny dropped. "I've more questions. Francisco Alcantra wasn't only your lover; he was your supplier?"

Dusty sunlight glinted on her curls as she laughed. "Yes to both. My bed was cold, and he was pleasing enough. Besides, men are so much more cooperative in a post-coital stupor."

"You sold questionable medical products to your neighbors." His words a statement, not a question. Ones that passed judgment. "For fun and profit. Don't." He held up a hand when she opened her mouth to protest. "I don't care if you were clear about the exact contents and origins of every pill and potion you peddled." Her shoulders stiffened and her eyes narrowed, but he'd not missed the slight shift of her feet or the discomfort that stiffened her neck. "Even sugar pills are far from harmless when misrepresented. Your lover died riddled with worms."

The blood drained from her face. "How revolting."

"Allow me." He turned her eyes toward the light and peered into them, but saw nothing that ought not be there, save a flicker of worry. "You appear to have escaped the worst of it."

"The trick, dear brother." She poked him in the chest. "Is to never sample the product that you convince others to try. As to sales? Create scarcity and charge a premium price. Wooster Square funded my escape. More, peddling my wares to the privileged few—whose scorn have made my recent years a living hell—provided a deep level of satisfaction." A wicked grin stretched her lips. "Selling to your purported grandmother was a particular pleasure."

He'd felt much the same on that last point. Immoral, nonetheless. He focused on his case. "Revenge served as tonics and tablets. But never ones you yourself ever consumed. Not even the peyote tea?"

"Serving tea was Cisco's idea. He knew my husband was low on funds and planned to keep Maria in his room, tied to the bed, as a guarantee. He might otherwise never be paid for items he went to great lengths to procure. Once does not casually raid the cellars of a foreign museum—it was only a matter of time before his actions drew unwanted attention from the authorities." The corner of her mouth kicked up. "Dumb luck —or was it?—that it was you."

He glared. "And your role in all this?"

She lifted a shoulder. "Double agent? I was to keep an eye on Cisco and the goods, to aid Maria if he grew uncooperative. A—presumably—drugged, befuddled, and unfaithful wife is easily ignored. I did not expect her to kill him."

"Why did she?"

"They've collected all the parts and pieces they require of the Americas." She took a step toward the door. "When you burst into the room, when she leapt from the window, I carried on with my role as intoxicated woman sprawled upon the floor. Anything to save my own skin. My life here, as Rodríguez's wife, is tethered to my usefulness. When I decided not to drip poison in your coffee this morning, I crossed the line from disposable to liability."

His eyebrows slammed together. "Is there nothing more you can tell me?" Twice today he'd dodged death. He'd like to prevent any further attempts on his life. Yes, even though he intended to kick the hornets' nest of whatever plot the Rodríguez siblings were hatching next door.

"From their hushed conversations, they believe themselves close to success," Rose answered. "And Maria never misses. Enzo sent a particularly nasty missive blaming me for the loss of Bixby and his work. That's how I knew it was time to flee. You've a target painted on your back, same as I do. Be careful." She rose onto her toes to peck him on the cheek. Chaste. "Goodbye, dear brother. And good luck."

She left him standing there in the empty room, stunned.

A drug-dealing half-sister married to a smuggling mad scientist brought into the family by way of a shared parent who wanted nothing so much as he desired to discover—no, create—a winged serpent with his son's help.

And to think he'd accepted the assignment with no plans to involve himself in family affairs beyond the level of a polite parlor visit. Instead, he was neck deep, the only one willing—capable?—of setting things to rights. A sister saved, a sister lost. Connections with a brother re-established, with bonds to that of an unknown brother-in-law left to sever.

The distant sound of the front door closing snapped him out of his reverie.

A *cuélebre*. The whispers were right—and so very, very wrong.

Time to put a stop to the creation of a Frankenstein monster of a dragon.

# CHAPTER FOURTEEN

The knock at the front door launched Glory into guard mode. She tore away from Charlotte barking as if the end days were upon them, her yelps and growls muffled by the leather gas mask covering her muzzle, by the hoses that ran from its sides, stretching backward to side-packs filled with activated charcoal that would filter and neutralize airborne threats.

A glance out the front window confirmed that Ryan had arrived, dinner in hand.

Grinning from ear to ear, she jumped up and hurried to the door.

Was it wrong of her to be glad he'd not taken the time to shave? Two days of scruff darkened the angles and planes of his jawline, scruff that brought to mind past activities undertaken on dark, moonless nights beneath scratchy woolen blankets wherever they could scare up an hour's privacy. Scruff she had every intention of reacquainting herself with. Intimately.

"Friend," she instructed the dog, as she pushed her own mask up onto her forehead and cracked open the door. "I hope there's something canine appropriate inside that brown-paper package you're holding."

"But of course." He set down two bottles to peel back the edge of waxed wrappings and pluck out a lump of sausage. The delightful scents of warm bread, red tomatoes and cheese wafted past her nose as he knelt to offer this tidbit as an overture of friendship. In turn, the dog permitted him to sink his fingers into her ruff for a neck scratch.

A tentative camaraderie thus established, Charlotte opened the door wide.

"Why is your dog wearing a gas mask?" He paused, foot on the step.

"Don't worry. Hiram gave me two of his own gas masks. There's one for you."

He frowned. "Because?"

"Because my handy pathologist of a brother suspects, from my overly in-depth observations of coughing fits and desperate dashes into the bushes to vomit, our targets have contracted parrot fever."

"Parrot fever?" His eyebrows drew together.

"An infectious bacterial disease transmitted from birds to humans via inhaled feather dust or powdered excrement." She snorted at the look on his face.

"Too much detail." Ryan held up a hand. "Airborne bacteria would have sufficed. Must you overshare right before we eat?"

She grinned. "Whatever you've brought with you smells wonderful."

He stepped inside. "I'd planned for a fancier meal, but family matters erupted, and my hasty exit precluded a kitchen raid. So, to avoid tinned beef and hardtack, I stopped on my way here to pick something up and stumbled into a bit of luck."

Pizza. A rare treat, especially during the hot summer months. Baked in the stone-fired brick ovens of Italian bakeries and not always on the menu, stores quickly ran out of the flat-bread pies when word of mouth carried news of their baking—sold before they even came out of the oven.

Fine dining—china, linen, silver—was well and good, but for an evening at home surveilling the neighbors' odd behaviors, was there anything more suited to the task?

"Come. The kitchen window provides the best view of the aviary, of their backyard activities. And if you lean to the left, a pair of binoculars directed at the street will let you analyze any crates they carry in." Her mouth watered as she led him through her front room. "Which bakery? Marino's?"

"Better." He carefully slid the package onto her table. "Catalano's."

"He ought to open a bakery dedicated entirely to pizza. No, a restaurant. Both? Endless lines would form outside his door, all willing to wait for a chance to sit at his table or begging for the chance to carry one home."

"Begging?" His voice teased as he tossed her a wily glance that sent ripples of anticipation across her skin. "I'd planned on that. But later, after dinner." He turned and pressed a dark brown bottle into her hand, one wet with condensation. "From Richter's bar."

She held it to her forehead and trailed it down the side of her face, purring. "Cold beer. Hot pizza. You won't need to beg."

His hands shot out, caught her hips, and dragged her close. Licked away the droplet of water that trickled down her neck. "Keep that up and it'll be cold pizza and warm beer."

A nip at the corner of his mouth—she'd only intended a quick taste—became a heated kiss that not even the cold glass pressed between their chests could douse. His presence in her kitchen alone raised the mercury without firing the stove. But his touch? That set her skin on fire. Yes, even through layers of ruffled skirts.

Heart fluttering, she pulled away. Ran a hand down the side of his face. Pure indulgence for the many nerves of her fingertips. "Threat or promise?"

A low growl rumbled in his throat. "I sent a bat to Tetzopa. Half an hour after sunset he'll arrive with reinforcements."

Anticipation and excitement left her breathless. "You're planning on going in? Tonight?"

"I am."

"That leaves us plenty of time." Hours, in fact.

She flicked the wire lever that held the bottle stopper in place, then took a long, slow drink of the cold, bitter brew, letting the flavor roll over her tongue. It had been a seemingly endless day, one that wasn't close to over, but she'd been looking forward to this moment ever since they parted. Five years of longing and regret as they both chased dreams, one that had left a corner of her heart empty and aching.

Today, she'd earned this moment. Both of them had.

"Charlotte, my willpower will only last so much longer." Ryan's voice held a note of warning as his fingers plotted a course up her spine, marching across the lacings of her corset until they found the knotted bow that held them tight. He tugged at the loops, raised an eyebrow.

"I'd hoped I might convince you to eat later." Smiling, she set aside the beer bottle and focused all her attention upon his neck, delighted he'd not bothered with a cravat. His informal attire allowed her to easily reach the top buttons of his shirt. One button fell free. A second. Then a third.

Sliding her hands beneath the cloth, she pushed it away, pleased to see he'd applied a fresh bandage to his neck, that no fresh blood seeped through the gauze. "The bullet wound?"

"Sore." He slid the gun holster from his shoulders and set it aside. "But a mere sting compared to the torture you seem to have planned."

"Oh, are you in agony?" She pressed a kiss atop a most enjoyable anatomical feature, the notch at the base of his throat formed by muscle and bone. A seductive, male trait too often kept hidden by those nooses men termed a cravat. She scraped her teeth across skin, downward, catching the fabric of his waistcoat between her front teeth and tugging. "A bit hot for layers, wouldn't you say?"

With a growl, he grasped her waist and turned, lifting her onto the kitchen table. "It's too damn hot for clothes at all." Large hands landed on her knees, then slid upward, gathering ruffles at her hips and nudging her thighs apart that he might step closer.

"Watch out—"

He dropped a kiss on the edge of her jaw.

"For the—"

Scruff scraped the side of her face as he nibbled her earlobe.

"Fossils."

He nuzzled the hollow behind her ear and whispered, "Do you ever stop thinking of them?"

"Only when they're not irreplaceable specimens from a giant oviraptorosaur that might forever alter our knowledge of dinosaur evolution."

"Seriously?" He leaned back, locking eyes.

She twisted, reaching backward to grab the best of all the fossils from its cotton-padded box and held it before his face. "Look. Do you see them?"

"Are those feathers?" He took the specimen from her, cradling it in his palm. Turning it about, marveling at its existence. "Not on an archaeopteryx, but a raptor?"

"Most definitely a raptor. Feathers only on the tail and arms. Bipedal. A crested head. About ten feet tall. With vicious claws. A kind of chicken-from-hell." Fitting, as that had been the week-from-hell.

His jaw dropped. "From where?"

"The Dakota Territory. Cretaceous."

"I heard you lead a team out. Brave of you."

*Or stupid.*

"Several. Each more successful until... Well, my last expedition wasn't going well at all—until I found this specimen."

"I'm sorry I couldn't stay, that I wasn't with you." Regret crept into his voice. "If Doc Jones hadn't tossed away my note—"

"Shh." She dropped a finger atop his lips, silencing him. "We've been over this. Our goals have always been at cross purposes, you chasing after strange living creatures, me excavating the dead and long gone." And they always would be. "In this case, I made the mistake of heading out too late in the season. Fall was just around the corner. I had to promise those men a graveyard of *T. Rex* bones. It was the only thing that convinced them to sign on."

He cringed. "You *promised* fossils?"

"I know, I know." Luck played a larger portion in many discoveries than any paleontologist wanted to admit. "But my source was good. The fossils *were* there, right where I'd been told. Only the site was already occupied." Claimed by a rival who had no intention of sharing.

"But you pushed on?" He returned the fossil to its box.

"The geology of the region was perfect. Absolutely perfect. And I'd paid my men plenty."

"Let me guess." He kissed the edge of her jaw. "There was dissension in the ranks. Grumbling about women being bad luck. But you refused to back down."

Gender hadn't factored into her self-doubt. Not one iota. But she'd certainly begun to doubt herself, her instincts, her nose for finding fossils. Hour after hour, day after day, they'd failed to find anything but the most meager of fossil beds.

Certainly no bone-rich dinosaur graveyard stretched before them.

And the weather was growing nippier by the day.

Oh, how she'd wanted to admit defeat. Only pride kept her going. "I nearly did. Had I not sunk my last dollar into supplies…" And what had been her other option? Let go of her academic dreams and pan for gold alongside her parents?

No. She'd been right. They'd found a magnificent fossil bed. But for her frustrated, pig-headed insistence, would she have stumbled across the giant, beaked raptor? No. Her men had gotten their terrible lizard and a triceratops to boot. Sales had netted them so much that not one of them had objected to her keeping the raptor fragments all to herself. In exchange for additional cash, of course.

"Most people don't bother to look beneath the surface." He tugged at the thin ties that held the neckline of her blouse closed. "But from the moment I first laid eyes on you, I could see the passion burning behind the heat-tempered steel armor you present the world." He let the backs of his fingers run over the dark embroidery as they traced the swell of her breast, then dipped behind the edge of her corset. "I always thought you were more suited to the ivory towers of academia than the Wild West."

"And how did you figure that?" Her breath came faster now, scattering her focus.

"You knew too much about the fossils, had too many fact-based hypotheses."

"As opposed to your wild imaginings?"

"Some of us work the other way around," he protested.

"Start with a crazy theory, then try to find evidence. Proved that Tommyknockers exist, did I not?"

She inhaled, ready to resume their old argument, but his lips caught hers and the heat of his mouth, the dance of his tongue were entirely too mind-melting a distraction for her to object. Hands cupping either side of his jaw, she surrendered to the moment.

Glory heaved a sigh and flopped onto the ground.

He pulled away, leaving them both panting. "Now, as much as I want to hear more about your fierce, feathered raptor, about the most spectacular find of your career, I'd prefer to focus first on human anatomy."

*Flick.* A single curved catch slid free, loosening the metal bands that braced the corset about her ribcage. Three more followed and the last of her hard shell fell away. Not that his skillful fingers were done. They quickly found the clasps of her skirts and petticoats to unhook them—one by one—then pushed them downward about her hips.

"Hmm." There was so, so much more to tell him, particularly about the iridescent feather. But, for a little while, she greedily wanted all his attention on her, not creatures that may or may not qualify as birds. "Agreed."

"I love it when our interests align. Now, where were we? Oh, right." He nuzzled and nipped at her throat, sending a shiver rippling outward over the whole of her body. "Our plans went astray when a certain fossil chicken raptor entered the conversation. And the only place feathers belong at the moment are beneath us."

"A mattress would be a novelty," she hummed, plucking

loose the last button of his waistcoat. He shrugged it to the floor as she yanked his shirttails free. "It was only ever packed dirt or dried grass before." Accompanied by the occasional unwelcome sharp stone.

Not that she'd minded, not when his roughened hands moved over hidden skin scorching every nerve ending until she felt as if she might combust if he didn't peel away every last stitch of clothing. Not that they'd ever quite managed. Not when too wide a variety of insects would take immediate advantage to sting or bite. Or when a team member could wander past their bedroll, glimpse bare skin, and find it an invitation to whistle or shout suggestions. There'd been talk of a taking a hotel room when they returned to Cheyenne, but then her ankle had been injured and a rider appeared with uncommon—and from her perspective, unwelcome—news of a singular discovery.

"Something to rectify this very moment," he said. "I always wanted to do this."

Her breath left her lungs in a giant whoosh as he lifted her, wholesale, from the table, to sling her over his shoulder, an arm wrapped behind her knees. With a tug, her skirts slid down her legs and landed in a froth of ruffles upon the floor leaving nothing but short, lace-edged bloomers tipped toward the ceiling.

"To carry me away like a caveman?"

"Isn't that a thought." His boots clomped as he carried her

upstairs. "We could have made something of a cave. Found a ledge for a lantern that my eyes might drink their fill."

Which was exactly what he intended to do now. Clothing out in the territories had been functional and practical. Coarse cotton, rough wool, raw linen. Much like their heated couplings. Certainly, he'd done his best to focus on the finer details of her anatomy, but their environment hadn't leant much to comfort. Hadn't permitted him to study her every feature, to map the contours of her body. A deficiency he would rectify now.

He tossed her onto a brass bed topped with a feather mattress and feather pillows, as predicted, fitted with fine, creamy linen sheets. At the foot of her bed was a white Marseille corded quilt, folded away in deference to the oppressive summer heat. She'd constructed a cloud one could sink into and pass the night in blissful comfort. A glaring contrast to a camp bedroll.

A light breeze drifted in from the open window, gauzy curtains drifting in its wake. On the floor, a braided carpet. A chair upholstered in chintz printed with red tulips sat before a dressing table. Her entire bedroom was a sanctuary of simplistic comfort. All taken in with a quick glance for it wasn't the furnishings that held his rapt attention.

Instead, it was the short, frilly underthings that only pretended to preserve her modesty. Cotton, perhaps, but their gathers arced over generous hips to reconvene as flirtatious ruffles encircling her thighs. A brief stretch of dark, satiny skin —one that teased and threatened his self-control—plunged back into hiding behind the tops of lacy openwork cotton stockings. Though didn't that make the view all that more seductive, not quite revealing the entirety of what lay beneath? Were that the goal, then mission accomplished. Already he was as hard as a rock and struggling to pace himself.

"Beautiful." He swept up her booted and once-injured ankle and traced a finger along the zigzag pattern worked into her stocking. "Yet ever so practical."

"There's no reason that form serving function can't also be pleasing to the eye."

"Like your boot?" Embossed leather encased her feet, ankles, and calves. Quite pretty. But the boot he held possessed custom features. Two concealed iron bands ran down the sides of the boots. They hinged at the ankle before continuing on to fuse with a metal plate embedded in the heel. "Clever." The bow gave way beneath his finger, and he set to work tugging and pulling at the laces, prying back the reinforced leather to yank the boot from her foot. Only then did he pull the stocking from her leg that he might examine the faint, raised scars that traced lines on either side of her ankle, memorizing their shape, their length.

He should have been there.

"There's not much pain anymore," she said. "So long as I keep it braced." Her words answered the question implied by his frown. "Though it's not as flexible as it once was." She held up a finger. "Don't you dare apologize again. There was no knowing how badly broken it was."

Perhaps not, but he would always regret leaving her behind even if their separate paths had advanced their careers.

But for their separation there would have been no

pigheaded marching through the Dakota Territory, no feath-ered raptor fossil which was certain to make a loud splash when her paper was published. No finding a Tommyknocker, no position within the Smithsonian as a Special Agent in charge of chasing down cryptids with the power of a gold badge to back his demands.

Now their worlds had re-converged. Could they manage to fuse their futures? Was that something she would even consider?

He lifted her leg, pressed a kiss to each scar, then set about freeing her other foot from its leather confines. Then he caught the edge of her stocking between his teeth and tugged it down-ward, inch by inch while she hummed her approval.

From the intoxicatingly smooth skin of her inner thighs to the warm hollow behind her knee, to the curve of her calf and the turn of her ankle, he lavished attention in the form of gentle bites soothed by soft kisses and murmured praise. By the time he tossed the stocking aside, if handed charcoal and paper, he might unerringly sketch an artistic study of her leg from memory alone.

"Ryan."

"Yes." He looked up.

"Come," she beckoned, her heavy-lidded gaze offering him no alternative.

He reached behind his head and pulled off his shirt. Dropped—briefly—onto her chair to shuck his shoes. Only then did he join her on the bed, thinking to continue his explo-rations. A notion that she quickly struck from his mind.

"My turn." With a push to his shoulder, she toppled him

backward onto the cloud of feathers. A second later she straddled his knees, her fingers working the fastenings of his trousers free.

The open slit of her bloomers parted ever so slightly, providing tantalizing glimpses of the dark curls beneath. Fingers curled into linen, he fought the urge to slip a wicked finger past their opening, to trace a teasing circle around her center.

At the very moment his restraint cracked, she backed away out of reach, dragging his trousers down his legs before returning, palms pressed to his bare thighs. "So strong. So big. And so very ready." Her hand wrapped about his rock-hard cock, reducing him to groaning, throbbing need. And then she bent and closed her lips around its head.

"Charlotte!" He arched back into the mattress as white fire shot through him, setting every nerve ablaze and threatening to fuse the vertebrae of his spine. Blind need reverberated, promising to shatter what remained of his self-control with each tug and pull from the hot, wet silk of her mouth. "Too much, too fast." His words rushed out on an exhale.

"We could stop." Releasing him, she crawled over his body, leaned forward, nipped his earlobe. "Go back downstairs." Her teeth scraped along the side of his neck. "Surveillance *was* tonight's official goal."

"Not a chance." He snagged the hem of her blouse, swept it overhead and cast it aside. Filled his hands with the twin globes of her breasts, brushing the pads of his thumbs over each dark nipple, watching as her own blood caught fire.

Knees on either side of his hips, hands on his chest and

wearing nothing but the thin teasing cotton of her distractingly short bloomers, she kissed him. Softly at first, then issuing demands with teeth and tongue that sent sparks flying between them. The soft press of her breasts drove him to distraction, but his palms were equally eager to shape themselves to the curve of her lower back, to smooth over the dip of her waist, to cup the breadth of her hips. A gentle reacquaintance that swiftly grew more insistent.

A demanding burn settled into his chest. What had been a mere ember now smoldered hotter than a white-blue flame. He'd missed this, missed her. Not only the sparks that flashed between them with every touch, but the partnership they'd struck. One where they each spoke their mind with ease, challenging each other. Pushing and shoving and tugging and pulling, ultimately arriving at places, at thoughts that neither could manage on their own. Both physically and mentally.

His flesh grew tight, harder with increasing desire and growing need.

She tore away, her breath rasping over his heated skin. Their gazes caught, held and in her eyes, he could see this was more than sex. Their connection ran much deeper. One strengthened by their joining, but never broken even when they were apart. He adored her and no other.

Slowly, deliberately she pushed backward. Her pelvis sliding over his. With a flex of hips, the blunt head of his shaft nudged against her damp opening, and she sank onto his hard length, drawing him into her body, inch by tortuous inch, until he was fully seated, encased in the soft, wet warmth of her sheath.

For a long moment, their eyes locked.

Her eyes sparkled with what he guessed were dark and delicious thoughts even as light from the window streamed inward setting her skin aglow. Never before had they come together during the daylight hours. One night lodged in his memory, when they'd snuck away from the campsite, blanket in tow, to a grassy hollow for a little privacy. He recalled how her silhouette had been backlit by the moon. A glorious sight. Though he much preferred the one above him now.

She began to move, lifting away. A slow kind of agony relieved only by her return. Then faster, their breaths scraping from their throats, hearts pounding, as they found their rhythm. As she dropped her hips, he drove upward. An ever-increasing pace that coiled tension at the base of his spine and drew a long moan from her lips.

# CHAPTER FIFTEEN

Close, she'd been so very, very close when he caught at her wrists, pushed as he twisted, and rolled her onto her back. A motion that separated them and caused her to cry out at the cruel sensation of loss.

"I need to see all of you." Tension gripped his body as he struggled for control, his finger fumbling with the waistband of her bloomers. A rending yank pulled them from her hips and down her legs, leaving her bare, nothing left between them. "There. Beautiful. Everything I could ever want."

And then he was done with speech.

Rough, masculine hands slid up her inner thighs, pushing them apart, spreading them wide as he dipped his head, opening his mouth and pulling her within as he stroked her center with his tongue and toyed with a most appreciative knot of nerves with incredible effects that all but drove away rational thought. Skills she hoped to revisit another time.

"No more. Not now." She wanted him inside her when she climaxed.

Hands fisted in his hair, she dragged him to her mouth. Glorying in the rough scrape of his beard, of the feel of masculine skin beneath her palms, she let them roam free over the rippling strength of his shoulders, arms, back. Propped on one elbow, his full weight suspended above her, he ran his palm over her rib cage, over the side of her breast, teasing, caressing, possessing.

She knew a moment's sadness that they'd not wandered the West side by side, hunting for forgotten creatures, for the bones of ancient reptiles, for hints that mysterious creatures still walked—slithered, swam, flew—among them. But there was no sense in regretting lost time. Instead, she wished to turn her thoughts to the future.

Did they have one together?

Ryan was the only man for her. She knew this with a bone-deep certainty. He filled a certain emptiness in the hollow of her chest. More, he didn't run from her single-minded passion for the mysteries of the past. Better, he reveled in it. Prodded her, challenged her to look beyond the obvious, to consider new angles, no matter how strange, how outlandish, or improbable.

She hooked a leg about his hip and hauled him closer still. She wanted him. He wanted her. For the moment, it need be no more complicated than that.

"In." A simple word, if one laden with a pleading note. "Don't make me wait."

His knee pushed at her thigh. His weight shifted. And his

gaze caught hers. All his intensity focused on her, his utter devotion. An undeniable connection hummed between them, a live wire burning red-hot. And then he slid inside her, filling her, stretching her. Her entire world concentrated, reduced to the point of their joining.

He drove into her, again and again, hard into soft, both a welcome invasion and a possession. Tension coiled, knotting tighter and tighter until it snapped in a shower of sparks, in a bright flare that radiated outward in all-consuming waves of pleasure. She screamed something that might have been his name, might have been a primitive cry of ecstasy. Frantic now, he chased her orgasm, pounding into her once, twice, then shouted his own completion, pulsing and throbbing inside her.

Arms locked about each other, hearts still beating hard as the aftershocks echoed and hummed, she knew he was her match, the one person who filled the empty space in her heart. Which meant she was in deep trouble. How could they possibly build a life together? Her in New Haven, him hours away by train, both of them dedicated to passionately pursuing their chosen professions? It was both terrifying and exhilarating to pin so much as the tiniest portion of her happiness on Ryan.

*Not now*, she told herself. No overanalyzing, no worrying about solving impossible problems. For now, it was enough to be wrapped in his arms and limp with fulfilled desires, to spend these precious hours of sensation and adventure together, at each other's sides.

She nuzzled his neck, breathed in soap, spice and his own unique scent that brought back memories of campfire smoke, open plains, and star-studded night skies. And thought of cryptids.

Which meant it was time to tell him, to explain what she'd learned about the green iridescent feather that Bixby had in his possession, one that looked like the many Professor Tetzopa had set aside as "quetzal feathers". Some had been perfectly normal bird feathers, true. But not all. Those she'd carried home had a different tale to tell. Much like her fossil raptor feather impressions, they were a rare find that could also rewrite the history of—

Birds? Reptiles? What *was* the creature that had sprouted the unusual feathers? In the kitchen, a handful of those very feathers rested in a tall glass beside her microscope. Beside the field glasses that made spying on her neighbors an easier task. Beside cold pizza and warm beer. Hard to regret those last items.

Outside, the sun hung low in the sky.

"We should dress," she exhaled on a long, drawn-out sigh.

Much as she wished to linger, to drag her hand over the planes and ridges of his chest and stomach, to follow the short, silky hairs downward, to encourage a repeat performance until they were again wrung limp with sensual gratification, such behavior would not solve the problem that were her neighbors. Hard to forget those who were willing to fire a weapon at the man you loved on the streets of New Haven.

*Loved.*

She rolled away, unwilling to examine the sentiment this very moment, but her heart lifted with hope for the future. Later, when there was time to think about it, to turn it over in her mind and consider every angle. Certainly, now was not the time to give it voice.

Half her clothing was on the kitchen floor, the other half tossed willy-nilly about her bedroom. None of it suitable for raiding a house filled with exotic birds possessed of a possible airborne pathogen. No, her loose canvas trousers paired with a plain cotton blouse and topped by a short-laced leather over-vest would best satisfy the demands of tonight's proposed raid.

Ryan threw her a heated glance that threatened to tempt her back between the sheets, but slid out of the bed to reach for his own clothing. A process not without its charms—she'd not had the opportunity to admire his backside for far, far too long.

He caught her ogling and winked.

Despite their recent activities, her face heated. Flustered, she asked, "So, did you find anything at the captain's house?" She tugged on a boot and set about lacing it tightly for maximum support.

"My half-sister."

She choked, gaped. "I'm sorry, your who?"

"Rose."

"Your former fiancée?" Her voice climbed to a horrified pitch. Charlotte knew she'd not been the first to his bed, to his bedroll. He was no monk. There'd been women before her. "Did you ever—"

"Never." He grimaced, fastening his waistband. "A peck on the lips. Quite innocent. Nothing more, thank aether."

She gave a sharp nod, echoing the sentiment. Glad there was no unwitting incest to add to the rat's nest of a tangle that was his family. "And how did you learn... your father? Another deathbed confession?"

Ryan pinched the bridge of his nose. "Not quite."

She knotted the bow of her boot and quirked an eyebrow. "Start explaining."

"It's a long and twisted story. We should eat. In lieu of normal conversation, I'll supply the tragic tale."

They traipsed back downstairs. Charlotte tossed her abandoned ruffles and laced stays onto a chair while Ryan peeled back the brown paper wrapper, revealing the magic produced in a wood-fired brick oven.

Her stomach growled. By the time she'd joined the princess's tea party, a certain unicorn had licked out the insides of every remaining sandwich. She'd waved away her sister-in-law's dismay and offers of less saliva-ridden treats in favor of a quick visit with her niece over cold milk and sugar laced tea.

"Eat." He handed her a slice of pizza. "My brother strong-armed me into visiting the dying patriarch." He flicked open his own beer bottle and took a long swallow. "Gathered about his bed, we held what amounted to a tortured family gathering, wherein my grandmother informed me that Rose called off our wedding, not because of my illegitimacy, but because we share the same father."

"The captain?" Charlotte whispered, mouth agape, pizza still uneaten in her hand. "And now she's married to Professor Rodríguez. That makes him your brother-in-law?"

"Worse." He cringed. "Maria is Rose's murderously inclined sister-in-law."

Another twist she'd not seen coming. "A bit like falling into a nest of pit vipers, discovering you've new relatives in such a manner." She sank her teeth into pure Italian genius.

"From the frying pan into the fire." He closed his eyes and shook his head slowly. Then dragged in a long breath. While she ate, he launched into a convoluted tale spanning years, wherein two Spanish—no, Asturian—siblings hatched a plan to create a *cuélebre*, seemingly from scratch. "The captain, enamored of tales of a family *cuélebre*, invited them into our city, into his life, and purposefully set about encouraging a match with his illegitimate daughter. I'm told Captain Donovan thought to saddle me with Maria as a wife."

"*That* is a tortuous plot worthy of a performance in ancient Greece."

"Both tragedy and comedy, yet to result in anything resembling catharsis," he agreed.

She frowned. "But why here, why base their operations for a dragon hunt in New Haven? Certainly, there's the professor's academic appointment, but if the cryptid—and a very specific one, at that—isn't even located on this continent, then—"

"Not a hunt in and of itself. Instead, it appears the effort is directed at creating—or recreating—a *cuélebre*. And to do so, they've established their laboratory lair mere yards from the home of my long-lost love."

*Love.*

There was that word again.

Her heart skipped a beat. Not a declaration, his comment. But it had slipped easily from his lips, casually without thought. She pushed away the swirl of emotions that sketched rainbows and hearts overhead. Tonight's focus needed to be on planning a raid, on uncovering the strange goings-on next door, on stopping whatever unscrupulous experimentation went on behind locked doors and shrouded windows.

Sentiment could be addressed *after* the dust settled.

She would *not* be distracted. Not now.

Slamming her eyebrows together, she focused on this flood of new information. "Creating," she repeated. "From scratch? Presumably using all those eggs he's imported, but how does one go about such a thing?" Her mind began reviewing all she knew of reptile and bird developmental anatomy.

"Rose implied her husband was attempting to create a living chimera, a dragon formed by surgical means. Perhaps by joining an alligator to the wings of an ostrich soon after the birth of both creatures in the hopes that such a graft might not fail?"

Her stomach turned. "I cannot fathom any success would come from such a method." Those poor animals. Subjected to pain and torture that a madman might perpetrate such a hoax. "Still, both creatures you mentioned have legs. And, correct me if I'm wrong, but didn't you say the *cuélebre* was a winged serpent, without benefit of any limbs?"

"So goes the legend."

"Then every so-called dragon under discussion has been of the feathered or winged variety. Nothing of the quadrupedal or bipedal variety. Unless—" She sucked in a sudden and deep breath. "Snakes."

"Eggs." Ryan reminded her. "Our other theme. The Tzabcan rattlesnake bears live young."

"Perhaps. But in dragon terms, they are of relatively small size. Perhaps they are not directly relevant." Eyes closed, her mind recalled all the delivered crates. So very many crates. "Pythons and boa constrictors are known for growing very, very large. And long." Did such creatures slither about behind her neighbors' walls? She rather thought they might. It would certainly give the groundhogs reason to flee. "How large are their eggs?"

"Wonderful." A muscle in Ryan's jaw jumped. He ran his hand behind his neck. "More exotic animals to worry about. Creatures upon which they've spent every last red cent—theirs and the captain's. Money is tight."

Open-mouthed, she listened to his tale of two houses stripped of anything and everything to scrape together funds. A picture of their scheme began to take shape, though the end results were almost too horrifying to contemplate. And yet...

"We're missing something." She paced back and forth. "What is the motivation, the why?"

"All clues point to an intent to restore the grandeur of their pedigree by returning a serpent-dragon, a *cuélebre*, to the caves that riddle the mountains behind their family's castle."

Charlotte gaped. "Are they hoping the creature will flap about, pilfering the countryside to amass a hoard of silver and gold, of rubies and sapphires? That seems..."

"Demented?" Ryan jerked his head in a nod. "And outright impossible. Infection. Rejection of foreign tissue. The entire process smacks of animal cruelty. They'd have more success hiring a taxidermist to assemble a facsimile and a clock-maker to animate the chimera insomuch as is possible. But selling tickets to a side show hardly seems worth this extreme level of underhanded effort."

While he spoke, she nodded in full agreement. Wealth. Power. Acclaim. Rodríguez would want them all. To claim them, however, a declaration would have to be made. Not a public one. That would draw too much attention to the illegal aspects of their endeavors. But if they only advertised to the upper crust... what? Stuffed and dead, mechanized or not, such creations wouldn't hold the interest of the wealthy for long, let alone convince them to reach into their deep pockets.

*Unless...*

Years ago, beneath the starlight of a distant territory as they'd leaned against the giant femur of a saurischian dinosaur, she'd gently—or so she'd thought—verbalized her doubts as to his chosen career. Her argument, that most cryptids were nothing but myth and legend, fairytales or tall tales. That there couldn't possibly be so many hidden creatures as yet undiscovered given the fervor for exploration, not to mention the rate at which humans were rapidly populating every corner of the globe.

He'd countered with a detailed history of the rise of the kraken in the Thames, of the pteryformes that regularly cast their shadows over London's streets during their nocturnal flights, growing excited as he listed all the evidence and indications that pointed to the probability of dragons existing.

Now, here they were, with him casting doubt upon the possibility her neighbors were in the process of resurrecting a *cuélebre*, but were instead simply following the grand tradition of circus and carnival side shows wherein there was just enough truth in the oddities they presented—bearded ladies, snake charmers, impossibly tall men—that the crowd peering through glass partitions into shadowed cages would believe—insist upon it, actually—that their eyes did *not* deceive, ignoring the sole voice of reason that might scoff, might attempt to point out that the creature within didn't move, didn't blink, didn't so much as draw a single breath.

In a stunning reversal of roles, she found herself about to argue *for* the possibility of a flying serpent. And hers, according to legend, didn't even possess wings.

Unease curled low in her belly.

It fit.

Just.

If one used a shoehorn and gave it a solid shove.

CHARLOTTE TAPPED her chin as she paced the kitchen floor, pizza and beer forgotten. "Extant—living—crocodilians are impressive, as are the palaeognaths, the giant wingless birds. But not dragon impressive. Not knight-in-shining-armor-battling-a-creature-so-enormous-that-it-might-terrorize-the-countryside-for-centuries impressive. Even a full-grown python with ostrich wings couldn't be passed off as a serpent-dragon, not if constructed from new hatchlings."

"Go on." He glanced out the kitchen window. There was no activity yet next door.

"But there's no evidence the *cuélebre* might, in fact, be a cryptid. Let alone that it might still be extant, living some-where in the Asturian hillside?"

"None."

"What if they're striving to engineer something alive, something that will continue to grow. Something that might even manage to reproduce?"

"They can try." He almost couldn't believe his ears. Char-lotte, arguing on behalf of a cryptid, if a human-created one. "But we've all read about Frankenstein's monster. A composite creature—and that was without mixing species."

"Parts and pieces from graveyards reanimated with elec-tricity." She waved a hand, dismissing such a possibility. "Maria wasn't concerned with reclaiming the contents of Bixby's box—rattlesnake skin and a feather and bone cells growing on collagen. I'd submit that's because she—they—have more such supplies already in their possession. Replaceable, if not easily so. Killing Bixby, however, prevented him from spilling any secrets about his project." A smile stole across her face. "Except she didn't bet on an ornithology expert taking custody. There's not so many of us wandering about the streets, especially in skirts."

Skin tingling, he leaned forward. "It's the feather, isn't it? What have you discovered?"

Charlotte plucked the iridescent plume from a glass that rested beside her microscope and waved it in the air. "This is not a feather ever before documented." Passion crept into her voice. "On the surface, its morphology screams 'bird' but not when you take a closer look."

"How exactly is that?" To him, it appeared to be a

perfectly normal green feather. A pretty one. Perhaps a little banged up, as if it had fallen from a lady's hat, blown across the street, and been stepped on once or twice before a curious child snatched it up.

"Its structure is all wrong for a bird's feather—from the manner in which it grew from an animal, to its shape, to the mechanism by which it achieves its coloration." She threw her hands in the air. "Moreover, the iridescent green hue is achieved via an extraordinary process, one unheard of. It's as if it sprang from an entirely different branch of the evolutionary reptilian tree. A branch never before documented. It's a kind of protofeather, a phylogenetic experiment—if you will—that, had you shown it to me in fossil form, I would have told you failed."

A gratifying warmth spread through his body. Not only had his instincts proved true, listening to a dyed-in-the-wool paleontologist convince herself cryptids might exist was a satisfaction he'd never expected to witness. "If not a bird, then what?"

"An evolutionary branch snipped off and lost to time." She began to pace, threw up her hand. "A fascinating undocumented intermediary that might tell us much about nature's trial and error, a discarded failure from the path ancient creatures like the archaeopteryx took en route to achieving flight."

"Except you're holding an actual feather, not a fossil." He frowned. "Anything as old as what you're describing would have decayed and disintegrated long ago."

"Exactly!" Charlotte thrust it into his hand. "Look at it. There's no true quill. The kind of tip our grandparents used to write on paper—letting ink flow via capillary action—is not present."

He nodded. "You're right. To begin with, it's not round." He'd certainly held enough feathers in his time to note a few oddities. "Nor is it hollow. There's no way for it to hold ink. It would serve no better than a twig as a writing implement."

She nodded. "Precisely."

"Why is the tip flat?"

"It shouldn't be, not if it grew from the body of a bird. Instead, the tip has exactly the same structure as a reptilian scale. This *feather* shouldn't exist, so I took it to my brother's house to take a look at it under the aetheroscope."

"You left your house? Alone?" He dragged his hand across his face. "Charlotte..."

"I know. Maria. With a gun. Precautions were taken. I exited via a hole in the back of my fence that allowed us to cut across a few backyards, unseen, to reach their street." She dropped a hand atop his arm, a move that failed to soothe him.

Shaking his head, he relented without further comment. "And found?"

She bounced on her toes, dark eyes glimmering. "*More* novelty."

He listened to a complicated account of parts and pieces, barely managing to follow all the detail but enjoying her passion. One particular fact stood out head and shoulders above the rest.

*Flight.*

In an unexpected turnabout, Ryan listened in stunned amazement while Charlotte argued a case for the existence of a cryptid that could fly. His heart—which had earlier flopped over and sighed heavily at the disappointing likelihood that he was hot on the trail of a collection of sewn and sawdust-stuffed composite carnival displays—sat up and blinked, then began to pump adrenaline through his veins and arteries.

*Could it be?*

Eyes wide, Ryan dropped onto a kitchen chair. He ran a hand across his face. "Has my hearing failed, or did you just suggest we might hold in our hands evidence of the existence of a cryptid? Of a Mexican feathered serpent, not to be confused with a Spanish winged serpent?"

"Don't be racing ahead of the data, now." She wagged a finger. "We have only a few feathers, ones with vague and unclear origins. And not a single scrap of any other proof to suggest the creature lives."

"But it's biological evidence that such a feathered animal *existed*," he insisted. "Therefore, it might still."

"Might," she agreed. From the expression upon her face, it was a huge concession on her part to make such an intellectual leap.

"A creature that could fly." He held up a hand.

"One that is *capable* of flight," she clarified. "It's not quite the same thing."

One minute she constructed an argument in favor of cryptids, the next—backed into a corner and asked for a definitive statement—she executed a decided backpedal. But that was one thing he loved about her, wasn't it? How she always challenged him, pushed him to back up any flights of fancy with cold, hard evidence. Evidence they just might lay their hands on this very night.

"It is when you're hunting flying serpents. *Living* flying serpents." He waved the protofeather in front of her face. "So what exactly do you think is going on next door?"

"Something that ought to be impossible. We've a series of items. The carved bone eyes of a carnyx, the war trumpet. A stolen codex constructed of baffling parchment, strange feathers, and Mexican rattlesnake skins." She counted them out upon her fingers. "All biological material, if not technically alive. Yet Bixby was able to culture collagen-producing cells from snakeskins that he might grow bone."

He raised his eyebrows. "You think—?"

"I think..." She took a deep breath and closed her eyes. "That they're attempting to raise the dead by developing a technique to reanimate the cells of dead tissue before injecting them into embryos forming inside viable eggs."

# CHAPTER SIXTEEN

They gathered in the moonlit yard behind Charlotte's house, standing in a half circle surrounding a freshly killed groundhog. An odd assembly that was part postmortem, part funeral ceremony. The critter was missing the better part of its hindquarters.

Was Glory wholly responsible for the slaughter? Had she merely dealt the final blow—er—bite?

Impossible to know.

A full-grown alligator or a large python would have swallowed the rodent whole, leaving behind no living evidence of its meal. But if Charlotte's supposition was correct, if her neighbors were working with hatchlings developed from cultured cells, then the creatures within their walls might still be juveniles and not yet capable of eating an entire groundhog.

Nonetheless, the sheer quantity of groundhogs that had met a grisly end in her backyard this past week was worrisome.

On the other side of the tall wooden fence that divided the

properties, a cacophony of soft chirps and clucks was accompanied by the occasional high-pitched whistle. No roars, thank aether. Birds from the sound of it, small and medium-sized ones.

Eyes fixed upon the mangled, furry carcass that lay on the ground, Carlos Tetzopa shook his head. "Are both of you insane? Five of them, three of us. Those odds might be acceptable in a normal raid. But add in this?" He waved at the gas masks that hung about their necks. "Oversized lizards and birds are bad enough, but airborne disease puts this far above my pay grade."

Ryan frowned. The man had a point and wasn't an official agent. He was more a visiting guest, working within the agency for a time. Though he'd been issued an Eagle B29 sidearm, he'd received only minimal training and, by his own admission, was no marksman. Taking Tetzopa inside the house with them was a bad idea. The professor was at his best *after* chaos subsided when it was time to analyze and present an opinion upon confiscated archaeological objects. And they hadn't enough gas masks to hand him one. The two of them were on their own.

Well, three, if you counted their canine assistant.

Glory, similarly outfitted to her mistress, wagged her tail, enthusiastic about her presumed inclusion. The dog was not officially invited, but given Charlotte refused to lock the dog in a closet and, given their proposed entry route—prying away rotten fencing to sneak in through the back—it was almost certain the pooch would burst through her dog door into the backyard, then worm her way through the gap to join them, barking loudly the entire time. Grudgingly, he'd agreed to the canine's participation as part of their opening strategy. Hence Charlotte's insistence upon the additional protection of a gas mask modified to accommodate a snout.

"Besides," she'd added. "It covers her jaws, and we don't want Glory clamping her teeth down on any chimeric creatures. She'd destroy them with a single bite."

Which led them to this moment.

"I don't like the look of that steam cart parked in front of their house," Ryan repeated.

"They're planning to transport something." Charlotte nodded her agreement. "If we wait much longer, we'll lose any chance of stopping this here in New Haven."

While waiting for Tetzopa to arrive, for dusk to fall, there'd been a significant increase in activity next door. Through field glasses, they'd watched as dark shapes passed behind drawn curtains, listened as doors opened and closed, as the woman Charlotte identified as their cook departed carrying an armload of copper cookware.

Add to that Bixby's murder, Rose's defection, the certain knowledge that the interest of a Custom's Special Agent threatened their activities, and it appeared Professor Rodríguez and his sister, Maria, were on high alert and preparing to move their base of operations. He expected them to flee under cover of darkness.

Were he in charge, the most precious items would be moved to a safer, new location as quickly as possible. Stolen archaeological material of a biological nature. Valuable equipment. Essential laboratory supplies. But what worried him most of all was the possibility that they would also move any successful experiments.

"Which is why I need you out front, Tetzopa," Ryan continued. "Keep an eye on what they load into the steam cart. Watch for cages, incubators. Anything that looks like it might transport live animals. We're going to do our best to put an end to their shady enterprise beforehand, but we don't want them driving away with live specimens. Don't ask the driver any questions, don't tip him off to our presence. Don't engage directly in any manner. Just drop him—or her—with a dart, slap on a pair of handcuffs, toss them in the back and call for help."

Charlotte frowned. "Toss? No. Not if there's any chance of live animals, including eggs. You might cause harm. Any creatures they've been manipulating are likely to be in fragile health." She pointed at the street. "Drag them behind those bushes or haul them over here and prop them against the fence out of sight."

Tetzopa grumbled, muttering about ancient Aztec gods meddling in the affairs of modern humans far from where they belonged. But, in the end, he gave a sharp nod. "Fine. I'll do my best to drop them one by one. But I'm not setting a foot in that house until an additional gas mask is located. All this over a quetzal's green feather..."

"And a missing codex," she reminded. "They'll have wanted a close look at that parchment, hoping it belonged to a winged serpent, to the *koo savi*."

"You're certain it's inside?" His mouth hardened into a grim line.

The ancient Mixtec manuscript motivated Tetzopa's assistance beyond all else. While they'd filled the archeologist in on the situation, they'd skimmed over the scientific details, stating only that the chance of the criminals producing a live creature was unlikely. Not that the archaeologist was worried, as he considered their story exactly that, an utterly illogical and highly improbable tale better suited to tabloids.

"Something tells me," Ryan said, "that they'd not willingly part with any biological material they thought belonged to a mythological quetzalcoatl."

Tetzopa sighed, then turned and headed back toward the street, keeping to the shadows and muttering, "I never realized protecting the past would involve so many insane people..."

Crowbar in hand, Ryan stalked over to the eight-foot-high fence. As quietly as he could manage, he pried off three boards and tossed them aside. Not that such an accomplishment provided them ready access to the neighbors' backyard. They still needed to traverse the thick tangles of shrubbery, bushes that hadn't seen the sharp edges of clippers in a full decade or more.

"Ready?" he asked.

"Very much so." Charlotte grinned, bouncing on her toes. "I've wild hopes of stepping into a Cretaceous wonderland even though good sense suggests I hope for their utter and complete failure. Still, finding a primitive creature sprouting protofeathers would shatter the preconceptions of every last paleontologist."

"First we catch the criminals, lock them down." Excitement and anticipation buzzed, setting his heart pounding. He'd not felt so energized, so alive an ages. "Then you can feather hunt to your heart's content."

"Promise?" She tipped her head, tossing him a coy glance. "It won't merely be a fevered search for anything dragon?"

He hauled her close. "Need the two be exclusive?"

Glory sighed and sank to the ground as her mistress grabbed his collar, planting a lingering kiss upon his lips. When she broke away, worry filled her dark eyes.

"Maria will shoot to kill," Charlotte whispered.

"I know."

"I've enjoyed our reunion and would hate to lose you." Her expression sharpened, reminding him of the knives hidden within her boots. "If she so much as points a gun at you, I'll be aiming for her throat."

"Keep yourself safe first." His hand fell to the curve of her lower back. The past few hours spent peering through field glasses while keeping watch over her neighbors had been anything but dull. They'd swapped tales of family and travel over pizza and beer, each of them carefully avoiding all topics that touched on their futures. Dare he hope she contemplated one in which he featured? "I want us both sitting at your brother's table tomorrow, telling Princess Aileen about how we saved her kingdom from marauding dragons."

A necessary first step to winning over her family in hopes that one day soon marriage might become a very real possibility.

"I'd like that too." She pushed at his chest. "Let's go. Time to find out how much of a fairytale we'll be spinning her."

He laughed and ducked into the bushes. Behind him Charlotte followed, her hand tight upon Glory's leash.

On the other side of the shrubs, they encountered tall ornamental grass. Crouching behind its blades, they sized up the aviary. Brick walls rose from the ground, transitioning into arched windows that were fitted with hinges and screening, a concession to northern climes. As was the four-sided tiled roof that joined to form an elongated peak decorated with an overabundance of decorative wooden fretwork.

Given this particular June had brought near-tropical weather to Connecticut, the windows were all cracked open, allowing the warbles and chirps of songbirds to escape into the neighborhood. A sunny, innocent, and cheerful sound. Concealing, perhaps, the darker motivations within. As did the woven grass mats tacked up and covering the lower half of the windows, an extra impediment for any curious eyes that dared venture so close.

He glanced at his pocket watch. The long hand was just short of the hour mark. Almost nine. The hour when, so Charlotte informed him, there was always a loud ruckus, a suspected feeding time. A task seen to by the group's muscle, the coughing, vomiting umbrella man. Given the probability of alerting those deeper within the house to their presence by stirring up a flock of birds, entering through the aviary wasn't his first choice.

But Charlotte's counter argument made sense. Neutralize a known threat at a time when the aviary normally erupted into squawks and tweets. Scan the feathered residents for indications of what the professor may or may not have accomplished to minimize any surprises they might encounter.

"It's time," he whispered, pulling his gas mask over his mouth and nose and adjusting the straps.

Charlotte did the same, then tugged one over Glory's snout and buckled it in place. A brief whine indicated the dog's displeasure, followed by a low, grumbling sigh of resignation.

*Clang.* A metal door opened within. With the faint hiss of gas, light poured forth from the windows. All while the creatures inside clucked and hooted in happy expectation of a meal.

"No dinner tonight, chickies," growled the umbrella man. "It's soup pots for all... well, most of you."

Wings flapped and a loud squawk was cut off with a dull snap.

The door leading to the backyard flew open and the ugliest chicken he'd ever laid his eyes on landed on the dirt. Were those claws on the tips of its wings?

Not the time to wonder.

He gave Charlotte a nod and she released the hound, an agreed upon distraction.

Glory looked up at her mistress. *Freedom?*

"Go!" Her reply hissed through the mask. "Catch!"

The dog needed no more encouragement. She took off like a shot, barreling into the aviary like an undisciplined kid turned loose in a candy shop, her excited woofs muffled but surprising enough to toss the fancy henhouse into an uproar.

"What the—" The umbrella man only managed those two words before dropping the wire cage he held with a crash, its door popping open. Flat on his back, an oversized, masked dog braced her front paws upon the man's chest. A cloud of chicken feed and coop dust hung in the air above them.

A sight Ryan took in as he rounded the corner, weapon drawn.

But Glory's moment of triumph was to be short-lived. The hulk of a man pulled a pistol and pointed it upward beneath the dog's jaw.

Ryan pulled the trigger, launching a poisonous dart that pierced the oversized zookeeper's pant leg to lodge in his thigh, and the umbrella man's pistol fired wide—*bang!*—failing to dispatch his canine conqueror.

Glory, dazzled by the vast array of not-quite-chickens, spun about. And chased after the not-quite-a-bird that had escaped its cage and ran for the doorway in a mad, flapping dash to avoid the cook pot. Rather disturbing, the speed with which the creature moved.

The dog, hot on its feathered tail, paused as she reached the threshold. With a great shake, she lowered her face to the ground and applied an oversized paw to the canvas and leather of the gas mask and pried it from her snout. She spared them both the briefest of glances, then blatantly ignored Charlotte's hissed commands of "sit" and "stay" to resume her chase after the lizard chicken.

Both disappeared into the dark, into the shrubbery, leaving only ominous silence in their wake.

Charlotte swore a blue streak as she joined him in the aviary. "She'll come home when she's ready. Probably bloody and covered in scratches. Possibly with feathers stuck in her—"

Her eyes grew wide as she turned about, taking in the captives. "Aether, what a horribly wonderful collection of—"

Birds was the easy answer, the classification that first rose to mind, given every creature possessed feathered appendages that approximated wings. But when peering closely, a number of those "wings" ended in three claws—could they even fly?

And he'd yet to see a chicken—or hear of one—that possessed a tail. Modern chickens sported a kind of clump of feathers on their rumps, but these reptile chickens had actual tails extending a good foot behind their bodies, tails of visible substance the animal was capable of whipping about. Yes, plumed. The feathers that ran along the tail's length were also bizarre.

Thus not-quite-chickens.

And the deeper into the aviary they moved, the stranger things became.

Wire cages stacked two deep held the oddest motley of not-birds. Escape attempts had been made, judging from the damage done to the wires. Some pecked at the wires even now. Others bit them. None seemed quite capable of muscling up and prying the bars apart—thank aether—for they were the stuff of barnyard nightmares.

Bags of corn, of chicken feed sat against the aviary walls. Alongside them rested cages of glass. One held crickets. The next, earthworms. A third, mice. Perfect for young carnivores, avian or reptilian.

Gas masks had been a good call by Charlotte's brother. Each step they took sent up a plume of questionable gray dust. The floor was strewn with feathers and feces and fur and the gnawed bones of rodents. Among them, groundhogs? Perhaps. Though there were no overt signs of these local backyard inhabitants being held as prisoners. Yet.

A point not without its own concerns given a single groundhog would feed several of the aviary's occupants. They didn't appear capable of hunting as a coordinated pack, which left the possibility they'd yet to discover a larger, single creature not housed within the aviary.

One not-quite-a-chicken cracked open its not-quite-a-beak, hissing at him from between a mouthful of needle-like teeth. A creature that was decidedly a carnivore and a good candidate for preferring groundhog meat to chicken feed. Another captive the size of a goose appeared to have scales running across its rib cage, down its flanks to merge with the scales covering its clawed feet—hard to see clearly, given the creature crouched in the back of its cage, hissing. A third not-quite-a-bird possessed a horny red crest and golden slitted snakelike eyes that reflected the gaslight in such a manner as to suggest they glowed with thoughts of mayhem and murder.

Double the size of these creatures and turn them loose in an open yard and a grown man wouldn't be faulted for running as fast and as far as he could to avoid an attack.

Hands pressed to her chest, Charlotte moved from cage to cage, quietly exclaiming her delight with each new oddity she discovered. When she reached his side, her hand fell upon his arm in a tight grip. "Dinosaur chickens!"

"Or would that be chickenosaurs?"

Amusement danced in her eyes as they shared a moment

of excitement at the utterly ridiculous zoological collection surrounding them, one that defied definition.

"All appear to exhibit at least partial atavisms, throwbacks to ancestral conditions." Wonder filled her voice. "Still, not a one of them bears any resemblance to a serpent-dragon, winged or otherwise. We need to find the Rodríguez's work-space, the laboratory in which they've been manipulating the chicken eggs that produced the inhabitants of this aviary. If they've moved on to ostriches and alligators…"

He slotted a new dart into the empty chamber of his Eagle B29 sidearm. "Have your knives at the ready. The teeth and claws worry me. If any of them can fly, we're probably going to regret this raid."

"It wouldn't be pretty," she agreed, pulling a wicked-looking blade from her boot. "But try not to injure any of the creatures unless you absolutely must. The Rodríguez siblings, on the other hand, I'm not so much attached to… but, if they cooperate, we might pick their brains for the techniques applied."

# CHAPTER SEVENTEEN

Amazing. Atavistic chickens.

All this time, she'd thought the noise that rose from behind the wooden fence was nothing but birdsong. Instead, it was... well, wasn't that the question?

These creatures weren't lizards. At least, not as humans would categorize them. Neither, however, were they quite birds. Possibly they were something that fit in-between, a kind of missing link. Except they'd been created by humans, not evolved in nature. Which meant somewhere inside this house they would find a laboratory—the basement, she guessed—and there, they might find answers.

The aviary alone, though filled with an array of jaw-dropping creatures, was meaningless without knowing how the creatures had been bred.

*No*, she corrected herself, *created*.

Though that did beg the question of their reproductive fitness. A question for a later time.

It might well be determined that the dinosaur chickens would need to be culled. Or they might become the subjects of intense scientific research when a gathering of world-wide cryptobiologists descended upon New Haven. There would be close scrutiny intent upon uncovering the mystery of their developmental origins with an eye toward illuminating how creatures such as the kraken, pteryformes and other strange cryptids arose in the recent present or reemerged from the distant past.

Now, if they discovered dragons inside, *cuélebre* or otherwise, not to mention anything approaching the fabled plumed serpent Quetzalcoatl, then New Haven—Yale in particular—would become a Mecca for all things related, however peripherally, to dinosaurs.

Was that Rodríguez's goal? To establish some kind of zoological park for which he could charge entry? Had he thought to generate the exhibits first, then beg forgiveness for his less-than-ethical approach? She was certain there were many wealthy men who would be keen to invest in such an enterprise.

Quietly, she and Ryan slipped from the aviary, leaving the secured umbrella man behind, and crept alongside the rear of the building, careful to stay out of line of sight from any of its windows lest they step into the yellow squares of light cast out onto the grass.

*Clang!*

One of the angled metal doors of the hatch leading into the basement crashed open. They jumped backward, pressing their backs against the stone foundation as the second door pushed up and outward with a rusty squeal.

But nothing emerged, save the light that poured out into the dark night and the voices that echoed up the stairwell.

"Why would you do that, send Romano to slaughter all the raptors?" Professor Rodríguez barked, anger infusing each word. "Each variety represents years of work. There's plenty of room on the dirigible. Not that I'm convinced we need to leave. Feed is easily arranged. Stop him."

"He's already begun," an obstinate, annoyed female voice replied. Maria. "A transport cart waits out front in the street. We'll take the most recent and valuable creations."

"Absolutely not," Rodríguez's voice rose a full octave as he shouted. "Evacuate the hatchlings if you must, but we've far too many fragile embryos. Those cannot be transported without risking all my progress."

Ryan and Charlotte exchanged a knowing glance.

"We've two portable incubators," Maria shot back, angry and irritated. "If those fail, so be it. Pack your favorites, most promising cell lines. If there's a disaster, we'll begin anew, elsewhere."

"Do you have any idea how ridiculous you sound? We've invested all available funds here. Years of time and effort. If we leave now, it's all for naught."

"If we don't abandon the premises, the authorities will find us, shut us down," Maria argued. "I told you Rose was a liability. The stupid woman failed to seduce that Customs agent at the hotel when she had the chance. Couldn't manage it the next morning either. She's weak and sentimental. Worse, she informs me his grandmother knows she's his sister and is likely to hold it over his head. He'll be angry."

"Because society rather objects to incest?" Rodríguez cracked a brittle laugh. "You can't blame the man and you're only angry because he's not yours to control. Regardless, the problem is easily solved. Kill her. Kill him."

"There are now more who are peripherally involved," she shot back. "How many dead need pile up before you understand our location has been compromised?"

The professor launched a counterargument, but this time in Spanish. Or was that Asturian?

With the gist of the Rodríguez siblings' conversation lost, all but the contentiousness that threaded through their words, Charlotte's ears focused on the sounds of packing that echoed upward. The thunk of boxes dropped onto the floor. The soft rustle of straw and crumpled paper. The banging of nails violently driven into wood. All as background noise to their increasingly loud dispute. Every so often, as an undercurrent to the commotion taking place below, she caught a low rattling accompanied by a hint of a whistling trill.

"Do you hear that?" Charlotte asked in a soft voice.

He nodded. "Some kind of animal, but I can't quite pin it down. Whatever it is, it's worrisome."

Her thoughts exactly. Given what they'd discovered in the aviary, she hesitated to make any firm predictions. Could be birds. Possibly groundhogs. Even reptiles weren't entirely out of the question.

The quarrel erupted into a shouting match. Unintelligible words were hurled like verbal daggers and must have hit their mark, for both Maria and the professor abruptly fell silent. Charlotte imagined narrowed eyes and dark glares as they packed... what exactly? Ancient artifacts? Cultured cells? Altered eggs? Entire animals, newly hatched? Juveniles, soon to be moved to the aviary?

Any creatures in the basement laboratory would, necessarily, be restrained. Yet the low grunts and whistles worried her. Even a turkey, sufficiently angered, might attack with a savagery and violence that made one reflect that a bird, sized to stand eye to eye with a human, was a formidable opponent. Take cassowaries, for example. Some six feet tall, they were not-so-affectionately nicknamed "murder birds" for good reasons.

Charlotte's patience stretched thinner and thinner. Why throw the basement hatch doors wide, if they were not ready to carry items to the cart? Was the cart's driver a part of their ring, expected to arrive at any moment to assist with the relocation? Had Tetzopa knocked him out and tucked him behind a bush? If so, how long before the driver's absence was marked as suspicious? Or was it Romano, the group's muscle, they waited for?

"Something's not right," she breathed through her mask.

Ryan shifted on his feet, nodded. "We should—"

*Whoosh!*

Inside the aviary flames burst into life, burning with an intensity unexplainable by the contents. The not-quite-chickens squawked and screeched an alarm that would grab the neighborhood's attention. But would anyone dare investigate? Or send for the fire department?

*Bang!* A gunshot!

Ryan pushed her forward. "Run!"

But before she could take two steps—*bang!*—the dirt exploded at her feet.

Charlotte froze.

"Not another step," Maria ordered. She jumped from the small, covered porch affixed to the kitchen entry, making her way toward them, pistol at the ready. "Drop the weapons and remove the masks."

When Charlotte hesitated, a second bullet punched a hole in the dirt before her—an inch from the toe of her boot.

"That's your last warning."

Charlotte tossed her knife away, shoved her goggles up and unbuckled the gas mask. She held it out, hanging from her fingertips. Ryan bent, slowly placing his sidearm upon the ground, before doing the same.

"Kick them away. Then raise your hands where I can see them." Behind Maria, the flames licked higher, casting an orange glow into the sky. Glass cracked and shattered as, one by one, the dino chickens fell silent. An unholy stench hung in the air, the scent of charred flesh and feathers overlaid by the malodorous stench of dung.

*Sterilized dung*, Charlotte hoped. She prayed Glory wouldn't return to investigate all the interesting sounds and smells.

Arms raised, Ryan toed his dart gun away. "We have to stop meeting this way."

"You're too late. Again."

"At least I didn't miss."

Charlotte shot him a glare. *Good aether, why was he egging the murderess on?*

"True, yet you failed to stop me. Handing the advantage of surprise to me." Maria snatched up the weapons and the masks, then raised her eyebrows and scoffed. "I expected more of the Americans, but it seems they neuter their agents as well. Darts? Really? How many to stop a woman?" Derision filled her voice. "Not that you'll have the chance to find out this evening. You're persistent and quick, though. I'll give you that. I thought we had more time than a handful of hours."

"If I understood Rose correctly, the captain planned for us to spend far more than mere hours together."

A ridiculous exchange, though Charlotte recognized it for what it was. Ryan was stalling.

"Ah, yes." Maria tucked away her knife and shoved Ryan's sidearm into a deep pocket. "The captain and his arranged marriages. Stars filled his eyes when he mused about the advantages of having an IBIS agent to assist us. I had my doubts, though you are a handsome one." She tipped her head. "I might have married you, taken you to my bed."

"Only to kill me in my sleep?"

Maria snorted. "It's as if you read my mind." With a dismissive shake of her head, Maria turned to squint at Charlotte, studying her closely as if she were an exotic, pinned butterfly. "Ah, now I see why you're a familiar face. I certainly didn't expect my own neighbor would bring Customs agents nosing around our property without first knocking upon the front door, all prim and proper, with complaints about the noisy chickens out back."

"Chickens?" Charlotte lifted her eyebrows. "Is that what you're calling them?"

Maria's answering smile held a sharp edge. "We keep the most interesting specimens underground. Which is where you'll be heading now, one careful, slow step at a time."

"Reinforcements are on their way," Ryan warned.

But would they arrive in time? Charlotte and Ryan exchanged a quick look. Would the backyard noise be enough to nudge Tetzopa to send for help?

"Is that why you've recruited a paleontologist to serve as your second-in-command?" Maria scoffed, then gestured with her pistol. "Move."

Step by step, Charlotte and Ryan trudged over to a set of rickety, wooden stairs, then descended into the basement, a space that was quickly becoming a seventh circle of hell. The mercury was rising sharply, but such wasn't the reason beads of sweat broke out on her forehead.

This was an underground laboratory. Only a few remnants of the basement's past remained—a furnace and boiler, a coal chute, an assortment of garden tools tucked into the rafters, wicker baskets filled with root vegetables. The majority of the space was dedicated to mad science.

On the right wall stretched a bank of egg incubators, their internal temperature regulated by a series of pipes connected to a boiler that gurgled and hissed—the water that ran through its copper pipes kept at a low simmer by a bed of smoldering coal embers. On their left, stacks of wire cages. Most—but not all—contained a single, panicked groundhog, curled into tight, furry balls as if they might shrink themselves beyond the notice of their captors.

Which left the distant recesses of the basement. Cut off from the rest of the space by floor-to-ceiling iron bars, there was a central door secured by a large padlock and a length of chain.

Despite the many gas jets that burned, the rough stone walls swallowed every ray of light, leaving the back half of the enclosure shrouded in dark shadows. Upon their arrival, the animals within had fallen silent, but not before a few low growls and strange whistles emerged from the oversized coop.

Squinting did little to resolve the contours of the creatures locked inside, but she thought she counted three separate large and bulky forms. At the front of the cage, there were a handful of feathers scattered upon the hay-strewn floor. One of them a bright, iridescent green.

She snapped her gaping mouth shut. Any chimeras were locked away and a secondary concern. If—no, when—the fire spread from the aviary to the main house, they were all in trouble. Better to take in the whole of the space, to plan a hasty exit the moment an opportunity arose.

In the center of the room, a wide work surface was covered with an array of bottles and jars and tubes and flasks. Silver implements—scalpels, tweezers, probes among them—gleamed with wicked intent beside microscopes, both of the light and aetheric variety.

Upon the table, colorful figures painted in red, yellow, orange and black danced across the white, chalk and gypsum gesso-covered surface of an ancient, folded book.

The missing Mixtec codex.

A small square section had been cut from its parchment and placed into a Petri dish to soak. Professor Rodríguez, in no hurry to pack up and leave, was bent over the fragment, carefully scraping pigment away from the underlying surface. She was torn between fascination at what answers it might provide and horror at the defacement of such a historic document. What about the parchment so raptly held his attention? Was it reptile skin? *Koo savi?*

"Both of you, over there," Maria pointed to a corner in the room. "Stand next to the pipes. Keep your hands in the air." As she marched them past her oblivious scientist of a brother, she slapped the backside of his head. "I'm done arguing with you, Enzo. Pack it in. We need to move. Now."

Charlotte hitched her step, a slight pause to crane her neck and observe what, exactly, Rodríguez had discovered. A subtle movement, but Maria hissed at her, which opened the slightest of opportunities for her other prisoner.

*Crash!*

Ryan toppled a groundhog cage to the ground. As the animal within screamed its fear, he ducked, lunging for the table and grabbing a fistful of sharp implements. Charlotte dropped into a crouch, reaching for the remaining knife hidden inside her other boot.

But her hand wasn't past her knee when Maria's fingers sank deep into her hair, flexed with an iron grip, and forced a bend in her neck to expose her throat. Before Ryan could turn around, the muzzle of Maria's pistol dug into her skin. A deadly gunshot with no chance she would miss. Charlotte barely dared to breathe, let alone move.

"Drop them," Maria ordered him.

Ryan's jaw clenched, his eyes darkened, and his face hardened into granite. But the scalpels clattered to the floor. He would not trade Charlotte's life for his. She'd placed her trust in the right man.

"No sudden moments," Maria commanded.

"Could you not simply kill them quietly outside?" Irritated, Rodríguez shoved his chair backward with such force it toppled over. His gaze leapt from Ryan to her, then fixed. "Miss Reid." His words passed through gritted teeth. "Never content to leave well enough alone. Always asking too many questions."

"As should any well-trained paleozoologist," Charlotte retorted. She ignored the pain in her neck and scalp to force the words out, refusing to be silenced, hard as it was to initiate a conversation with her neck twisted in an unnatural position. "How else does one make discoveries such as these?" Looking past her nose, she swept her gaze across the contents of the room. "Most impressive," she said. "And that's merely judging from what I saw of the work you consigned to the aviary."

From the corner of her eye, she saw Ryan shift his feet, ever so slightly, into a bracing position, readying himself for a chance to act. If Maria would only lower the gun.

"Impressed, are you?" Rodríguez tossed back. He did his best not to look interested, but his expression all but begged her to fawn over his work.

The professor had always struck her as a prideful man,

enjoying nothing more than preening in the limelight. Though the first tendrils of smoke curled into the room and fire threatened the building, would he instruct Maria to loosen her hold that he might enter into an academic discourse?

"I am," she answered. Reasoned conversation wouldn't save them, but it was her turn to stall for time. Time for Ryan to find a chink in their armor, for Rodríguez to countermand his sister. For a neighbor to summon the fire department who would arrive, alarms ringing loud enough to wake the dead. Something, anything that might provide them with the slightest of advantages. "Is that a cathode ray vacuum tube? Have you been subjecting fertilized eggs to X-ray emissions? I've heard rumors that it can disrupt and alter the microstructure of biological tissues."

The effects were largely detrimental, such as the variety that might explain the strange blisters on Rodríguez's hands. Yet X-rays were a tool that could be used to create mutations. And while that usually resulted in an alteration that was a turn for the worse, occasionally it produced startling and enlightening results. For example, if those not-birds in the aviary were mutants...

The villainous herpetologist forced a smile that failed to claw its way into his eyes. "Perhaps I should not have rebuffed your efforts to collaborate with such force. But I've no need or want of an assistant that arrives in the company of government officials."

Charlotte sighed internally. So much for her hopes of distraction and delay.

"She's not here for a job interview, idiot. Now make yourself useful." With a quick movement, Maria reached into a pocket and threw a pair of handcuffs at her brother's feet. "Lock your brother-in-law to the pipes."

Rodríguez's gaze snapped to Ryan. "This one is—"

"Rose's ex-fiancé. Our brother-in-law." She slashed a hand through the air. "Now hurry. Romano is dead. There's a fire in the aviary. I estimate five minutes until the flames jump to the kitchen. An additional ten minutes before we *must* evacuate. However, I cannot account for any fire department inter-ference."

"Those pipes are gas lines!" Rodríguez objected. Not that it stopped him from retrieving the restraints.

Maria rolled her eyes. "We wouldn't want to give our pris-oners access to water pipes, would we?" She jerked her chin at Ryan. "A few steps closer to the wall."

"Not even a few polite words to spare for a family member?" Ryan asked as he backed up, palms out. A dark light flared in his eyes. "For the man who might have been your husband?" His lips pulled into a faint sneer. "Were his stan-dards and morals a little looser?"

Charlotte's eyes widened. Was he mad, attempting to provoke her at such close range? Martyrdom was the last thing she wanted from him. They would leave this underground lair. Together.

Her answering smile was that of a vicious predator. "I find myself relieved you never answered any of Captain Donovan's letters. As it stands, the only courtesy I'm inclined to provide you with is a bullet to the brain." She tipped her head in the direction of the shadowy cage where one of the dark forms had begun to stir. "But I'm guessing curiosity and an intense unwillingness to capitulate will win out." She waggled her gun —easy, quick death versus a painful one via flame, fang, or claw.

Scowling, Ryan held out an arm above the pipe. "You'd be correct. What are we to expect of Rodríguez's monsters?"

"Impossible to say." Rodríguez clipped a cuff about Ryan's wrist, threaded the linking chain over a pipe then snapped the other cuff into place, locking his prisoner's hands uncomfortably high above his shoulders. "Those creatures are imperfect. Mere practice. And yet complete with primitive animal instincts. They are positive proof of concept—resurrection of extinct animals as art applied to biology. Alas, we were working within a confined period of time. Which is to say brute force is useful, but less than ideal."

A cold ball of fear dropped into Charlotte's stomach. Nothing good ever came of rushing science. They'd kept these animals alive, but carefully locked behind bars. Worse, the creatures were not included in their evacuation plans. Because they were too large? Too dangerous?

"That's enough pontificating, Enzo." Maria shoved at her shoulder. "Every moment you spend blathering to these two is a moment of lost packing time."

Thrown off balance, Charlotte careened forward, stumbling to a stop beside Ryan where the professor repeated the process of locking her wrists to an overhead pipe, effectively sealing their doom. The metal dug into her skin. She swallowed hard and blinked back frustrated, fearful, and angry tears. Instead, she turned her face toward Ryan whose answering expression promised her their evening did not end here in a dark, dank basement. She took strength from that and stiffened her spine.

"We've much to do and won't be keeping watch over you." Maria set an oil lamp down upon a nearby table and struck a match, lighting it before replacing the glass chimney. There would be no blowing out the flame. "But I'm confident an open flame is inducement enough to convince you not to yank over hard on those gas pipes." Turning, she shot a piercing glare at her brother. "Hurry up, we're almost out of time."

Dropping her forehead to Ryan's shoulder and taking what comfort she could in his nearness, Charlotte whispered, "What now?"

# CHAPTER EIGHTEEN

Her innards quivered. Out West, death had stalked her via storms—with both lightning and snow. There had been floods. There had been landslides. Upon other occasions, dehydrating heat that sucked every last drop of water from her pores suggesting mummification might be her end—or the wildfires that raced across the land. Occasionally food had spoiled, threatening famine. Guns, arrows, and other weapons had been pointed in her direction. But not once since she returned east had she contemplated the imminent threat of certain demise.

Until now.

Resist, and they would bleed out upon the floor. Or they could choose immediate incineration. Alternatively, they could wait for the beams and struts of the wood-frame house to catch fire and fall in on them.

Even now, the first whiffs of smoke met her nose.

"No panicking," Ryan reminded her. "This is *not* the end. Keep watch for opportunity."

Rodríguez rushed about the makeshift laboratory, gathering those items he must deem irreplaceable. Historic artifacts went into a canvas satchel along with the codex. A rack of test tubes filled with a reddish gel-like substance and bottles of what must be essential reagents were packed into a wooden crate.

Weapons holstered, Maria heaved the crate, already nailed shut, onto her shoulder and—tossing a careful eye in their direction to assure herself the prisoners were of no immediate threat—carried it up the basement stairs.

But the eggs? Those required more time and effort to ready for travel. Rodríguez transferred each one by one into portable incubators built of wood and covered in nobs and dials and tubing, much like the one they'd confiscated from Bixby. One egg was ostrich, and two were of a size and texture that screamed alligator.

All eggs had been worked upon, the tips carefully cut off and pulled away to expose the developing embryo. For X-rays. For physical manipulation. For transplanted grafts. Then the shell cap had been replaced, its rough calcium carbonate edges sealed once more against the external environment by means of paraffin wax such that the embryo might continue to develop, to become a hatchling.

*Sizzz. Snap.*

Sounds hissed and crackled overhead, then faded. A soft moan came and went. She tipped her head, straining to categorize the noises and ignore the strain of her arms overhead. Had sparks leapt to the house? Did dry wood even now catch fire? It seemed likely.

Hard to hear over the hiss of the boiler and the gurgle of hot water running through the pipes that kept the incubators at a preset temperature. No wonder the professor grumped about having to leave this property. There were many incubators, all large enough to contain dozens of eggs resting within. Each modified egg representing hours upon hours of work. Had he traveled to Florida himself? Charlotte doubted it. Rather, she suspected he'd been in the basement these past weeks. That he'd sent an assistant herpetologist in his stead to collect and ship raw material in the form of alligator eggs for his efforts here in New Haven.

Rodríguez handled the largest egg with most extreme care, biting his lower lip as he carefully stuffed soft scraps of flannel into every corner of the box to ensure the oversized egg would suffer not the slightest of jolts. Finally, he closed the lid, snapped the latches shut and tossed a glare at his sister who had returned, barking at him to hurry.

"They're in a fragile state," he groused, lifting the incubator, handling it as if it contained vials of unstable nitroglycerin. "And more than a month out from hatching. If the dragon embryo dies during transport without its heart ever having a chance to beat, all the blame falls to you."

Charlotte's gaze snapped to Ryan's. *Dragon?* she mouthed the word.

A tentative smile tugged at the corner of his lips as a spark flared deep inside his eyes. A trick of the light, perhaps, but they seemed to blaze a bright blue.

Before today, he'd never quite managed to convince her such cryptids existed, even though every cryptozoologist—reputable or otherwise—swore themselves blue claiming the creatures existed in the Ural mountains of Russia. But now, after today? She might not be ready to set her skepticism entirely aside, but she was open to possibilities. Whether or not they'd live long enough to chase after conclusive answers remained to be seen.

"Me? You're blaming all this on me?" Maria placed a hand on the incubator with the two smaller eggs. "If you'd allowed me to dispose of Rose at the Sea View Hotel along with that traitorous Spaniard, we wouldn't be having this conversation." She glared at her brother. "You bought me in as security and have proceeded to ignore almost all my advice. From the beginning, I told you that involving Captain Donovan—not to mention his house—in any capacity was a bad idea. Better to have set up our laboratory on our ancestral soil."

"Perhaps. Which is why I agreed to transport a few of the creatures to Spain. Fertilized eggs are ill-suited to international overseas travel. Jar the egg badly enough, you'll rupture the yolk sac. But as you've set the property alight, the discussion is moot." His gaze sharpened. "You have the eyes?"

Maria pressed a hand to a velvet pouch that hung about her neck. "Safe and sound."

"Hmm. Bring the rest of the carnyx." He tipped his head toward the missing war trumpet, now seemingly sightless without its carved bone eyes in place. "It's part of our cultural heritage." The professor slid a look at the two prisoners as he stuffed a few final items into his pockets. "Let's go." He hoisted his own incubator and took to the stairs, disappearing into the night. With any luck Tetzopa had hobbled the steam cart, ruining their plans for escape.

But Maria didn't follow. Not even as the overhead sounds of crackling flames grew louder, as something snapped and broke off above them. Instead, she strode to the back of the basement and dug in her pocket.

"You've another knife in your boot?" Ryan murmured under his breath. "Not only are we going to survive this brewing inferno, I want those bone eyes. Tonight."

Charlotte nodded. "Agreed." On the off chance they really were from an extinct *cuélebre*, they could not be allowed to stay in the possession of a mad scientist and his sister.

"Be ready." He shifted, sliding the short length of chain that bound his hands together along the pipe. "We'll pry the links apart."

An escape plan that didn't involve creating a gas leak, yet one with an emerging and yet more worrisome complication. She jerked her chin. "We've additional problems." *Understatement of the decade.*

Ryan twisted to follow her gaze to the back of the cellar, to where Maria stood before the door of the large cage, padlock in hand. He dropped a sting of curses as she turned the key.

*Clank.*

The chain dropped against the iron bars, loose. A sound that roused the interest of the shadowy creatures within. Skin —or were those scales?—slithered over stone.

"I did promise to satisfy your curiosity." Maria sauntered closer, pulling Ryan's Eagle B29 sidearm from her pocket to place it upon a table just beyond his reach. "It seems only sporting to give you a chance, however minuscule, of testing your dart gun. Though I expect it is calibrated for human—mammalian at best—physiology. What are the odds it might work upon birds or reptiles?"

Doubt flickered in Ryan's eyes.

Maria smirked, a corner of her mouth kicked up. "No? If you ask nicely, I'll shoot you both now and put an end to any prolonged suffering you might endure. After what I've seen them do to groundhogs..."

Yellow eyes with slitted pupils appeared at the iron bars, blinked. Set in a small head atop a long sinuous neck and behind an oversized beak, they seemed to belong to nothing more worrisome than a full-grown ostrich. Trouble enough if the animal was abused and angry. It pecked at the door—a swift, lashing movement that shifted the iron bars upon creaking hinges. Another peck, then the creature opened its mouth and hissed. Rows of sharp teeth gleamed in the gaslight. Patches of gray-green scales ran across its torso.

For a moment, Charlotte could do nothing but stare as dread walked up her spine, one icy finger after another. She swallowed, forcing herself to focus. To take a deep breath, to be ready to confront whatever happened next.

Ryan swore.

Maria laughed and turned on her heel. "And so ends our strange little family gathering." She snatched up the carnyx war trumpet and left by way of the cellar hatch. Two loud clangs echoed through the basement as the iron doors fell shut, sealing them inside.

With a kick worthy of a Can-can girl, Charlotte landed her booted ankle atop Ryan's shoulder. The effort strained and twisted her knee but when the alternative was certain death? She bit back complaint. "Can you reach my knife?"

Uttering profanities the like of which she'd never heard, Ryan contorted himself into a position worthy of a circus performance, struggling to reach the knife sheathed in her boot. At last, his fingertips managed to pinch down on the tip of the hilt and gradually slip it from the leather casing.

But mostly her gaze was fixed on a second set of eyes that emerged from the darkness. Ones closer to the ground. Ones that sent her heart rate soaring. A shining pair of eyes. No, reflected. The creature possessed a tapeta lucidum, a reflective surface upon the retina. An adaptation improving vision in low light, one that tended to characterize carnivorous species, including the crocodilians. True to her prediction, the luminous paired eyes advanced with an ever-so-slight sinuous shift as the creature walked, its movement complicated by an odd limping gait.

*Limping?*

She squinted. The forearms of this second, shorter creature were malformed—from their posterior edges sprouted structures not unlike feathers. Not quite an alligator.

The ostrich-like animal lashed out again and the door opened a few inches. Encouraged, it stepped forward into the light and gave a shove with a clawed foot. No. Not claws. Talons. The likes of which had no business on the toes of a great, flightless bird.

Free to explore the subterranean level, the not-quite-an-ostrich began to strut about the underground laboratory. Which was when she noticed the scales that ran down its neck. Aether, a boney crest protruded from its skull and claws did indeed mark the terminal tips of each wing.

Adrenaline shot through her system, elevating her blood pressure so quickly spots flashed before her eyes.

One such monstrosity was bad enough, but behind it galumphed the not-quite-an-alligator. The shortened and malformed forelimbs were not an asset to movement, forcing the creature to belly-crawl more than it walked.

But even more terrifying was the large snake that half-walked, half-slithered between and around the ankles of the two first monsters. A forked tongue flicked, sampling its environment, passing judgment on this new freedom. Then it reared back, propping itself upon rudimentary forelegs and hissed with cold and cruel eyes.

"Ryan," she croaked. Voicing his name was a struggle, lodged in her throat as it was. *Thud.* Somewhere above them something fell. A beam? Her heart could beat no further, yet their situation continued to rapidly deteriorate. "You need to hurry. Look behind—"

"Hang on. I've almost got it." From the corner of her eye, she could see he struggled with the blade. The angle required to pry himself free was proving difficult.

"You *need* to see this." The air she used to force the words past her lips wheezed from a tight chest steeling much needed oxygen from her lungs. The room tilted ever so slightly. Studying the mineralized bones of long dead dinosaurs, or the tiny fledglings of modern birds had not at all prepared her for the reality that flapped, strutted, and hobbled.

The not-an-ostrich crossed to the caged groundhogs, striking out at the wire bars that trapped the rodents inside with powerful force. Over and over, until the cage was utterly and truly destroyed. The rodent within screamed, bared its teeth, and fought bravely. But it wasn't enough. The toothed not-a-bird grasped the thrashing groundhog and tore it limb from limb, eating the choice bits before flinging the remains to the ground. In a flash, the not-an-alligator was upon them, tossing the mangled rodent into the deep recesses of its throat.

"Almost there." Metal scraped against metal as he forced the knife into the links of chain that joined the bracelets of his handcuffs.

"Ryan? We have a problem. Three of them." The ground-hogs in her backyard must have escaped from the aviary, from the smaller dino chickens that couldn't quite finish them off. Any of the oversized rodents hauled into this basement never stood the slightest chance.

"Just a second." Again and again, he wrenched and twisted and pried, finally mangling the link such that his bonds fell free from the overhead pipe.

Immediately, he spun about, lunged for his weapon, and snatched it from the table, registering in a single glance the monsters, their activities and the reason her voice was hoarse with dread.

"Shit." An oath muttered as he spied the open cage door and the three creatures now beyond its threshold, casting nightmarish shadows that would strike terror into anyone's hearts.

Under any other circumstances, that single word might have been one filled with awe and excitement. But for the direct threat made to their lives by these toothed, clawed and oddly feathered chimeras, he'd be scratching notes and formulating plans for publication, for naming the cryptids...

Except these weren't mysterious creatures re-emerging from the past from parts unknown to reclaim their place in the natural world. Their existence wasn't supported by a branch that sprang from either the reptilian or the avian family trees. They were manmade monsters. Unique specimens created in a laboratory by a mad scientist, unable to reproduce more of their kind.

*Thank aether.* She'd hate to think what it would be like to encounter an entire flock of these not-birds marauding through the streets of New Haven. Or to learn of not-alligators residing in trees beside countryside ponds. Of the not-snakes—

Her head whipped about, eyes searching and finding nothing. The temperature was climbing rapidly and the heat in the room was stifling; perspiration had her blouse stuck to her back. "The not-a-python has slunk off to parts unknown," she informed him as, swearing, he frantically pried at the links of chain that held her prisoner. Her voice might sound calm, but her heart was anything but. It leapt and soared, beating at an ever more frantic pace, the situation made worse by her bound wrists, her arms still stretched overhead, useless.

Beads of sweat broke out on Ryan's forehead. "Best bet is

that Maria threw a bolt on the basement hatch, otherwise it's the most direct exit. Option two, the kitchen stairs."

The floorboards above them let out a series of ominous moans.

"That door leads into a burning building with no knowledge of the floor plan." *Clink.* Her arms fell free. A brief moment of relief before she grabbed her knife from Ryan's hand, crouching to point its tip at the not-an-ostrich as it hissed and bared its teeth while strutting toward them, the creature she judged the most immediate threat. "Both options involve passing three unnerving monsters, one now hidden from view. I vote we attempt the more direct exit into the backyard."

Beside her, Ryan also raised his weapon and took aim. "The body of the not-a-bird makes for a good target. When I fire, we make for the table, scramble over it, and run for the basement hatch. Ready?"

As good a plan as they were likely to have, not that they had time to develop an alternative.

"Ready."

*Whoosh. Thud.*

His dart found its mark in the breast of the two-legged beast, and they ran.

Charlotte leapt onto the table, half sliding, half crawling across its surface, scattering bottles and boxes and various pieces of equipment. The not-an-ostrich screamed and struck out, its snakelike neck lashing at her thigh. Needle-sharp teeth pierced the thick fabric of her canvas trousers and lacerated her skin. Pain lanced through her and she sucked in a sharp breath.

Ryan kicked out at its body, shoving it several feet away, before lobbing reagent-filled glass bottles at it. Glass shattered and noxious fumes filled the air. Backed into a corner, the monster hissed and warbled a birdlike sound as—thank aether—the poison released from the dart took effect and dropped the creature to its knobby knees.

Ignoring the pain in her leg, Charlotte snatched up the Petri dish holding the Mixtec parchment fragment and stuffed it into her pocket.

Waiting at the other end of the table was the not-an-alligator. Its eyes gleamed with predatory anticipation.

"Wings," Ryan muttered. "The damn thing has wings."

Not quite, but now was not the time for an academic debate. "Insufficient to fly. Our main threats are its sharp teeth and its lashing tail. Stopping it? I don't like our odds." Her voice was tight. "What are the chances of a dart piercing its armored skin? Those scales are too thick."

Ryan unbuckled his leather belt, re-threading the tip through the buckle to form a loop. "If I can manage to land on its back..."

Hand upon his arm, Charlotte shook her head, horrified that he'd even suggest such a stunt. "You've little chance of success. Better to distract it, make it run in a different direction while we try for the hatch."

The not-an-ostrich opened its maw and screamed. A horrible sound that, for a second, froze them both in their tracks. Then the creature lifted a clawed foot and kicked over a chair, prodding them back into motion.

Ryan jerked his head in agreement. "Phase two, then." He

stood on the table, reaching overhead into the rafters to pull free a shovel and a garden hoe.

She slid her knife into her boot and accepted the shovel. "Wait one moment." She scanned the shadows for the limbed snake. "I can't locate the not-a-python."

He cringed. "We've little choice but to move."

They both crouched upon the table, ready to spring into action. Ryan reached out with his hoe, catching the wire cage of a groundhog, and toppling it to the ground. The rodent within screamed and Charlotte's heart squeezed, knowing the doomed creature was their only hope at escape.

Its attention and interest caught, the not-an-alligator walk-slithered forward, it jaws opening, widening, reaching—

"Go!"

Charlotte leapt from the table, running full speed to the stairs, to push and shove at the steel hatch doors. As feared, their exit was blocked from the outside. Frantic, heart racing, she turned, glancing at the kitchen stairs. But any hope of that exit was forestalled by billowing smoke that hung low in the air above them.

And Ryan? Against all reason, the insane man *had* tossed aside the hoe and leapt on the back of the lizard-monster and had his belt looped tight about the not-an-alligator's jaw, the muzzle of his pistol angled against the back of its skull, directly above the brain, the most vulnerable location of an alligator's skull. A desperate, calculated bet.

She'd smack him later. If he survived.

*Whoosh. Thud.*

The dart fired from point blank range. The creature jerked

—the only indication anything had happened—then resumed its fight to free its jaw. Not a good omen. Had the dart needle penetrated the creature's skull?

The monster thrashed. Threw its head from side to side. Lashed its tail. Growled as it heaved itself toward the bottom of the basement stairs. An impressive show of power given the not-an-alligator carried a grown man upon its back. All while Ryan held on with all his strength.

Hoping poison seeped from a needle into the not-an-alligator's brainstem in time, Charlotte turned back to the doors, confronting an imminent threat of death by smoke inhalation, or building collapse. Tightening her grip upon the shovel, she struck at the overhead, angled doors. Over and over and over until the damn things exploded outward.

# CHAPTER NINETEEN

"Ryan!" Charlotte shouted.

He looked up from the back of the still-strug-gling alligator monster and saw stars.

Real stars. Stars set in a dark night sky above a flickering yellow glow. Behind him, above him, everywhere around him, flames leapt higher as the house took a deep breath of fresh air and redoubled its efforts to burn itself to the ground, not at all deterred by last night's rainstorm.

Abandoning his belt as a lost cause—the creature might be half limp, but he wasn't risking a bite during his exit—Ryan shoved to his feet and ran up the stairs into the relative cool-ness of the warm summer night, weapon drawn. Where he found their battle against monsters not yet won.

"Woof! *Woof woof woof!*"

The relief of his escape quickly turned to worry over the scene before him.

"Glory! No!" Charlotte yelled as she ran, her voice

scarcely audible over the crackle of flames that climbed the wood cladding of the house. But the dog refused to heed her calls. Instead, the canine leapt about the backyard alternately lunging then backing away from something hidden in the over-tall grass.

Charlotte's arrival, shovel held aloft, only emboldened her dog.

What did Glory have cornered? Escapees from the aviary? Those were terrifying in their own rights, but as he scanned for both dino chickens and native rodents, he spotted instead the unmistakable flecked pattern of python skin.

Not a groundhog, but rather the missing limbed serpent raised its head from the overgrowth. Somehow the not-a-python had slipped out the basement hatch when they weren't looking. He gaped at the fully formed front legs that bent at elbows and ended in four digits on each hand. A most impressive experimental result that begged further study and explanation.

Glory growled, her hackles raised and her ears pinned back.

The legged snake lashed out. Missed. Then recoiled for another strike.

The dog leapt into motion, dancing about the bizarre serpent, testing various angles. Lunging, then jumping backward, again and again, until she'd forced it backward into a dark corner of the yard.

He lowered his gun. Like as not, he'd miss. Or the dog would leap in front of the dart, midair.

The limbed-snake dropped back into the weeds on all

fours and walk-wriggled toward the bushes—the dog's cue to launch an attack. With fierce, focused attention, she seized the atavistic snake's throat, whipping the creature back and forth with a violence that must have snapped its sinuous spine in several places for, by the time he and Charlotte drew close, the battle was won.

Glory tossed the limp, unsettling not-a-python onto the ground at her mistress's feet, tongue lolling.

Charlotte fell to her knees, dropping the shovel, and wrapped her arms about the canine, burying her face in her fur, murmuring words or rebuke, relief, and praise in succession.

"Most impressive." Glory wagged her tail, accepting his attention and congratulatory scratches as her due.

But their night was far from over. The sound of approaching sirens met his ears—the fire brigade would arrive at any moment and once their first priority was attended to, scores of firemen would comb through the wreckage, walk the property, and find the inexplicable remains of bizarre creatures. There would be no hiding them. Too many of the not-quite-chickens had escaped alive into the bushes.

They needed to move. There was a dirigible to ground and a pair of Spanish siblings to haul into custody for questioning. Only then would he and Charlotte have the luxury of time to unravel the zoological complexities the mad herpetologist had engendered.

"We should keep this for further study," he said, snatching up the legged snake and tossed its broken body over his shoulder. He'd not be leaving the bizarre tetrapod snake laying unattended upon the ground. The Mexican archaeologist could keep this particular experimental creature in custody while they pursed the Rodríguez siblings. "Charlotte?"

She looked up from her dog. "Yes?

He jerked his head. "We're about to have company. Time to go."

Ryan left her tying a length of rope to Glory's collar, intent on assessing the exact situation they now faced. He strode past the burning building toward the street, hoping Tetzopa had somehow managed stop Maria and Enzo Rodríguez in their tracks. Alas, it appeared they would not be so lucky.

Neighbors wearing confused expressions gathered about a handcuffed form laying prone beside the street—an unfamiliar face that Ryan guessed was likely the hired driver. The steam cart was gone. As was Tetzopa. The archeologist must have been caught by the Rodríguez siblings mid-effort.

"How many people departed?" A question he put to the crowd at large.

A man answered. "Three, if you count the man forced to drive at gunpoint." His eyes narrowed. "A man dragged from his vehicle, his attacker kidnapped. A house fire threatening the neighborhood. And that's before we mention the awfully strange bird that ran behind a bush or that snake you've got about your neck." He squinted. "Are those legs? What the hell is going on here?"

"Illegal import of animals and associated biological materi-als." Ryan flashed his badge. "Please, sir, for your own safety, do not approach any bird roughly approximating a chicken or any other unusual animals you may encounter."

The man blinked. Opened his mouth, but before any words could slip past his lips, Charlotte appeared, dog at her heels.

"Charlie, remember how I told you the bird songs from their backyard weren't right?"

"Miss Reid? You're involved in this?"

"Unfortunately. And the goings-on inside that house were far worse than we could ever have imagined. I'll tell you every-thing, but right now we need to follow that cart to the docks, stop them before they can untether. They're the ones behind all this chaos. Can you keep Glory?"

He nodded. "Consider it done."

She turned to the canine, her voice firm. "Sit. Stay."

With a mournful and resigned sigh, the canine sat. Then turned inquiring eyes toward Charlie.

"Bacon," he promised.

Charlotte handed the makeshift leash to Charlie.

Ryan cast about looking for likely transportation as sirens sliced through the night, heralding the arrival of the great steam pumper fire engine that now tore down the street. The fire wagon with its coiled hose followed mere feet behind. Galloping in their wake, a clockwork horse. One with a glinting gold badge welded to its flank. "Customs," he told Charlotte. "Our ride is here."

Brakes slammed and the firefighters leapt from the vehicles and immediately set to work, ignoring the gathering crowd. As water arced through the air, dulling the dry roar and crackle of the burning house, Ryan waved down the rider, flashing his badge.

The mechanical horse slid to a stop and an agent jumped down, his brow furrowed. "Tetzopa sent a bat requesting help?"

"And Customs sends only a single man?" Ryan shot back.

The agent shrugged. "Night staffing."

Cursing, Ryan grabbed the reins and passed them to Charlotte. "Send another bat," he told the man. "Request assistance. Direct all available agents to the Water Street docks, near Harborside Park. Our target set this house afire and is making a run for it." He waved at the smoldering house. "Strange biological material and laboratory equipment will be discovered, much like this creature." He shoved the legged serpent into the stunned agent's hands. "This operation falls under the domain of IBIS. You understand what that means?"

The agent's eyes widened at Ryan. "Dragons?"

"Only if we're very lucky." He leapt into the saddle behind Charlotte where she waited, holding tight to the reins, and gripping the clockwork horse's flanks with her knees, leaving him the stirrups. "In the basement are incubators with eggs. If any survive, make them a priority. I'll loop you into details of the investigation later. For now, document it all. Nothing leaves the property."

The man gave a sharp nod. "On it, sir."

Charlotte reached for a lever at the horse's side and re-engaged the escapement, allowing the wound spring to send the clockwork horse into a sedate walk. "Settled?" she asked Ryan.

He wrapped his arms about her waist, grateful to have a partner so poised and level-headed even in the face of danger.

The perfect companion for this wild ride of an assignment. "Let's move."

Charlotte pulled the lever down two notches, taking them quickly into a fast trot. "You think they've a personal dirigible?" she shouted over her shoulder. Over the pounding of steel hooves against packed dirt.

"Yes," he yelled back. "One for hire. There's no chance it's one of the North-East Airship Line's vessels. Staterooms and storage bays must be reserved, and departures follow a strict schedule. Everything points to a private rental. If Spain is their destination, they'll want to head north or south, land at an international harbor and travel from there."

They rounded the corner and Charlotte shoved the lever down, sending the mechanical horse into a full gallop. Ryan leaned forward, chest to her back as they raced through New Haven along Franklin Street, a straight shot to the boat and dirigible slips of Northern New Haven Harbor.

Three city blocks to go. Rodríguez and Maria had a head start, true, but they carried precious and fragile cargo.

There was a section of Harborside Park affectionately known as Dovecote Dock. Its specialty was offering tethering points along with refueling and catering services to those smaller, private dirigibles that fell into the pigeon class—transport designed for short hops between cities.

Many such dirigibles tended toward luxurious, at least when privately owned and maintained by business tycoons and other members of society's crème de la crème. Others, those rented by the day or week, were comfortable, but were more serviceable.

Not that there were many pigeon class airships in New Haven. Most luxury airships floated over the Connecticut city without stopping, preferring to tie their ropes down in New York City or Boston. A fact that attracted characters of the more questionable sort to local shores, possibly a point that the professor and his sister counted in their favor when they'd established a base in Ryan's hometown.

Two city blocks.

"They'll go north," Charlotte yelled. "To Iceland, where they can ferry to the Faroe Islands, then points south."

"Possible. But an obvious route. Better to stop them before they lift off."

One block.

"Your leg?" he called out the question. He didn't care for the dark streaks of blood that marred the canvas of her trousers. That not-an-ostrich had possessed a vicious beak and alarming talons.

"Stings. But it can wait. Don't even think of leaving me behind on the ground."

Ahead of them, aether-filled balloons bobbed above the briny waves of the harbor, their silver fabric glinting in light cast by streetlamps. Individual vessels were marked by the flickering of red and green port and starboard lights. From a few occupied gondolas the blue-white light of Lucifer lamps seeped out from around the edges of pulled blinds.

Which vessel was the one where Rodríguez and Maria stashed their nest eggs, both literal and figurative, in hopes of escaping the reach of US Customs, IBIS division?

The shabbiest of all, given their sudden departure and

their depleted funds. Sure enough, third berth to the left floated one of the oldest pigeon class models. Its balloon bore numerous patches and many coats of paint—now flaking—had been applied to its hull over the years. Its captain—judging from insignia sewn onto the front of his shabby overcoat—unwound tethering ropes, readying for cast off.

Most telling of all, however, was the familiar steam cart parked beside its cargo bay door.

Charlotte hauled the control lever upward, locking the clockwork horse's legs. Steel hooves skidded over the wooden boards of Dovecote Dock. They jumped from its back and ran to the cart to find the wagon bed ominously empty.

"Tetzopa?" Ryan called, searching.

A groan directed their attention to a piling a few yards away where the archeologist sat, his fist wrapped about the long pipe of the carnyx, his leg bent at a strange angle. Broken.

They hurried to the archaeologist agent's side. His leg needed medical attention. The more immediate the better.

"Agents are on the way," Ryan told him.

"That bastard Rodríguez ought to be walking with a limp." Tetzopa fixed Ryan with a determined glare. "I hooked him with this... odd trumpet. But he still has my codex."

Charlotte knelt by his side. "We found Rodríguez studying a fragment cut from the parchment for microscopic examination."

Tetzopa stared at her in horror. "Cut! They cut an ancient document!" His next word emerged as a furious growl. "Go," he ordered. "This is not a night for history to repeat itself with more cultural theft. Stop them. Put an end to their vile plans."

Charlotte frowned, even as her gaze shifted to the dirigible. "Your leg—"

A pump roared to life—the dirigible's air extractor. A machine that pulled ballast oxygen from the balloon to send the vessel aloft.

"Will wait." Tetzopa waved away her concern. "I'm not in immediate danger. Go. Hurry."

Charlotte glanced at Ryan, uncertain.

Neither option sat right. But much as he hated to abandon the archaeologist, if they didn't climb aboard the gondola in the next few minutes, there would be no retrieving the artifacts or the mad scientist's creations.

He ran back to the clockwork horse, digging into the saddlebag and hauling out a flare gun. Back at Tetzopa's side, he pressed it into the man's hands. "Wait as long as you can, then send up a signal." He looked to Charlotte, his instincts battling inside his chest. Much as he wished to leave her safe upon the ground, he needed her. "Let's go."

Ryan ran toward the gondola as it lifted away from the dock, launching himself at the docking ladder affixed to its side. Nails scraped over paint, but he caught the very last rung. Legs kicking, arms straining, he hauled himself upward and flung himself onto the deck. But there was not a moment to spare laying prone. Charlotte was not with him. He leapt to his feet, grabbed a nearby coil of tethering and tossed the entirety of the rope over the railing, watching it unfurl.

Charlotte, running alongside the dock, leapt into the air and caught its swaying length. In mere seconds, she dangled over water.

His heart pounded in his ears, the sound of blood roaring eclipsing even that of the dirigible's clanking engine, as she climbed upward hand over hand while he hauled desperately at the rope. Below, the streetlamps rapidly became pinpoints of light. A moment later, Charlotte caught at the docking ladder with both hands and placed her boots securely upon its lowest rung. Then she began to climb. A few tense moments later, her feet hit the deck.

But before his pulse had a chance to drop, there was a loud click. The sound of a pistol's hammer locking into place.

*Dammit.*

Charlotte lifted her hands overhead, as did Ryan. Wind whipped the air as he turned to find himself, once again, staring down the barrel of Maria's pistol.

"Most impressive." Maria smirked. "And yet so very disappointing. My ostrich exhibited a preference for live groundhogs, a taste I expected would transfer to human flesh. I'm tempted to try once more, but your presence is problematic."

The woman had hoped for their demise. Regretted her inability to be present as her creations stalked human prey. Not once had her actions even hinted at the possibility that somewhere, buried deep inside her, remained the slightest remnant of something that might be termed ethics or morals. How twisted must a person's soul be to set a trio of nightmare creations upon two people, expecting them to be torn limb from limb by a toothed bird and a winged crocodile?

"Why?" he asked, wanting to know. Needing to know. "Why go through so much trouble?" Marriage. Murder. Theft.

"Why work with Captain Donovan? Was there no business tycoon who would fund your project?"

Insult rippled across her face. "Hand over the rights to my family's *cuélebre* to some rich American?" She spit the last word as if it left a bitter taste on the tongue. "Surrender my family's legacy, one that stretches back centuries? I would never." She drew another breath. "I found the cave, the coins. Without my discovery—my efforts, my hard work—our land would be lost, my brother nothing more than a common laborer. This project, the restoration of a *cuélebre* in the cave it —and others of its species—once inhabited will be my crowning achievement."

"To what end?" he shouted. "Who installs a winged serpent upon their property simply for the sake of recreating history?"

"Is it not obvious?" Her eyes narrowed. "How much would you pay for a glimpse of a living, breathing dragon? A small fortune. Compound that over time and my family's future is secured. And if my brother manages to restore a breeding population? How many young boys once dreamed of becoming a knight in shining armor?"

"Hunting?" Bile burned the back of Ryan's throat. "You'd let men shoot at a dragon for a fee?"

"Now, now." She waggled a finger as her mouth stretched into a mocking grin. "We'll only allow one man at a time—or a woman—but swords only. Keep it a fair fight."

"And prevent the stock from depleting too quickly."

She barked a hard, callous laugh. "Ah, now, it's moments

like this I wish you were more mercenary like your father. We could have managed so much more with your help."

"But you don't have a *cuélebre*, do you?" Charlotte challenged. "Just a collection of mutated birds and reptiles."

"I don't recall claiming success." Maria's eyes narrowed. "It's a multi-stepped process."

While her brother might be induced to lecture, to swagger like a peacock and showcase his knowledge to a trapped and doomed audience, not so his sister. A disinclination to converse further betrayed by the slightest twitch of a muscle in her finger.

He dropped onto his hands a moment before Maria pulled the trigger, thrusting out his leg as he spun. A surprise move that swept her legs out from under her and sent her sprawling. Her weapon clattered across the deck—an advantage that would not last more than a few heartbeats.

"Grab it," he yelled. "Run!"

Charlotte threw a desperate, pained glance at him, but snatched up the pistol and darted away, disappearing into the main hold.

Ryan flung himself after Maria, grabbing hold of her wrist. The solid swing of her clenched fist connected with the angle of his jaw. Stars exploded across his vision, but he managed to keep his grip. Tumbling in a tangled fury, they grappled with each other, each struggling to gain the upper hand. In a last-ditch effort, Ryan redoubled his efforts.

Though she wriggled and squirmed like a slippery sea monster, he landed on her back. Gritting his teeth, he captured her other arm and pinned it behind her. Beneath him, Maria bucked like a wild animal desperate to break free. A frustrated, animalistic screech tore from her throat.

"That's my inheritance you're wearing about your neck." He would grab the pouch from her neck, save he needed two hands to hold her thrashing form. As long as he had control of her, he had possession of the carved bone eyes she and her brother had pried from the carnyx.

"Yours?" she spat, struggling against him. "You're nothing but Irish scum. Celtic, perhaps, but of the wrong sort."

He gave a derisive snort. "Yet you feel you've every right to claim the inheritance of the Mexican people?" he countered. "Are your family's old conquistador habits dying hard?"

They both jerked at the sound of gunfire that discharged inside the gondola's hull. Maria laughed—or was it more of a sardonic cackle?

Was he concerned? Yes. But Charlotte had spent years upon years in the Wild West and knew her way around a sidearm. The sooner he subdued Maria, the sooner he could run to her side. He cast about for a means of restraining his prisoner.

The door to the bridge slammed open. An angry airship captain stormed out. "What is the meaning of this? Are you trying to send us to kingdom come firing off live rounds?"

"Return to port!" Ryan ordered him, flashing his badge. "This woman is a wanted criminal."

"Wanted, you say?" The captain's gaze hardened. "For transporting a bunch of strange birds? I don't think so."

"For murder," Ryan answered. "On two counts."

The airship continued to rise. A process the captain

seemed disinclined to reverse.

The man didn't even blink. Instead, the shifting move-ments of his shoulders were one step short of a shrug. "Can't think why I'd have any interest in cooperating with Customs. The minute they climb onboard, I'll lose my license."

Ryan followed the drift of the man's eyes, noticed the backup fuel tanks lashed to the cabin of the gondola and cursed. Their labels had been stripped away. True, many diri-gibles re-used tanks perfectly legally. But testing those tanks for the presence of hydrogen instead of aether was as simple as lighting a match. Hydrogen use in such large quantities might be banned in the United States, but there were those who flaunted the rules in favor of turning a sharper profit. And, given the guilt and fear that stiffened the captain's shoulders, this particular gondola hung beneath a giant, flammable gasbag.

Which explained the man's concern over live rounds of ammunition. The slightest spark could ignite the airship and send it up in flames.

Of course the siblings would rent from the unscrupulous.

"Help me. Hand me a rope," Ryan ordered, praying the man would see reason, lest things go from bad to worse. "Land the dirigible and I'll pretend I never saw those."

"Help *you*? Not a chance." The captain snatched up a mop and smacked Ryan's shoulder, once, twice. With enough force behind the blows to leave bruises and threaten his grip upon Maria. "Now take your hands off the lady."

As the man raised the stick high for another blow, Ryan twisted about taking his captive with him. Placing her between them in self-defense. The handle's downward arc now directed itself at Maria's midsection. The captain reeled, his every instinct rebelling at striking a woman.

A poor choice that was his undoing.

For in that very moment before he recoiled, Maria, all sinew and muscle, reacted instinctively. She curled and kicked —her booted feet striking the airship captain's chest and toppling him backward.

The mop flew from his hands as his arms reeled and spun, tracing circles in the air in a mad attempt to regain balance. But to no avail. The captain's hips struck the railing and momentum pitched him over, his shouts fading away. Cut off by a distant, faint splash.

No time to worry about kraken or wonder if the man could swim, for Maria jerked her head backward, smashing her skull into Ryan's nose. Pain exploded in a dizzying array of flashing lights as his captive became all sharp angles and claws. She yanked free and ran.

A heartbeat later, he leapt to his feet—blood pouring over his lips and chin—and gave chase. But three steps ahead of him, she dashed into the bridge and slammed the door. Ryan grabbed hold of the handle and wrenched. Locked.

Another gunshot rang out from inside the gondola's hold.

Charlotte. *Dammit.* He wanted this dirigible down, out of the sky. Now.

But not via an uncontrolled descent beneath a blazing ball of fire.

Abandoning hopes of securing the helm, he raced for the hold.

# CHAPTER TWENTY

Professor Rodríguez howled as blood dripped from the tip of a finger that was no longer quite all there. Not because the bullet had caused him injury, but because he'd almost lost his grip on the portable incubator. Had it fallen to the ground, it might have jarred the precious eggs within.

"The first hours, days of cell proliferation and migration are critical to proper development. All taking place atop a most fragile structure, the yolk sac. After I've gone to such lengths to procure fertile ostrich eggs all the way from Africa! Why would you do such a thing—you know that better than most!" Bewildered, he stared at her. Unable to grasp the evilness of the horrible things that had been done in pursuit of his demented attempts to hatch a *cuélebre*.

Everything he'd done to reach this moment was beyond wrong. And still, yes, she *was* mortified. Not that she'd admit as much to him, not even with the tiniest alteration of her expression. These altered eggs ought not exist at all. Did that mean she was duty bound to ignore a mad scientist's groundbreaking research techniques and destroy them? She'd yet to make up her mind.

Smoke drifted up from the pistol in Charlotte's hand. It had been some time since she'd last fired such a weapon, even longer since she'd pointed a gun with deadly intent at a man, and her aim was off. But only a little. Not bad considering it wasn't her own gun.

When she'd burst into the belly of the dirigible, he'd ignored her. As always. Though after her warning shot, she grabbed his full attention.

"You were supposed to die in that fire," Rodríguez yelled. "How are you here?" Annoyance morphed into hopeful suspense. He leaned forward, clutching his hand, uncaring that he'd lost half a digit. "The incubators. Did the fire brigade arrive in time to save the incubators? Please say yes."

Unlikely. But let him wonder.

She narrowed her eyes and chambered another bullet. "I won't ask again. Next time, I won't miss." The time for warning shots was past. She'd aim for dead center, for his stomach. Even if the unfamiliar weapon drifted a touch.

The longer this went on, the higher the dirigible would rise and the longer it would take to return to port. She wasn't keen on extending this voyage, but neither would she rush and chance a mistake.

He gasped. "You wouldn't. These may well be viable!"

Deep down, she too wished to see what strange creatures might hatch from his altered eggs. But any chance of that rested upon taking control of this dirigible—and that included everyone on board. If that meant cracked eggs... Well, she'd learn to live with the disappointment of never knowing what kind of embryos grew within.

Priorities.

She tipped her head.

He huffed. But, grumbling, he bent at the waist. Slowly. Carefully. Cringing as the incubator touched down at his feet.

"Your sister mentioned stowing live birds aboard this dirigible." Her mind flashed back to the nasty bite the not-an-ostrich had delivered. Even now her leg throbbed. "Where are they?"

That elicited a harsh bark of a laugh. "Birds? We've many creatures hatched from eggs. Wouldn't call any of them birds."

She tightened her grip on the weapon. "What then?"

He shrugged. "Would you like a tour? Let me go and I'll lead you to their cages."

A quick glance about informed her there were no live animals—only eggs—in the hold. "Thank you, but no. I'll find them myself. Now return the stolen Mixtec codex," she ordered. "Toss the satchel at my feet." She gestured with the muzzle. "Gently. No need to do anymore damage to a priceless artifact that belongs in a museum."

Where was Ryan? Had he run into trouble? Should she abandon her quasi-diplomatic approach, shoot Rodríguez, confiscate the codex and incubator, and go find him? Yes. Still, she didn't move. Curiosity had nailed her feet to the ground.

"The Mexicans have no use for it," Rodríguez protested, wrapping his fist about the strap of the canvas bag slung over his shoulder, the bag that held the codex. "They'd left it locked up in a dusty basement, ignored for decades. No one in the entire country has the slightest idea of the creature hidden beneath all that white paint, beneath pictographs of presumed myths. The living descendants of its scribes have forgotten the stories and abandoned their heritage." His voice rose with each statement and a feverish mania entered his eyes. "Better the parchment remains in my possession. I alone possess the skills to raise the dead."

His ego was no small thing. Then again, she'd witnessed with her own two eyes the proof that he'd accomplished what no one before him had ever managed.

"This?" She tugged the soggy square of parchment from her pocket, wondering if he would confirm what she suspected. "You're telling me..."

He nodded, smiled at her in approval. "Precisely. Parchment. Skin. The very cells of a once-living, deified creature preserved in the dusty, forgotten archives of a once-great civilization. My ancestors were conquistadors—"

"Invaders." She stuffed the fragment back in her pocket.

His smile fell away and his countenance darkened. "Call them what you will, but when they heard tell of a great feathered serpent that flew through the skies—part bird, part snake—worshiped as a deity representing both death and resurrection, they did not brush aside the myths as nonsense. My ancestors wrote down their stories, carried them home. I grew up on those legends, told as they were alongside those of the Asturians, also a once-great people, now thought of as mere Spaniards."

"So you thought to return to the New World, to once again

plunder, to steal their history from them outright?" History repeating itself? Not on her watch. She motioned with the gun. "Toss it. Now."

The stars flew from his eyes as his fingers dug into the canvas and his mouth flattened into a harsh line. "I wish I could. But I must refuse. Insurance you see. If these eggs fail to hatch, I will start again. But if our experiment meets with success, I will gladly return the artifact—along with the creature itself, alive once more. All I need is a little blood—"

"You intend to hatch a quetzalcoatl that you might *bleed* it?" A bewildering plan. Then again, she recalled hearing stories of Mayan blood rituals and Aztec sacrifices. "To what end? How on Earth does any of this help you restore a *cuélebre* to the caves on your family's land?"

"Maria told you about that, did she?" He frowned. "Research takes time. It's expensive. You know that better than most."

None of his logic—or his work—seemed to run in a straight line. Her mind skittered over the events of the past day and landed squarely upon the not-worm infestation of the smuggler and the so-called pharmaceuticals Rose had peddled throughout the neighborhood. Perhaps she'd been more involved than she'd admitted to Ryan? "Do *not* tell me this is all about developing some kind of high-end medicinal treatment."

Irritation clouded his face. "Such is—was—the domain of my wife. Scratching in the dirt, chasing after pennies by peddling Alcantra's ridiculous cures." He set his jaw. Lifted his chin. "No. The *cuélebre* is the ultimate goal. The quetzalcoatl will not be harmed."

"Save for your theft of its blood."

His eyes narrowed. "If all goes as planned, we will only require a single animal, a single vial of its blood. Once we achieve our end, I have every intention of returning this codex —and any live quetzalcoatl—to the Mixtec descendants."

As if such an empty promise made it all better.

"Blood," Charlotte repeated. While he clutched a bloodless parchment to his chest. He sought to resurrect a *koo savi* only to bleed it? She shook her head. It made no sense. To create a hybrid animal, a chimera of sorts, one grafted solid tissue. But that wasn't what he was after. "What purpose, exactly, will blood serve?"

"To bring back the dead from their bones."

And wasn't that the exact phrase Professor Tetzopa had used during his recounting of one of many myths attributed to the feathered serpent god? A final puzzle piece to complete the picture.

Dragon bones pried from the eyes of an ancient war trumpet soaked in blood collected from the veins of a quetzalcoatl that had, in turn, been resurrected from an ancient document.

Myth mixed with science and touched with a little insanity.

Blood by itself couldn't revive an animal from bone fragments. That much was nonsense. But if one could somehow fuse the desiccated remains of cells from long-dead animals with those of the living, and transplant those cells into a cluster of rapidly dividing cells inside an egg, could a viable hybrid be created?

Based on the residents of the aviary and the creatures Maria had released from behind bars, Charlotte was forced to the answer that yes, yes it could. And Rodríguez had managed exactly that.

It boggled the mind, the lengths to which he'd gone, the long, complex, and twisted path he'd followed, all in hopes of recreating his family's mythological winged dragon.

"All to generate a *cuélebre*."

His answering smile was beatific. Rapturous. And downright alarming. *Madness.* That devout flickering light dancing in his eyes was pure insanity.

Was it too many years spent working in a subterranean laboratory, nose to beak with ever more bizarre chickens as he manipulated their eggs, their offspring, to draw forth prehistoric phenotypic features, characteristics thought to be irretrievably lost in living creatures, now accessible only through paleontological studies?

The science he'd employed—cathode rays, embryonic manipulations, coaxing the dead cells of an animal back to life—to create his atavistic monsters was impressive.

Above board and funded, his work might have drawn much acclaim. Fame, even. Zoologists would have leapt at the chance to restore extinct species such as the dodo, the great auk, the quagga—the list was long—all wiped from the face of the planet by overzealous hunters. Among them, countless avian species, birds valued only for the brilliant plumage, killed, their feathers passing briefly through the hands of a milliner to adorn a lady's hat, then forever lost.

But the greater good did not figure in his plans.

No. Instead, Rodríguez was solely focused on accomplishing the—all but?—impossible by means of some ill-defined sorcery. Blood to resurrect the dead? He sounded like a man in need of a soapbox and a street corner where he might spout nonsense verging on the fanatical. How had the man risen so far in his field?

She lifted the pistol and pulled back the hammer. "The codex. Now."

"Fine." He moved as if to haul the satchel's strap over his head. Then threw the bag at her. *At* her. Not at her feet.

And that was when the benefit of having an older brother handed her an advantage. Snowballs. Mud clods. Buffalo chips. All employed as elements of distraction in childhood battles. And she'd given as good as she'd gotten. Forewarned was forearmed.

The satchel smacked into her hip and slid to the floor, but she didn't so much as flinch, knowing more would follow in its path.

Sure enough, Rodríguez reached, grabbed, and threw item after item—a Lucifer lamp, an empty chamberpot, a handful of netting—in quick succession.

Charlotte dodged them all as she took aim and fired. This time she didn't miss. Even better, she hit the leg already damaged by Tetzopa's expert wielding of an Asturian carnyx.

He screamed. An exceedingly satisfactory sound that accompanied his collapse, a fall that landed him in the remnants of his tantrum—a tangle of twine, scattered shards of porcelain and puddles of faintly glowing bioluminescent bacteria—clutching his leg.

Justified, as he'd likely not ever walk again without the aid of a cane. His leg was a bloody mess. Lucky him, she'd aimed to miss his knee—if just. A kindness to ensure that the limb would at least still flex. Provided he didn't bleed out. In which case, her care was irrelevant.

She twisted the chamber, lining up another bullet. Not that Rodríguez looked capable of any further resistance, but better safe than sorry. And there was still Maria to worry about. As she bent to grab the satchel, to sling the weight of his notes and a Mixtec codex over her own shoulder, the floorboards beneath her feet pushed upward at a steep angle and a sudden roar of the engine met her ears.

Though they'd been on the rise for several minutes now, this sudden acceleration combined with a sharp rise likely meant Ryan had not seized control of the dirigible.

Speaking of, where was—

Ryan burst into the cargo hold, feet skidding through the glowing bioluminescent pool. "Hold your fire! The balloon is filled with hydrogen."

Mouth agape, hand loosely wrapped about the pistol, she turned toward him. "What!"

The airship rose at an ever-steeper angle—a shift that sent the portable incubator sliding across the floorboards. She lunged, saving it from a violent collision with a stack of unsecured crates.

"Worse," he added. "The captain fell overboard, and Maria

has the helm."

The words hit her like a barrage of coprolites.

If they couldn't seize control of this airship, the further from land they floated and the more likely they'd have to swim back to shore. Not an appealing prospect. The Long Island Sound didn't have *much* of a kraken problem. Which wasn't to say they weren't there. Still, most people preferred to swim at the netted beaches. Particularly the ones where great care was taken to maintain the integrity of the wire mesh.

All considerations before she factored in eggs and ancient manuscripts, items she wished to carry back to shore intact and uncompromised. Not that the possibilities of such were looking all that favorable at the moment.

Was it time to abandon ship before they couldn't make land?

"The escape glider." Her words were half statement, half question. "The codex will not survive a plunge into seawater," she pointed out. "Nor will the eggs be viable if they sustain much of an impact—assuming we wish to preserve them?"

"Do they possess any value, beyond satisfying our curiosity?"

"An excellent question, one I'm hard-pressed to answer. What if they're the key to restoring extinct animals, ones destroyed by human hands? What responsibility is upon our shoulders?"

One hundred yards was about as much range as they could hope for off of a coast-hugging pigeon class vessel. Open to the skies and capable of seating six, it wasn't built to do more than carry passengers back to the nearby shore.

Ryan looked torn. "We take the eggs. Save the philosophical debate for later." He frowned, ignoring Rodríguez's wailing. "Abandoning ship now is the wise move. But Maria still wears the bone carvings about her neck."

The velvet pouch which held the war trumpet's carved eyes. The only known bone items with a direct link to the Iron Age beginnings of the Principality of Asturias when a *cuélebre* might possibly have existed. An item the siblings had both double checked was in their possession before abandoning the burning house. An item Maria kept close to her heart. Without it, the only biological connection to a once-living *cuélebre* was lost.

Ryan wouldn't leave without the carved eyes. Not until no other choice was left to him.

And she wasn't leaving without him. She tucked the pistol into her waistband. It wasn't safe to use onboard, but neither would she abandon a perfectly good weapon.

Charlotte swallowed hard as her gaze fell uneasily upon the parachute packs that hung on the wall. None of them looked reliable or inviting. Were they all in working condition? Would they, if deployed, open? Unfurl? Catch the air and carry its wearer in a soft fall to the waves below?

Little hints of disrepair and disinterest were scattered about the hold—rusty overhead beams in dire need of a wire brush and paint, cargo ropes with far too many spliced sections to be trustworthy, piles of dirt and debris so compacted and consolidated it rivaled the caulking as weatherproofing.

Did she trust these parachutes? No.

Even the escape glider presented a sub-optimal prospect

and she'd yet to take stock of its flaws and shortcomings.

Yet, as predicted, Ryan snatched one of the parachute drop packs from a hook, carefully checked the pack and pronounced it safe and sound before sliding his arms through the straps and buckling it about his waist. "I'll stay. Handle Maria while you transport our prisoner and assorted items back to dry land."

"I'm not leaving you behind." Stomach churning, she grabbed a pack for herself. Thrust it at him. "Check mine please."

"But the codex, the incubator and eggs—"

"Wait. I've an idea." She grabbed another parachute drop pack and strode over to Rodríguez, bent to grip his tear-stained face. "Stop your caterwauling and listen carefully. One way or another your precious eggs are going overboard. They'll either travel in his hands beneath a parachute—" she pointed at Ryan, "—or in yours aboard the escape glider. Choose."

"My leg!" he cried. "You might as well force me to walk the plank!"

She dropped the parachute pack, turned away. "Guess he's staying."

"No! I'll do it. I'll do it."

Ryan frowned. "Leave him in possession of an irreplaceable artifact and the only remaining viable eggs?"

"The only unique items aboard this dirigible hang from a chain about Maria's neck." She shrugged. "There are other codices—and the embryos inside the eggs may fail to develop no matter what we do. Besides, Rodríguez is deeply invested in their survival. He'll see them safe. Insofar as he's able."

Conflicted, Ryan ran a hand through his hair.

"Charlotte…"

She tipped her head. "You really think you can retake the bridge and capture Maria alone?"

"The odds are low," he admitted. "I'll need a distraction at the very least."

She nodded. "And I'll not be much use with an ancient manuscript strapped across my chest holding a box of raw eggs."

He snorted. "That would likely present problems."

"Then help me wrestle him into the escape glider. We'll stash him there with the artifacts and incubator, then pull the wing pins so he can't launch. Not that he'll be going anywhere on his own with that leg of his. If we subdue Maria—no harm, no foul—we'll be back in port soon, tethering down." She glanced at Rodríguez. "He claims there are live creatures aboard. The best of all his work. If we take the helm—"

"Published papers. Scientific acclaim. Yes. Fine. But if the situation deteriorates, if we can't take control of the vessel, you need abandon ship with this madman in tow."

A chill ran through her. Abandon Ryan? She frowned. "I won't—"

"Promise you'll glide for shore if Maria swings the airship to starboard, alters course to head over open water out of range of the glider's ability to land." Though his voice was thick with emotion, his expression brooked no argument.

Charlotte opened her mouth. Closed it. "Fine," she acquiesced, knowing that an argument about the specific conditions that would negate her agreement would only waste more time. "Let's move."

# CHAPTER TWENTY-ONE

Though he'd much prefer to see Charlotte safely off the dirigible this very minute, he knew she wouldn't leave him. And her promise wasn't fooling him either. The set of her jaw and the determination in her eyes told him they were in this together until the end.

Aether, he loved this woman. Loved her intelligence, her insight, her resolve and—there was no denying it—time spent wrapped in her arms. If they survived this situation, he'd move heaven and earth to stay by her side.

A deep shudder rumbled through the dirigible, shooting the vibration of grinding gears up through their feet.

"She's speeding up!" Ryan already had Rodríguez's arm slung over his shoulder and was halfway through the door, hauling the weight of a man he'd much prefer to dump overboard. The professor wasn't fighting him. Instead, the man muttered under his breath about the tragic loss of data and the years it would take him to recoup his losses. Charlotte, right behind him with the scientist's satchel slung over her shoulder and the incubator tucked under her arm, would remind him that the mad scientist's mind was worth plumbing. She would want to pick Rodríguez's brain while he rotted in jail.

There was little he wouldn't do for the woman he loved. And he'd be lying to himself if he didn't admit to a tiny flicker of hope that resurrecting a *cuélebre* from a pair of carved bone eyes wasn't as impossible as it sounded.

So for now the herpetologist would live.

As they crossed the deck fighting through the salt-laced wind that whipped at their clothing and scoured their skin, he kept a careful eye out for Maria, not quite believing she would leave her brother entirely to their mercy knowing he was largely incapable of defending himself. That Ryan was linked to them both as family, however tangled their relationship might be, did not sit well. The woman was a kind of monster in her own right, so perhaps she sought only to save her own skin. Or perhaps she was consumed with a struggle to steer the airship, regretting her hasty removal of its captain. He could only hope for the later and plan against the first.

Did she hope they would simply abandon ship? Did she arrange for her own escape, perchance to secretly return and fetch her brother?

That thought made him clench his teeth, that this drama would not reach its end this very night. He'd damn well see that it did.

With more haste than care, they lowered Rodríguez, moaning and groaning, onto a bench in the escape dirigible. The man crumpled with a whimper, collapsing forward to clutch his bleeding leg. At his feet, they tucked the incubator and the canvas-wrapped codex.

As they might need to make a quick exit, Ryan twisted the spring launcher, ensuring the propulsive force was at maximum power. Given the somewhat dilapidated state of the vessel, he also double checked the glider's folded wings to be sure they would deploy as expected.

All while Charlotte dug a roll of gauze from a medical kit and pressed it into Rodríguez's hands.

"What?" the man screamed. "You expect me to bandage this gaping hole on my own?" Then continued on, rattling about cartilage, tendon damage and the function of the patella as an anatomic pulley to increase the lever arm of the knee during flexion.

They both ignored him.

Frowning, Charlotte bent over to study the control panel. "Not the most self-explanatory of dials, knobs and switches, but manageable."

With the stomp of his boot, Ryan broke the casing covering the wing extension mechanism and pulled the locking pins free and handed them to Charlotte. "He'll not be going anywhere without this."

With a grimace, she tucked them into a secure pocket.

As neither of them fancied taking their chances with the kraken in the water, any decision to abandon ship needed to be made before they were out of the escape glider's range. The idea of leaving the task of apprehending Maria to the Coast Guard rankled. She might turn the airship back toward land anywhere along the coastline and leave the gasbag to float where it would before disappearing with the carved bone eyes.

Though the possibility they were carved from dragon bone was remote, it existed. To that end, they were priceless. He wanted those artifacts in his own hands. Tonight. And, for now, the coast was in sight and well within glider range.

Gripping railings and various items lashed to the deck, they fought their way up the inclined surface toward the bridge with nothing but a single weapon between them. How to enter without being shot upon entry? There were windows aplenty, but only one door leading to the deck. Was there time to dive into the belly of the gondola in search of a floor hatch?

He struggled to devise an entry that would not end in gunfire. A lead lump in his stomach warned him this would go badly. And if she turned the dirigible—

The airship canted, turning for open water.

*Shit.*

He opened his mouth, about to yell at Charlotte, to tell her to head back to the escape vessel, when a shuddering vibration passed through the ship's iron framework, rattling its wooden cladding. Maria, activating the coal hopper, dropping fuel into the furnace, readying the airship for forward propulsion.

Leaving them a small window of opportunity.

*Sabotage.*

An idea blazed. Why risk their lives when a much simpler possibility existed?

"Follow me." He flashed Charlotte a wide grin and spun about one hundred and eighty degrees, leading her aft, snatching up a long-handled telescopic pole with a hook on its end. A tool normally used to thread a rope through mooring rings, it would serve his purpose.

"Ryan?"

"The rudder." He pointed. "She's banking right. If we jam the exposed cable—"

"The ship will be unable to straighten again." She bent over the railing, analyzing his plan as the wind whipped at her hair. "Forcing the dirigible to circle around, to go back toward the city. The airship would pass directly over New Haven Green."

Where unwelcome questions would be asked about the audacity of a pigeon class to darken the city skies. An investigative balloon would be launched. Police dirigibles would arrive en masse. Unwanted attention for Maria. Aid for them.

"It could work," she decided. "But the cable is some distance down. Are you sure you can reach it?"

"Yes." But a knot of fear tightened in his chest. If he couldn't? The parachute pack strapped to his back brought little comfort. Still, his plans to lean that far over the railing in a blustering wind this high up in the sky made his heart leap into his throat. Where the organ stayed, pounding out a stuttering dispatch that telegraphed desperation. "If I fall—"

"You won't," she interrupted, her voice trembling with emotion. "I refuse to believe fate would be so cruel as to snatch you away from me." She inhaled and her gaze sharpened with determination, even if it failed to conceal the worry that he might slip from her grip and tumble into the dark waves below. "But if the unthinkable occurs, I'll launch the escape glider and meet you on shore. We'll bag Maria another day."

Charlotte wrapped her fingers about the pack's straps and held tight, anchoring him to the deck as he leaned outward, struggling to slide the steel sections of the telescopic pole past one another. Time seemed to stretch forever as he extended the contraption, foot by foot, toward the rudder. Every muscle in his arms trembled with the effort and a cold sweat formed on his forehead as he fought the wind and the weight of the pole itself and the knowledge that, at any moment, Maria might straighten the rudder, ruining their chances.

Finally, the last segment snapped into place.

He thrust the pole downward, wedging it between the steel cable and the mechanical machinery constructed by a complex network of toothed gears, cogs, and sprockets.

He'd barely exhaled his relief before the rudder began to move. Would the pole hold? Would it fracture and break, shattering their plans?

There was horrible grinding sound accompanied by a deep vibration. The vertical airfoil shuddered as the cable pulled, making a mighty effort to straighten the dirigible. But failed, unable to comply with the commands transmitted by the helm. Bolts strained. Overtaxed clamps failed. Then, with a final metallic twang, something deep within the mechanism broke, locking the airship into a tight right turn.

*Success!*

Releasing the telescoping pole with the arch of his back, he dropped onto his heels, and spun about to catch Charlotte in a brief embrace, kissing her with exuberance. Not only were they headed back to port, Maria—not one to surrender—would be forced from the bridge to attempt a fix.

There was no time to waste. He grabbed Charlotte's hand and pulled.

Together, they ran to the foredeck, stopping adjacent to the door leading to the bridge, where they fell against the side of the airship, chests heaving. Sharing a knowing and tense anticipatory glance. Then the dirigible accelerated and canted into a tight turn. "She's making a run for open water!" Charlotte yelled. "If she keeps this up, we'll only spin faster and faster."

How long before Maria realized she was doomed to travel in circles?

Not long, he wagered.

Casting his gaze left and right and overhead, aware she might well sneak out a side window and loop back, he tugged his Eagle B29 sidearm from its holster and readied three darts. He wished the woman dead but intended to take her alive. If incapacitated.

As soon as they had the Spanish murderess in custody, he'd locate the dirigible's gas release valve and give it a solid pull. A slow leak of hydrogen would collapse the airbag inside its netting, dropping their altitude by gradual degrees. Land or sea, the airship would touch down. Pigeon class dirigibles were watertight and quite capable of floating, though not particularly seaworthy. A ship would spot them bobbing in the harbor and sail to their rescue. Or, if the city was beneath them when landing became inevitable, he'd snag one of the airship's tethers to a rooftop landing pole. With the dirigible pulling constantly to the right, the rope would wind around the pole in a strange dance, drawing them into an ever-smaller spiral. Eventually, they would be able to shimmy down a rope to safety.

Ryan eyed the door. It was only a matter of a few minutes. His every muscle vibrated, ready to spring into action.

A faint overhead noise was their only warning. Ryan grabbed Charlotte's arm and pulled her sideways.

*Bang!*

A bullet whizzed past his head so closely he felt the breeze in his hair. Maria was on top of the gondola. Which meant the bridge was empty. He ducked, kicked at the doorknob. The lock broke and the door slammed open.

"Take cover inside!" he yelled, reaching for Charlotte, fully intending to take on Maria himself. But before he could push her to presumed safety, a screaming demon burst forth from the interior.

The high-pitched shriek accompanied a furious goose-sized raptor that flapped feathered arms—for the clawed appendages could not be called wings. The creature lashed its tail while stretching out a long, sinuous neck to scream its fury through an enormous not-quite-a-beak filled with long, needle-sharp teeth.

Teeth which clamped down upon his ankle, piercing through both boot leather and his skin. He bit back a pained howl, grimacing as he fought to keep his eyes on the enemy.

"Look out!" Charlotte yelled.

As he fell to the ground, Maria lifted her pistol, taking aim at his skull. At the same time, he aimed his own gun. There was no contest whose projectile would do the most damage to a human. But even if he died here and now, Ryan could at least cripple the vengeful murderess giving Charlotte a chance to escape.

He pulled the trigger and, remembering how a single dart had failed to drop her at the Sea View Hotel—held it down firing all three darts in close succession.

*Whoosh! Whoosh! Whoosh!*

"No!" Charlotte launched herself at Maria, shoving the woman's arm upward.

*Bang!*

Maria's shot had gone wild, but not his.

He and Charlotte froze, their gazes lifting to the massive hydrogen-filled balloon above. Had her shot pierced the silver fabric?

"We have to assume it hit!" Charlotte called. "We're out of time!"

Shock drained all expression from Maria's face. Three darts were a significant blow to the nervous system. After all, stunned immobile was the goal. Maria froze. Those he pursued often did. The toxic insult to their nervous system left them momentarily stunned.

An opportunity Charlotte did not waste. She snatched the pistol from Maria's hand, threw it overboard and drew her knife in its place.

He kicked at the goose-shaped creature still attached to his ankle. Yes, its pointy little teeth hurt like the devil, but separating it from his boot would only provide it with the opportunity to sink the fierce dentition into his flesh elsewhere. He'd rather knock the beast unconscious, then pry it free.

With stiffening fingers, Maria pulled a dart fired from his B29 lodged from her hip, glaring at the sharp tip. Pain and anger contorted the features of her face. "Tetrodotoxin?"

Most of his targets fell with but a single dart. A few times he'd fired a second one. But never three. This woman's physiological resistance to venom was unmatched.

He shook his head. Corrected her. "Conotoxin."

A cocktail of cone snail peptides, the dart's contents were formulated to induce a fierce stinging pain, swiftly followed by numbness and tingling. Not deadly, but decidedly incapacitating. Unlike the British dart favored by the Queen's agents, IBIS agents dropped their targets with potent venom and asked questions later.

"*Cagon mi mantu.*" Maria swayed on her feet.

Charlotte wrapped an arm about the murderess, pressing the sharp edge of her knife to the woman's throat while shoving her one stiff step at a time toward the airship's bridge. Then suddenly Charlotte stopped. "Ryan?"

"She'll drop in a minute." He kicked at the mini raptor again. But the creature only redoubled its efforts, flapping its poor excuse for wings and whipping its long tail. Sharp talons ripped through his trousers. Blood welled, soaking the torn fabric. Stitches might be necessary. "We take control of the helm, slow the airship before—"

"That's going to be a problem." Charlotte jerked her chin upward.

Hands wrapped about the throat of the atavistic goose gnawing on his ankle, he squeezed. Easier to snap its neck, but a living, breathing relic—

"Ryan!" She yelled over the howl of the wind. "We need to go. *Now.*"

Finally, deprived of oxygen, the creature fell limp, its

strange shrieks silenced. Which was when he became aware of a whistling hiss. His head snapped up, his focus narrowing to a small hole in the silver fabric of the dirigible's balloon. The results of Maria's stray overhead bullet.

*Shit.*

Not ten feet away a thick black smoke billowed from a crack that had opened in the overheated engine's exhaust piping. Worse, sparks sprang from inside the fractured duct, flying upward toward the balloon and the gaping hole in its side.

Age. Fatigue. Improper maintenance. Did it matter what had caused the breach?

So much for steering the airship back into harbor. This gasbag could blow at any moment. A surge of adrenaline shot through his veins. No time for terror, only action.

Escape dirigible it was.

He staggered to his feet, holstered his weapon, and yanked the velvet pouch from Maria's neck. Her fingers barely managed to twitch in protest. Beneath the fabric, he felt the bone discs shift under his fingertips. Satisfied, he shoved them into a deep pocket.

"Do you want this?" He nudged the not-quite-dead raptor with his toe, knowing beyond a doubt what Charlotte's answer would be. The striped red and orange feathers forming a crest upon its skull all but guaranteed the raptor would be traveling with them.

Charlotte scooped up the floppy not-a-bird. "Very much so."

"Time to haul ass." Ignoring the burning pain in his leg, he heaved Maria's drooping and all-but-unconscious form over his shoulder, ignoring the deranged laughter bubbling from her throat as they ran to the escape glider.

*Whoosh!*

Flames exploded across the surface of the balloon, engulfing the rear propellor in a flash of red orange. They had minutes at best.

Ryan all but tossed his prisoner onto the floor of the glider and set about freeing their moorings. The unconscious raptor landed beside her. Charlotte leapt in and yanked on levers, popping each wing into extension before sliding their locking pins into place. She dropped into the foremost seat, scanning the various instrument dials while Rodríguez cursed them for ruining everything.

"All systems go!" she called over her shoulder. "Ready?"

A horrible keening of metal sounded, a brief warning preceding the catastrophic failure of the smokestack as it collapsed onto the deck. Cinders exploded from its burst seams —a final act that sent a shower of sparks into the air, swirling in the wind to land upon the sessile ropes that bound the gasbag to the gondola, burning through the netting then spreading over the silver fabric.

"Brace for launch!" Leaving out the part where he wasn't going to manage to join them in the body of the glider, he wrapped fisted hands about a tethering rope tied to its rear side. Offering up a brief plea to any gods or goddesses who might be watching, he shoved the escape glider from its groove.

As the aircraft lifted from the deck and caught an updraft of air beneath its wings, he jumped. The fibers of the sisal rope dug into his palms, burning. But it held, dragging him away from the doomed dirigible.

Five feet. Ten. Twenty.

How far might they make it before—

*Whoosh-Boom!*

The gasbag exploded behind them. Heat licked at his heels. A momentary sensation quickly snuffed out as the airship—deprived of everything that held it aloft in one brief blast—plummeted nose first like a seagull intent on snatching away a beachgoer's carefully packed picnic.

# CHAPTER TWENTY-TWO

The floor seemed to drop from beneath her, taking her stomach along for the ride. A queasy and alarming sensation, as if she'd tumbled overboard and now plummeted headlong toward the dark water below. But her sweaty palms clutched the wheel in a death grip. Eyes pointed forward. Her spine ramrod straight in the pilot's chair.

Reason repeated over and again that the escape dirigible had been built to exceed engineering specifications—the wooden boards might creak and groan as they rubbed against the riveted steel hull, but they held. That it didn't matter if the silver cloth covering the airfoil extensions wasn't fitted tightly to the wing framework—they stayed in their fixed position spread out to her right and left and held them aloft. That if the pedals beneath her feet controlling the rudder felt a bit wobbly, it was fine because they responded to her movements. That if the braking mechanism rattled—

No. They were too far from shore to test that system.

Altogether, things were proceeding as they ought. The escape dirigible hadn't fallen from the air, had it?

*Yet.* An unpleasant internal voice drew attention to her heart pounding an alarm on her sternum.

"Ryan?" Her yell emerged high-pitched and panicked. Behind her—no, below and behind her—the dirigible burned on the surface of New Haven Harbor.

She hated dirigibles—none ever rose to her standards for flight—and symbols marking the various dials and buttons of the control panel resembled petroglyphs more than standard designs. Even worse? An escape glider. A co-pilot's advice and help would be much appreciated.

Clenching her teeth, she glanced over her shoulder and panic grabbed her by the throat. Maria and the not-a-goose lay unconscious on the floorboards, immobile. Rodríguez bent over them both, distraught. But no one else. No Ryan.

*Where was he?*

He'd launched them from the airship—but hadn't leapt aboard? Was there any chance of him surviving such a fall?

Every fiber of her being rebelled at accepting the obvious. Yet simultaneously worked itself into a froth of panic. An attempt at deep calming breaths failed, scratching in and rattling out as they did.

"Behind and below you!" Ryan's voice, though faint, arrived at her ear by way of some stray updraft.

*Behind? Below?*

Tears fell from her eyes and were snatched away by the wind. She struggled to hold the aircraft steady against large gusts that shoved the glider sideways and tossed it two feet in the air.

Which was when she caught a movement out of the corner of her eye.

Ryan, dangling from a rope.

*Shit.*

How could they land safely? They couldn't. He'd have to let go, drop to the ground.

*Ground.* She needed to steer for clear ground, then come in low and slow.

Could she slow down a glider before they touched down? There was a dial that might indicate such, but she wasn't certain exactly how—or when—it might slow or stop the aircraft. Did they need to be on land? Would it work while they were still midair? She glanced, dubious, at the fixed wings. And how, precisely, did one land an escape dirigible, for that matter? Certainly not like a sled?

She cringed, imagining the sparks that would spray from beneath the steel belly of this beast as it slid down a cobblestone-lined road. Packed dirt would be an improvement. Grass even better. Far, far less injury dropping onto something relatively soft. Water would be preferable, if not for the kraken.

Then again, they needed to land near help. Medical help.

And a few civic-minded bystanders would also be a bonus.

The airship, the rudder's control cable sabotaged, had circled back toward the harbor as hoped. For a few scant minutes. Not so expected was its explosion in a most spectacular manner just off the end of Long Wharf. News that was certain to find itself inked in large font across the front page of the New Haven Register tomorrow morning. As would details of their emergency landing. A landing she prayed would take place on New Haven Green. A wide-open space was her best chance of executing a safe touchdown. Even better, that location wasn't far from the medical school on York Street.

Ryan yelled from below, but whatever he wished to convey was lost on the wind.

She could see her target now. The park was a dark square outlined by glimmering gas lamps. She turned the wheel, adjusting their trajectory, lining up their approach as best she could with one of its crisscrossing pathways. Fingers crossed, such would serve as an acceptable landing strip. With that attended to, she focused her attention back to the control panel, searching for anything that might aid her cause.

*There.* A button with an icon she thought indicated wheels.

She punched it and felt the something fall beneath her. And then... nothing. Had a hatch opened? Had wheels dropped into place? Impossible to know, but she found it worrisome that her hands—tightly gripping the steering wheel—detected nothing different. Nor did her feet—solidly braced against the floor—register any additional mechanical vibrations.

There was no rumbling indicating a turning of gears, no sensations to indicate anything had happened at all. Broken?

Possible.

*Probable.*

Likely their best option was skidding to a stop. Better than an abrupt halt by way of tree, lamppost, or brick wall.

They left the water behind, then the docks. A few rattling seconds over the train tracks and then they were coming in fast over roofs and chimneys. People and vehicles were no longer distant and blurry ants, instead now possessed of discernible arms and heads. Many of which were pointing upward in her direction, tracking the rapid approach of an aircraft into forbidden airspace and exclaiming at the man that dangled overboard.

Tension tore through her, sending cries of alarm zinging along every nerve. Muscles in her shoulders, arms, hands, and fingers clenched, resulting in a death grip upon the steering wheel. Her heart squeezed and released with such force and speed the organ felt as if it might burst at any second. There was no room for mistakes. No second chances. With Ryan hanging below, she needed to stay high enough to clear him over buildings. She could not live with an ending where he'd smacked into an oversized window like a startled, misdirected bird.

*Honk.*

*Shit.* She glanced over her shoulder, hoping for a nocturnal duck or goose objecting to their presence in his airspace. But, no, it was the raptor, regaining consciousness at the most inopportune moment.

Upright with eyes open, the mini feathered demon craned its neck over the edge of the dirigible, striped red and orange crest feathers whipping about in the wind, then let out a louder, more panicked squawk that could—and did—wake the nearly dead.

Maria lurched into a seated position.

Charlotte cursed a long string of razor-edged oaths. IBIS needed to dial up the dosage of their darts.

"You need to take control of the glider!" Rodríguez—one hand holding blood-soaked gauze against his leg—slapped the face of his disoriented sister, shoved at her shoulder. "Do something! We've but minutes."

They were close to the green, but not close enough—even if she could now sight the corner of Church and Chapel. There was still plenty of time for catastrophe to strike as they passed above and between buildings. She yanked at the wheel, correcting the glider's course—always good to not tangle in a building's overhead telegraph wires—missing the first of many obstacles.

The aircraft rocked and shifted. Another glance informed her that Maria had her feet beneath her with her sights set on mutiny. A murderess without care or concern for anyone but herself. Charlotte could not surrender her post as pilot.

"Sit down!" she screamed in warning.

But the woman was lifting a leg to step over the bench seating, intent upon staging a coup. An act which left her no option.

Charlotte yanked at the wheel, sending them careening in another direction, but throwing Maria off balance.

Below her, Ryan shouted objections, but she couldn't respond, struggling as she was not to crash into the corner of a building as she approached the city's central park.

After skimming far too close to the stone facing and ducking beneath a hanging sign, she course-corrected a final time, then risked another glance.

And watched as Maria lurched sideways and fell. Atop the feathered, flightless atavism she'd reared in a cage.

The raptor-like creature screeched its displeasure and—with another glance—she caught a view of the not-a-goose sinking razor-sharp teeth into Maria's arm.

Behind her, Maria screamed. Rodríguez shouted. All the kicking and thrashing tossed the glider from side to side. Below, Ryan hollered, struggling not to fall as chaos erupted above him.

"Hold still!" But, of course, no one listened. There was nothing to do but land this contraption. An inevitability that rushed at them with increasing proximity.

Squinting, she lined up the nose of the glider with a diagonal pathway that began at the green's corner. Trees presented her with a final obstacle.

With grim hope for a different outcome, she smashed her hand down on the button that indicated wheels.

Nothing. A belly landing it would be.

She clenched her teeth and yanked on a lever adorned with an icon that looked to promise it would slow the glider. With a great creak, something dropped from the wings. Flaps of some sort. The glider slowed, no longer careening toward the ground. Instead, it seemed almost to float—a leaf on the wind.

A moment of peace soon interrupted.

"Maria!" Rodríguez yelled, lurching. Nearly tipping the aircraft on its side.

From the corner of her eye, she watched the atavistic not-a-goose—teeth clamped about Maria's bloody neck—leap from the glider, its primitive clawed wings spread wide—dragging along the murderess.

The shouts of onlookers rang out beneath.

Ryan hollered that he was letting go.

The glider's wingtips clipped leaves, tree branches. Holes tore in the silver airfoil fabric.

"Hold on!" she yelled at Rodríguez, bracing her feet against the front end of the vessel, ignoring the sharp complaints of her hardware-studded ankle.

The iron belly of the glider touched down, skidding across grass and stone pavers, scattering the pedestrians who'd believed themselves out for a calm evening's stroll through the park. Dirt and mud kicked up. Clumps of grass flew. Every joint in her body seemed to twist apart and slam back together before the escape glider spun to a sideways halt in the middle of Temple Street.

Rattled but grateful to be alive, Charlotte scrambled from the tattered remains of the wreckage and staggered to her feet, limping. She turned about, looking for Ryan. For Maria and the raptor.

"Miss?" A voice from a gathering crowd. "Do you need help?"

"A doctor," she gasped, searching over his shoulder for Ryan. "Alert Customs. This man," she pointed at the mad herpetologist, "is a wanted criminal. He needs to be bandaged and taken into custody."

Mournful, Rodríguez stared down at the incubator at his feet. "Everything is lost. My work. My sister."

She rather agreed. Hard to believe his precious eggs were

anything but scrambled. As to his sister... Charlotte turned away, hobbling along the path, cringing at the pain that shot from her ankle to her thigh with each step. "Ryan? Ryan!"

The small knot of a crowd parted on a gasp, and Ryan lurched forward, hand wrapped about the neck of a feathered creature none of them had ever laid eyes upon. Blood dripped from its needle-sharp teeth.

Ignoring all aches and pains Charlotte ran forward to throw her arms about him in a fierce hug. Tears streamed down her face as she held him close. With a sound kiss, she dropped back onto her heels and stepped away to assess his many injuries, every scrape and laceration, but focusing on the gash upon his thigh. "Your leg?"

"Will need stitches." Though his wounds must pain him, Ryan's voice was filled with relief. His clothing was torn and bloody. Scrapes and lacerations scored his lower leg, but the wound inflicted upon his thigh was the most worrisome. Given the length of the talons on the atavistic creature, stitches were in his immediate future.

Then it dawned upon her that—though he held the mini raptor—Ryan seemed unconcerned about the creature's latest victim.

"Maria?" A question, but she rather thought the answer was a foregone conclusion.

He shook his head, then tipped it backward over his shoulder toward a tight knot of onlookers. "Dead." He lifted the not-a-bird. "Impossible to say if the fall or this creature killed her first, but with the deep gash in her neck and the pool of blood beneath them both, I'm ruling it death by dinosaur."

Given the woman's murderous habits, she had been destined for a violent end.

Police whistles sliced through the air; the calvary had arrived.

Ryan tugged his gold Customs badge from a pocket, ready to confront all questions and cut through the red tape.

"You need to see a physician." She set her jaw, unwilling to countenance an argument. "Let them take Rodríguez into custody. Send Maria to my brother."

"I'd rather avoid the hospital." He tipped his head. "Two birds with one stone? How is your brother with a needle and thread?"

"Adequate." She twisted her lips and huffed a laugh. "If you're a corpse."

"Hospital it is."

# CHAPTER TWENTY-THREE

Every muscle in Ryan's body ached. Every ligament and tendon pulsed with a dull throb. Each step tugged and pulled at the many stitches in his legs. And his palms, raw and torn by the fibers of the rope, burned beneath gauze bandages.

But there was no chance that anyone could convince him to sit a moment longer in a wheelchair beneath a hastily erected canvas tent on scrubby grass, watching as IBIS agents combed through the wreckage of the blackened building. No matter that a pretty princess named Aileen and her unicorn canine sought to serve him tea and cake on fine—if chipped—china.

They'd pulled a number of chicken-like quasi-birds from the overgrown shrubs and grass, each eliciting gasps of horrified surprise. The princess's mother had, of course, attempted to convince her daughter to return home, but Aileen and Glory made their rounds among rescue workers who had dragged themselves over to the tent for refreshments whenever exhaustion struck.

Ryan pushed himself onto his feet and grabbed awkwardly at his cane with bandaged hands, crossing the soot-stained yard at half speed. At the cellar hatch, he descended steps into the sopping wet, charred and smokey remnants of the underground laboratory once dedicated to incubating monstrous feathered creatures that might or might not have resembled those of the Mesozoic.

From his interrogation, he'd managed to learn that Rodríguez and his sister had spent years plotting their attempt at restoring the *cuélebre*, the mythological dragon of European origins, to the caves of northern Spain. That they'd been—in the madman's mind—very close to achieving their ends. Until Ryan and Charlotte had ruined everything with their raid. After that, the herpetologist had snapped his jaw shut, refusing to speak to the man who had destroyed his glorious plans for his castle and family coffers.

Ryan had peppered him with questions. What were his techniques for creating the bizarre hybrids? Did he truly think a quetzalcoatl might have hatched from the egg in that incubator he'd clung to? Was he in contact with other scientists attempting similar experiments? Had reports of dragons hailing from the Ural Mountains of Russia influenced the herpetologist's work or had otherwise informed his approach to experimenting upon the eggs of pythons, alligators, and ostriches?

But the man had turned a blank face to the stone wall of his cell and refused to utter another word. Ryan had poked and prodded and coaxed and tried everything short of begging, all to no avail.

They'd raided the man's state-side residence, but his bare-bones home life had offered them nothing new, save to perhaps confirm Rodríguez had indeed depleted his resources in pursuit of his obsession. His Asturian relatives in Spain had been contacted by telegraph. They denied contact with the family's black sheep and stopped just short of disowning him. Nor was there any help from the Peabody Museum forthcoming.

Rodríguez and his sister had, for years, effectively pigeon-holed their efforts at dragon-building, confining all work to the windowless basement in New Haven.

With the mad scientist himself refusing to speak, any hope of understanding the process—laboratory protocols—by which they'd hatched the atavistic reptilian birds was buried in the charred, wet remains of this basement. Thanks to the competence and rapid response of the New Haven Fire Department, enough of the house remained to hold out hope that they might be able to infer something of his methods.

"You shouldn't be down here." Charlotte's words were clipped, even though a smile flirted along the edges of her lips. "But your timing could not be more perfect."

Was she thinking about the kiss they'd shared, bloody and beaten, in the middle of downtown New Haven? A triumphant kiss, but also one of fierce longing. Much as he enjoyed the adrenaline rush of chasing criminals, of tossing them behind bars, most of all he enjoyed these small moments of discovery, the revelation of truth surrounding the existence of unlikely creatures. Enjoyed sharing the moment with her. His had been a solo endeavor for far too long. This was the woman for him, bar none. Not a single doubt remained.

"As if I could possibly stay away." From her. From the final hunt for any remaining salvageable evidence.

Above them, new wood held up overhead damaged beams. In the far back, the iron bars of the cage tilted at a worrisome angle. Everything else existed in piles of varying destruction: wet ash and soggy papers with running ink. Occasionally, he spotted islands of glass and metal, some of it more or less intact.

For the first time in nearly two days, they were alone.

"We were right!" Charlotte flapped a handful of paper scraps at him. Torn. Singed at the edges. "Rodríguez began his work by subjecting developing reptile and bird embryos to mutagens. When he succeeded in creating animals with traits reminiscent of evolutionary throwbacks, such as the dino chickens and the feathered raptor we discovered aboard the dirigible, he collected cells from one species and inserted them into an early-stage embryo of another species to form a single, individual creature. With questionable levels of success."

"Chimeras created using alligator and ostrich embryos, much like those Maria let slip from their cages."

"Fascinating enough—if entirely unethical." She shuddered. "They ought to have been biologically incompatible, given their divergent positions on the phylogenetic tree. Alligators are an archaic reptile that branched off on a different evolutionary pathway long before dinosaurs exploded into a variety of forms. Birds are the remnants of a tiny branch off the very tip of the tree. Millions of years separate them. Still, alligators and crocodiles are their closest living relatives."

"And snakes?"

"Closer to crocodiles than birds. Not that such reasoning stopped him."

He grinned. "To think Glory hunted down and killed the first snake to walk on North American soil in millennia."

Charlotte rolled her eyes. "Rather a habit of hers, hunting animals in backyards."

"So an atavistic snake with legs. Atavistic birds with teeth, wingtip talons and more scales than plumage. And reptiles—crocodiles modified to sprout feathers. Yet still no quetzalcoatl, no *cuélebre*. No feathered serpents—flying or otherwise." He thought of the incubator they'd retrieved. Of the shattered egg within. A shame. He'd rather hoped to see it hatch.

"Rodríguez was certainly working on it." She held up a hand and ticked off items. "Ancient bone. Ancient feathers. Ancient skin. Bixby's assigned task was to revive—resurrect—ancient cells from the biological material stolen from the National Mexican Museum that it might be transplanted into these atavistic embryos."

Ryan's eyebrows slammed together. "Is that possible?"

"No." A definitive answer. "But that's not to say the technique would not have worked, if not in the manner expected. Ernst Haeckel has written extensively about the presence of heredity material in the nucleus of a cell. Friedrich Miescher demonstrated that this substance, which he called 'nuclein', is a collection of nucleic acids and protein. If nuclein is indeed how hereditary traits are passed from generation, then any such material Bixby collected from the museum relics and injected into the cells of developing embryos might well have provided instructions for ancient traits alongside more modern characteristics."

Downright astounding that such a thing might be possible. "Into python eggs to produce a quetzalcoatl?"

"As a proof of concept? Or perhaps he thought it a necessary intermediate step. He did rant about needing the blood of a quetzalcoatl to resurrect the bones of a *cuélebre*."

Ryan pressed his hand to the velvet pouch that now hung —safe—around his own neck. "Using the only known biological material rumored to have originated from an Asturian winged serpent." He sighed. "A shame we'll never know if his most recent experiments might have worked."

"Or might we?" Charlotte turned to pull forth a battered crate. "I found this in the corner beneath a collapsed tabletop." Shifting the lid out of the way, she pulled out handfuls of straw to reveal one of the mad scientist's portable incubators, still humming away. Carefully, she lifted the lid. Inside lay a single egg. "A python's egg. See this patchwork? The leathery, soft shell has been peeled away, then replaced."

"Do you think—" He was at a loss for words.

She grinned back. "We'll know in a little under two months. If it hatches. I'll write a report for IBIS, detail the upsides and downsides, and then it'll be up to them to decide if we continue to let the egg incubate or not. I do think the process ought to be studied in hopes of restoring any avian species humans manage to hunt to extinction, but it's work that needs to be carefully regulated."

He hoped they would agree. Ryan never wanted this adventure to end. Or if this discovery reached a natural conclusion, he wanted her by his side as they hunted for the next. Forever. His heart squeezed, filling him with nervous euphoria. He'd spoken with her brother, Hiram, shortly after Sunday dinner. Won his blessing and that of his wife. Then spent any time not wrapped in red tape, or pacing beside a certain herpetologist's cell, pondering how and where to ask the most important question of his life.

A burned-out basement was far from romantic, but he couldn't wait a second longer.

Slowly, with much help from his cane, he lowered himself onto a single knee.

"Ryan? I think it's best we not touch the—" Her hands flew to her mouth as he tugged a ring from his coat pocket.

"Life with you in it is richer, deeper and full of meaning." His heart raced as he gazed into her eyes. "These past few years apart were filled with a sensation of emptiness. Only when we're together do I feel whole. I'm hoping you feel the same." The fossilized cabochon of polished ammolite flashed with blue and green iridescence. "Marry me?"

The love in her eyes set her face aglow. "Yes," she said softly. "As soon as possible."

# EPILOGUE

The past two months had passed in a blur of activity.

A simple wedding, attended by his siblings and Charlotte's brother and family—with Glory and the Princess Aileen attired in finery befitting her royal station, complete with tiara. Her parents had sent their congratulations by telegram, with regrets that they would not be able to attend but promising to visit soon.

His wife's published paper, documenting the feathers of the fossilized dinosaur Anzu, had taken the paleontology world by storm, generating alternating waves of acclaim, disbelief, and argument. The latter mostly quelled by the American Museum of Natural History in New York City who examined the evidence directly, pronounced it sound—and quickly offered one Mrs. Charlotte Nolan a position as a Curator of Paleontology.

Rumors of their discoveries in New Haven were quick to circulate among the cryptozoology community. Their investigation, which now involved both Mexican and Spanish authorities, drew the attention of the International Cryptobiology Committee who sent a member to oversee the work of the United States Improbable Biologics Investigational Service. The man had gaped at the assortment of not-quite-birds and not-quite-dinosaurs—both dead and alive—before him and promptly filed a report filled with superlatives. More members of the ICC arrived to view the creatures for themselves. Impressed with his work, the ICC offered him a position in their New York City office. One which Ryan rapidly accepted.

Professor Tetzopa, now well on his way to recovery, had left for Mexico City to escort the Mixtec codex back to the safekeeping of professional archeologists who, along with a few select cryptobiologists, were keen to take a much closer look at the ancient national treasure that had been stolen from them.

The altered python egg, however, remained on US soil, safe and secure under his and Charlotte's care and supervision. Everyone had agreed the fragile embryo harbored within was far too precious to subject to any prolonged overland travel. All final decisions as to the creature's future would be made later, pending the outcome of the incubation period.

Fifty-two days after the egg was pulled from the remnants of a burned building, a tiny tear appeared in its leathery shell. Ryan launched a flurry of kinetic chiropteras into the city's airspace while Charlotte dispatched a series of telegrams announcing the imminent event.

Several hours later, a small knot of people gathered about the egg, all of them holding their breaths and praying that something other than a python would emerge.

At long last, the tip of a nose appeared, and a forked tongue flicked out and the hatchling slithered out to a chorus of gasps. Of wonder. Of disbelief. Of astonishment. For a ruff of green, iridescent feathers fanned out about the small not-a-snake's neck. An impressive ruff, yet purely ornamental. Incapable of conferring the power of flight.

But many fledgling legends could trace their origins to grains of truth, however tiny.

Charlotte squeezed his hand. "Is that—" Astounded, she looked up at him. "A juvenile quetzalcoatl?"

Awe filled his response. "That or a laboratory-created close approximation."

Manmade myth, perhaps, but it now existed.

His was the perfect job.

# ABOUT THE AUTHOR

Though ANNE RENWICK holds a Ph.D. in biology and greatly enjoyed tormenting the overburdened undergraduates who were her students, fiction has always been her first love. Today, she writes steampunk romance, placing a new kind of biotech in the hands of mad scientists, proper young ladies and determined villains.

Anne brings an unusual perspective to steampunk. A number of years spent locked inside the bowels of a biological research facility left her permanently altered. In her steampunk world, the Victorian fascination with all things anatomical led to a number of alarming biotechnological advances. Ones that the enemies of Britain would dearly love to possess.

www.AnneRenwick.com

instagram.com/anne_renwick

facebook.com/AnneRenwickAuthor

pinterest.com/AuthorAnneRenwick

www.ingramcontent.com/pod-product-compliance
Lightning Source LLC
Chambersburg PA
CBHW031312210726

48287CB00005B/1515